Mrs. Rosie AND THE ROCKSTAR

MAELYN BJORK

ISBN: 978-1-77883-409-7 (Paperback)
978-1-77883-410-3 (Ebook)

BookSide Press
877-741-8091
www.booksidepress.com
orders@booksidepress.com

Contents

Chapter One

Painfully, the little boy crouched under the hospital bed. He crawled up to the front of the bed and jammed himself in there as tightly as he could.

A medical aide came in to his room. "Jared." She called as she opened the bathroom door and found it empty. "Where are you? You'll miss your appointment for your morning scrub."

She bent down and looked under the bed. "I can see you. You're going to get stuck under there and then you'll really be hurting."

"No! don't want to go. It hurts too much. If you go away then maybe I'll come out."

Out in the hallway, Dr. Roselyn Rosenbaum passed by and could hear the nurse's aide. She stopped and walked into the room. She glanced at the aide as she pointed under the bed. The aide grimaced and shook her head.

Roselyn nodded and set her the files she carried on a night table. "Hey Jared, do I have to crawl under there to get you out?" She waited for a moment. "How come you crawled under the bed? I'll bet it's colder down there than in your bed."

She put her hands on her waist and sighed. "Okay, I haven't had any breakfast yet, and when they bring your lunch, I may just have to eat it."

She heard some scraping from under the bed. "In fact," She glanced at her watch "Maybe I'll send Ms. Ferandaz here, to go fetch it." She turned and winked at the aide. That was the first reaction she noticed from the aide other than boredom and irritation.

They both heard some sliding and slowly, on the far side of the bed, the little boy eased out away from it and pulled himself up. As Roselyn studied the small boy, she mentally she winced at the torn dressings and the ugly scabs on the child's chest and arms. They were both aware of the burns he had suffered in a neighborhood fire that had happened several days earlier. There had been several people who had been involved in a triple house fire. And three of them had been children.

Since this hospital had the best burn unit in the county, the three children had been brought up here to University Hospital. Roselyn had become involved, because she had just finished her doctorate in illnesses, accidents, and their effects in pre-teen children. She helped the suffering boy up on the bed. "Now why were you hiding under this bed? It has to be more comfortable than the floor, and much warmer."

Jared scowled at her, but she noticed a tear glistening on his cheek. "It hurts too much, the scrub. Can't they just leave the scars and scabs alone?"

"Okay, let's pretend that you were injured riding your bike. What do you do then?"

"I go home and my mother would clean me up and then up and put some medicine on the hurt places and some band aids on them. Then in few days they heal up and I take them off." He shrugged, but winced as he moved his left shoulder.

"There is your answer. But your burn wounds are much larger and deeper. By scraping them off and keeping the area clean. Then allowing new skin to grow over them, they will heal much better. The big problem is infection. If you get infection in those wounds they will not heal properly. So by scrubbing off the old damaged skin and allowing new skin to form, and hopefully by next year your whole body will be better. You must not skip a day of treatment. And being in the hospital is very expensive for anyone, and it takes lots people to care for you. You should not waste their time and energy. If you go home now who is going to help you there?"

Jared dropped his head. "I don't know?' There was a cry in his voice. "Is my Mom getting any better?"

"She is still quite ill. I'll tell you what. I'll make a deal with you. If you go up to your scrub appointment, then I'll go check on your mom. Is that a deal?"

He frowned, but then said. "Okay."

She stepped back and called upstairs for an aide to come and get Jared. Then she turned to Ms. Ferandez and spoke to her about lunch for Jared. "Save one for Jared, because they are coming to get him for therapy, Okay?"

The aide nodded. "Do you want me to save one for you, too?" She watched the doctor nod her head. "Okay, let me know how the boy's mother is doing."

Roselyn took the stairs one floor up to the adult burn unit. Luckily there were Jared's sister and mother along with sixteen people had been involved. So far six people had been released. Marian Conner, Jared's mother was still Critical not so much from surface burns. but inhaling smoke and superheat air. She was in and out of consciousness and had some lung damage. She had been a smoker, and even though she had quit the habit about the time she became pregnant with Jared, there was still some latent damage.

Roselyn decided to check the woman's chart. There was some improvement, but still some infection. Right now, the doctors were relying on antibiotics, and a new treatment they were trying; a fifteen-minute session in the oxygen pressure chamber. Roselyn hoped that would be effective for the woman.

She glanced at her watch. Maybe she had time to check on Benjamin Grey Feather. He was from a Native American tribe in Southern Utah. He was eight years old and had suffered a psychiatric episode. Or possibly had been born with brain damage. He had never really learned to speak. He hummed a flat tone when frustrated. Otherwise, he was silent, or once or twice a day would give out with piercing screams, then curl up a ball on the floor or in the rear of a vehicle in which he was riding. Sometimes he would go missing and would be found in the rear of a parked truck or nearby car.

He had been brought in by a doctor living in Northern Arizona. The medic's diagnosis: Severe autism. He was from the Navajo Tribe living near the Glen Canyon Dam in that area. Northern Arizona. He spent much of his waking hours twirling around gazing at a shiny rock, car keys, or gazing at his wiggling fingers. Then he would grow tired and fall down and lie on the floor. Someone would then pick him up and put him in some sort of bed.

First, they took him to the hospital at Page Arizona, but about a week later brought him to the main hospital in Salt Lake City. Roselyn had been sent in to observe him. The second day she brought in a large art tablet and a box of markers and some crayons. She set them on a small table. Then she opened the art tablet and took a marker and drew a line on the paper. A minute or two later he stopped twirling and stood still to watch her make marks on the paper. "Here, Benjamin." She held out a crayon. "Would you like to draw on the paper?'

He slowly moved closer and continued to watch her make marks on the art tablet. Then he suddenly walked close to her and, yanked the crayon from her hand. He bent down to make a long line across the paper. He spent several minutes making marks on the paper.

Roselyn folded the tablet to a clean page and began to draw a stick figure. He stood quietly and watched. She drew a woman with wide hips, and curly hair. "This could be a picture of me, or your mother or some other woman." she said.

For a long moment he studied the stick figure she had drawn. He stood there staring at her drawing. Suddenly he sat down across from her, pulled the art notebook across the table, grabbed up a crayon and began making marks on the paper. He picked up two more crayons and began making marks on the top page in different colors. It was as if he were deciding on which crayon he liked better. With both crayons in his hand, he stared at them, but then set one down and began to draw a crude circle with the green one.

She watched quietly as he filled the circle with a smaller circle, then a line down and he added legs to the line. He seemed to gaze at the marks he had drawn. But his next move was to stand up quickly and knock over the chair. He turned to her and the look on his face was of distress. He crawled over to the corner of the room and put his head between his knees and began to cry.

At that moment Roselyn realized that she had not studied his case notes long enough to become really familiar with them. She waited several moments and then said. "Benjamin, would you like to work on your drawing now or later?"

Perhaps a minute later he lifted his head and stared at the table and the paper he had made marks on. Slowly he stood up and walked back to the table. He stared down at his drawing. Surprising Roselyn, he sat down, picked up the crayon and gave the figure arms.

Roselyn took a deep breath and then asked. "Who is this person you drew Benjamin? May I write down a name?"

For a long moment, he stared at the paper. He placed his hand on the drawing. "Mo-m - -mother." Then he covered the drawing with his hand and began to cry.

She realized that this was a breakthrough for him. She had no indication when reading his notes that he had ever spoken (at least while here at the hospital). She quickly sat down and added this to her notes. A moment later there was a knock on the door. Roselyn jumped up to answer it.

"Dr. Rosenbaum your lunch is here." Another aide came in with the tray and set it on the desk. "If you want more than just water to drink, there is a coffee pot in the work room."

"Okay, thank you." She watched as the girl pushed into the room and set the tray on the desk. The girl glanced at Benjamin huddled on the corner of the room.

"How's he doing? Poor kid." She shook her head and backed out of the room.

Roselyn debated about eating in this quiet office, however, perhaps she could offer this little boy something to eat. Reading his chart, she recalled a note about him taking food in a dark corner or under a bed to eat.

A while later, he did come over to her and stood by her tray, which was closer to her. He indicated that he would like a quarter of her chicken sandwich. He would only take a piece of the section she had already taken a few bites.

Later that afternoon, she consulted with a new mother, who had given birth to a premature infant who had to be placed in the NIC-U. She went out to chat with the nurse on duty about bringing the premature infant to his mother. And on went her day.

About 4:30 p.m. Dr. Rosenbaum left the hospital, and made a stop at a supermarket. She knew they were out of milk, fresh fruit and needed a roast for Sunday dinner. When she finally drove into her side of the three-car garage in was nearly 6:00 p.m. It was then she remembered that she and her husband had some sort of dinner to attend.

Once she reached the garage and parked her car, she began to empty the trunk full of groceries. As she carried in the first sack of food, she remembered what the evening's activities were. She and Taylor were to attend some formal dinner for the American Psychiatric Association. Another trip to the garage for food, she glanced at the kitchen clock. She hurried into her younger daughter's bedroom. "Hey Shanna, Shanna could you give me some help emptying and putting away the groceries. I think I need to go upstairs and change for some dinner your father and I have to attend this evening."

"Well, okay. But can I decide what we're going to eat for supper tonight?"

"If the meal you decide on needs cooking, can you take care of that chore?" Roselyn asked.

The girl frowned. "Of course. I'll choose something quick and easy." They walked to the kitchen and began pulling food out of one of the sacks. They both heard a door slam. Shanna moved to the garage entrance. "Hey Ellie, we get to cook tonight. Mom and Dad are going out to some dinner."

Older daughter Ellie stood in the front hall way. "I wondered why the garage was still open. Okay, let me take my books and coat downstairs. Mom, you'd better hustle. Dad hates to wait for you. *In fact, he hates everything around here.* She thought.

"You speak the truth." Roselyn hurried upstairs. She began peeling off her outer clothes. Once she stood in the large master closet, she began searching for a dressy winter outfit. After all it was November. She dragged out simple, short sleeved silk blouse The shirt was black and calf length, with an easy fit, an A–line, she would wear that. Now, for a shower.

While Roselyn slipped on her black half- slip, Taylor came out of his closet. He stood for a moment in front of their valet mirror and fixed his bow tie. "I'm leaving now." He said.

"Can't you wait? Give me fifteen minutes. I don't want to drive to the country club alone." She begged.

"No. I'm leaving now, and I'm not coming back." He walked over to a dark gray suitcase that lay on their king-sized bed. "You must understand. I'm leaving you. I left you a letter. It's on your desk in your workroom. It should explain my feelings."

"Leaving! Where are you going, why?" What have I done? Or perhaps is it something you've done?"

She stood there with one arm in the sleeve of the black velvet jacket and watched him pick up a suitcase from their bed, and walk down the long hallway to the stairs and to the main floor and on down to the garage.

Chapter Two

The two Rosenbaum daughters watched their father walk past the kitchen and down the stairs to their three-car garage. "See, I told you he was leaving, I heard him on the phone talking to his latest feminine 'fling'. This time, I guess he'll move in with her, instead just sneaking around behind Mom's back." Ellie spit out the words.

"Yeah, I've known he's been cheating for quite a while. Right now, I need to go grab a coat. Janet will be here any minute now. We're going to the football game between Alta Canyon and River View. Tell Mom I'll be home around 11:30 p.m." They both heard a honk. "There's Janet now. See ya later."

The younger sister bounced down the stairs and left through the open garage. Ellie heard the ding of the oven and grabbed a hot pad and pulled out a pot pie she had decided to eat. She also grabbed a package of salad mix from the fridge. "Hey Mom, do you want a chicken pot pie?" She called up the open stair case. "The oven's still hot. I'll put one in the oven for you." She waited for a minute, but heard no response. She shrugged, and turned off the oven. She shook some salad mix in a bowl and added some ranch dressing. She tilted the pot pie on a plate and set her food on the large oak table sitting near the kitchen windows and the balcony beyond. Next, she grabbed a glass of water and began to eat.

Roselyn, still with her arm in the black velvet jacket just stood there. Finally, she actually tried to slip her other arm in the dangling sleeve, and realized she could not have worn this jacket. It was too tight. She stood there in mild shock. Taylor had left, with a suitcase.

He said he was not returning. Was he really leaving her?! She couldn't comprehend this. He just couldn't leave? Could he? She glanced down. She was wearing a silk blouse and a dressy black skirt. She took off the clothes and carefully hung then up. Now she was wearing a half slip and panty hose. If she was staying home, some sweats would be more comfortable. She worked hard to have a well- organized closet and so it was easy to find some comfortable casual clothes. Once she had changed, she sat down on the bench at the end of the king-sized bed.

Suddenly, she realized the house was very quiet. Roselyn could hear her own breathing. She could feel her heartbeat. She tried to swallow and her throat felt hot and dry, as if she had been running a long distance. She walked out of the bedroom, and continued moving along the open staircase and stood at the top of the stairs. She couldn't seem to think. *What should she do now?* She started down the stairs, but was still wearing panty hose and no shoes. She slipped on the second stair and had to grab the railing to stay upright.

That act brought her back to reality. First, she needed some shoes or at least slippers. Returning to her closet, she grabbed some shoes and slipped them on. But why did he leave? She couldn't understand that. He had a beautiful home and a wife of twenty-six years and three great children; Two beautiful, smart daughters, and a son on a Church mission in Mexico. Good children, and each in their own way; successful; The younger girl, a senior in high school, a daughter in college and a son on a Christian mission.

Taylor's father was Jewish; thus, the last name Rosenbaum. So their marriage was somewhat unusual. Taylor had been brought up in a loose Jewish tradition. So courting and marrying an LDS (Mormon) girl was not a problem for him. His family would not give him trouble.

But for Roselyn her family was surprised that she would turn away from the traditional Mormon family life to marry a Jewish young man. Both Roselyn and Taylor had discussed their unusual situation. They decided that they would allow their children to choose a religion as they grew older.

Eric their son, had friends that were involved in the LDS religion. So as a teenager, he decided to follow that rather strict lifestyle. Taylor was okay with the boy's decision. When Eric decided to go on a mission, it had not been a problem for his father. But now Taylor had decided to leave his wife? So he was not only leaving Roselyn, but also the rest of the family. But why? What had he said? He mentioned a letter. Something about a letter? To understand this whole weird situation she found herself in, she'd better go find that letter.

She started down the stairs, reached the main level, and walked into the kitchen. Some of the food she had brought home had been put away, but there were still a few sacks to empty.

She glanced in the sack and found some foods needing to go in the freezer in the garage. Allison must have left them for Roselyn to put out in the garage. Roslyn quickly completed that chore and left out a pot pie to eat. She studied the uncooked pie but had no appetite. Rather she set her tea kettle on the stove and made a cup of tea.

While she put away the last of the food, she dropped a teabag in her cup. Soon the water was hot, and she could sit down with her tea. Instead, she took the tea and turned back upstairs to her 'work room'. She often wondered why Taylor referred to this room across from the master bedroom as her 'work room'? When they had this house designed and constructed, he had the architect design his office close to the front door. At times he would have a client come to the house to have a 'session'.

However, her room was designed to be upstairs close to the master bedroom. Taylor always referred to that room as a 'work room'? Perhaps, it was because her sewing machine that in there.

But where were her daughters?" She listened very quietly and could hear a TV on downstairs. Ellie's room was downstairs. The house was loaded with TV's. There was one in Ellie's room, one in the family room downstairs. One in the master bedroom, and one in Eric's room, which she had closed off since he was out of the country at this time.

For a moment she thought about her tall, handsome son. He had inherited his dark brown hair from his father, and a trim strong body. He had been gone nearly eighteen months and would be home early next summer. What would he think of his father leaving the family? Roselyn had to find out why Taylor had left. She would go into her 'work room' (Why couldn't it be called it her den or office?) Taylor insisted that his *office be* near the front door of the house. There was no argument about that. Sometimes he had a client or a business friend come to his office.

She supposed that she was fortunate to have her *office* close down the hall from the master bedroom. What did Taylor say? He had left her a letter in her *work room*. She'd better go find it.

Roselyn refreshed her tea and walked back upstairs. She sat down at her desk and noticed a fat envelope on the desk. She always liked sitting at her desk. It had been her grandmothers'.

When the woman had passed on at the age of eighty-two, it was amazing she had lived that long. She had been an immigrant from Sweden and come to Utah just after the turn of the 19th Century. She and a younger sister had come and soon after that the whole Swenson family followed her and younger sister. Nearly all the family came to become members of the new Latter-Day Saint Church. All but her father. It was ten years before he decided to join his wife. She had emigrated earlier with the youngest daughter. and had joined the first four daughters who had also come to Utah; To be members of new religion; the LDS Church.

She picked up the letter. For a moment she just held it in her hand. Somewhat afraid of what it might say. She opened it and spread it open on the top of her desk. It read:

Dear Roselyn,

This has been a very difficult letter to write, however I feel it is imperative it must be done. I must clarify my thoughts and want to communicate my feeling as well I can. I want you to know how

I feel about our situation; therefore, I must proceed.

For the past five years we have been drifting apart. I started when you came to me and told me that you wanted to return to college and pursue an advanced degree in clinical psychology, I was amazed you thought you actually had the time to this. However, the children were at an age where they no longer needed your constant attention. You would now have the time to return to this academic pastime.

I had no idea how involved you would become in your studies. I realize that advanced degrees require serious work, but the zeal with which you 'attacked' this project astonished me. There was much to admire, but as you went after your 'dream', your family suffered. And in a way you did too. The extra weight you have gained has detracted from your appearance. And I am sure it has caused health problems as well.

I'm sure you are proud of your accomplishments, and I have heard many positive comments about the wonderful work you are doing at the hospital. I'm sure you are helping many children that are suffering from certain trauma as well as Autism and Downe syndrome. However, our marriage has suffered, and I have suffered to a great extent.

I still have needs, and lately I am not numb to kindnesses from a cheerful, attentive, attractive woman at my office. She says she loves me, so I have become involved, and am greatly attracted to her. We enjoy each to a great degree. I am going to share a condo closer to my treatment offices with her and see if this relationship will grow and become more serious.

Therefore, I have filed for a legal separation and in 90 days will make the decision as to whether I will want to further this relationship. You and I have had 26 years together and three attractive, intelligent, loving children together. I am so proud of each one of them. I will continue to support them financially. At the present time, Eric on his mission of course, and also, I have college fund accounts started for all three of them. You are and will continually be secure with your position at the hospital.

I do wish you well.

Sincerely, Taylor

Roselyn quickly folded the letter into a sleek paper airplane. She had become very adept at this activity. When Eric was a child and became restless at Sunday sacrament meetings. When he no longer could sit still, she would take him into the rear of the building and they would make paper airplanes and sail them in the empty hallways. Now she sailed the airplane letter off the open stairway to the front entrance to the house. She did it a few times, up and down the stairs. But when she could no longer find it, she decided to go back upstairs and watch TV.

While she stood on the stairs, she heard a faint whining. *That has to be Maddie. Roselyn thought.* She knew Taylor hated Maddie, her little dog. *He's locked her up somewhere.* "Here Maddie." She called. The whining only got louder. Next, she heard a frantic bark. The sounds came from somewhere downstairs. Roselyn hurried downstairs to the basement level. "Where are you, Maddie?"

As Roselyn crossed the large family room, the barking got louder. First, she looked behind the open bar in the storage room. No dog. She crossed the room to the solarium. Rather than a just a deck off the lower level, they had decided to close it off enlarge it, and build stairs down to a pool. The area down to the swimming pool was partially enclosed. But an individual would have to walk through an exercise room to reach the pool. The barking became more frantic. There near the small closet in the exercise room was a dog kennel, and her frantic dog.

She opened up the kennel and her dog jumped out and nearly knocked her down. "Okay, okay, you're safe now. Do you need to go outside?" The little black and white dog bounded up the stairs to the front Foyer and stood there barking. Roselyn hurried up the curved stairway and opened the front door, and quickly flipped on the porch light. The little dog 'shot' outside, did her business, and took a run around the front lawn, as if to let everyone know that 'this' was her territory. Then she came back to the front door, and as Roselyn opened it, she said. "Okay, let's go find some dinner for you." They walked back to the kitchen and Roselyn opened the pantry and pulled out a bag of dog food and filled a bowl with a generous serving. She also picked up the dog's water bowl rinsed it out and filled it with cool, fresh water.

Chapter Three

As the dog ate, Roselyn surveyed the contents of the refrigerator. "Maybe, I can find some supper, too." After eating a section of a pot pie, she cleaned up the kitchen, scrubbed out the sink, and ran the dishwasher. She carried the remains of her beverage and went back to her work room; office. One special piece of furniture in there was a tall bookcase that Taylor had given her several years ago. As she thanked him for his 'Birthday gift' to her, he shrugged and said.

"Well, you are always buying or checking out certain books from the library. So you need to organize them. Start a collection. You are always going off to 'book meetings' and many times you purchase the books you are presently reading. Now you have somewhere to keep them."

She did find the bookcase useful, and she appreciated the gift. But did he have an ulterior motive? Keep her involved with her books, during this time he was freed up to find other 'amusements'. Forget getting into a new book, she eased over to her bedroom to watch TV.

She took the remains of her beverage upstairs, got comfortable and turned on the TV. Glancing at the clock she realized it was past 9 p.m. and one of the shows she liked would be on. She settled in to watch and after that program the 10 p.m. news would be on. What seemed like a few minutes later, Shanna came upstairs and stood in the doorway of the bedroom. "Hey Mom, a bunch of us decided to go skiing tomorrow."

"Who is going to drive, and which canyon are you going to go ski?" Roselyn asked. The digital clock read 11:40 p.m. "Did you just get home?" She asked her younger daughter.

"No, I've been on the phone. We managed to get Kathy's Dad's

Jeep. It will go up the canyon just fine."

"What time are you leaving?" The mother asked.

"About 9:30 a.m. Will you get me up at 8:30? I'll get up in time for some breakfast. If, you wouldn't mind cooking something for me?"

"Of course, I will. Now get to bed."

Roselyn went back to her bedroom and tried to watch TV. Nothing on the 'tube' would cut through the sudden sadness she felt. Not necessarily that Taylor had left her, really all of them, the whole family. But it was a sad depression she felt. She lay in her usual position and just felt so drained of her usual energy. She closed her eyes, and sometime later she heard the water run in the bathroom next to hers. She dragged her eyes open and glanced at the clock on her nightstand. 2:32 a.m.? What was going on in the hall bathroom Shanna used?

She got up and knocked on the door. "Shanna are you okay?" finally the door opened, and there stood her younger daughter with her long, now wet hair wrapped in a towel.

"Oh, Mom, I'm so sick. I threw up in my bed, and this yucky stuff got in my hair, un all over me."

She let her mother come in the bathroom and Roselyn could see a mess of wet towels, pajamas, and a wet bathmat on the floor. As the mother surveyed and then smelled the results of an upset stomach, fleetingly she was taken back to raising three little children with all the triumph and troubles they could have.

She wanted to ask what Shanna had eaten, but decided that was a worthless effort at this moment. "Okay, you go in and lie down in my bed, and I'll clean up yours." Roselyn grabbed a robe and some slippers, and began to strip the Shanna's bed. She walked into her den, found a large plastic bag in the closet and stuffed the soiled bed linens into it. She dropped the bag, went back into her bedroom and covered her daughter. She began her walk down the stairs to the main floor and then on down to the basement level and carrying the soiled linens heading for the laundry room. Once she had a load running, she went back upstairs and searched the linen closet for clean sheets and towels.

Making Shana's bed was easy compared to the chore of making up a king-sized bed. She had been doing that for 25 plus years. When she returned to the master bedroom, she found Shanna had fallen sleep. But her hair was still damp, so Roselyn wrapped it in a clean towel.

There was plenty of room for both females, so Roselyn slid over into Taylor's usual place. For a few moments it felt strange to sleep so close to the tall windows. However, she settled in the spot and closed her eyes.

The next thing she heard was the ringing of a phone, then a few minutes later the house phone. That was picked up, and for a fair slice of time it was quiet in the house. Somewhat later she felt a touch on her shoulder.

"Mom, what's going on? The clothes in the washer are clean so I put them in the dryer. I answered two phone calls for Shanna. Is she going skiing?"

Roselyn glanced over at her bedmate. "She had an upset stomach about 3 a.m. this morning. Hang on." The mother got out of bed, and grabbed a robe. She gazed at her older daughter. "She had a stomach episode around 3 a.m. So, I cleaned her up and let her sleep with me." Roselyn walked out of the bedroom and closed the door.

"Okay, now I understand why you were washing in the middle of the night. I put the rest of the sheets and towels in the washer, and also the wet ones in the dryer. One of her friends called about going skiing. I suppose that's not the plan for today." Ellie put her hands on her hips and tilted her head. "Okay. When someone calls for Shanna, I'll tell them she's indisposed."

"Thanks girl." Roselyn put her hand on her daughter's shoulder. "What's your plan for today?"

"I'm meeting a couple of friends at the library. We're preparing for an exam. Last time we studied together, it worked out pretty well. I'll call if we decide to eat 'on campus'." Ellie watched her mother nod. (*This has to be rough on her, having her husband walk out the way he did. Such a bastard!)*

Ellie went downstairs and got ready for the day. Her plans were to meet two friends to study for an exam on Monday. One of her courses was Political Progression, or the long version 'History of Political Development in the United States' So far this Semester the class hasn't seemed too one sided. It was a rather fascinating and some of the 'Founding Fathers were fun to study. What she realized was how important Christianity was back then was in the scheme of things. That was one of the major areas some more modern FDS scholars believed. Nowhere else could the American nation flourish, but here on the American Continent? It allowed more freedom of thought.

When she went upstairs, Shanna was still in her mother's room. Could she have Covid 19 or one of the variants? Well, they all had had their shots, and so far no one had become ill. The rumors floating around campus were that a few of the students had been vaccinated, and yet had developed a mild case of the virus. What she had studied in Chemistry was that virus's do behave that way, and every individual would react to the vaccine differently. As time went on it each individual had a slightly unique reaction to the disease, and the vaccine. Time would tell. Maybe her father would get covid? Naah, an individual had to be *human* to react to the virus.

At home, while Shanna slept, Roselyn showered and applied some light makeup. She did dress carefully, because she needed to return to the hospital. At least to check on two of the children she had worked with the day before. She would need to be at her office by 1 p.m. and put in at least a half–time day. She also hated to leave Shanna. But she went ahead and dressed for a work day.

Again, she checked on Shanna, but found her up and standing in her room. "How are you feeling?" She asked.

"Weak, but not as miserable as last night. Do you think I can have some tea and toast?"

"Sure. I'll go make you a cup of tea." As the girl sat in the kitchen picking at her toast, and still feeling shaky from her tender stomach, she watched her mother. "You have to go to work, don't you?"

"Yes, I have two patients I should check on. One is a Navaho boy from the reservation in the Southern part of the state. I need to make an evaluation of his behavior. But I won't leave until later. I made up your bed, so you can return to your room."

"Yeah, I was looking forward to a day on the 'slopes." Oh well, it's just past Thanksgiving. I have the whole winter to ski." The girl stirred her tea. I think I'll go back to bed."

Ellie sat down and watched her mother make breakfast. Finally, she stood up and walked down to check on her younger sister. Shanna was lying in bed, and seemed to be half–asleep. "Hey girl, do you want anything to eat this morning?"

Shanna yawned and rolled over. "Mom already fixed me some tea and toast. I guess in a little while later I could eat some cereal."

Ellie shrugged. "I'm going to make some French toast. I'll make you some too, and leave it for you. I'm meeting some people at the library, later. So I'm making breakfast now."

"What's Mom doing?" Is she going to the hospital?" Shanna asked.

"Yeah, I think she has a half-day planned. She usually has to leave by 12:30 p.m. So you'll be left alone. You okay with that?"

"I think so. I'm better than I was early this morning. Don't fuss about me, I feel like I'm over the stomach *thing.*" An hour or so later Shanna got up and stood gazing out the window. *Wow, it snowed a bunch. I'll bet four or five inches.* She turned and walked into her closet, and dragged out a sweat outfit and decided to get dressed. When she went into the kitchen, the coffee was perking, and her mother was making French toast.

She turned as her daughter brushed by to open the refrigerator. "Are you feeling better?" Roselyn asked." And while I have my head in here is there anything I can find for you?"

"No. Right now I'm going to have some of this." Shanna pulled a glass from the cupboard and filled it with ice, and in it she poured diet coke. She took her drink and sat down at the table and took a sip of her drink.

"Good. The coke will settle you're stomach and help replenish the fluid you have lost." Her mother said.

"Thank you, Doctor Rosenbaum." Shanna said and sat down. "Are you going to the hospital?"

"Yes, I have two possibly three patients I should check on. I have to leave by 12:30 p.m. Will you be okay here alone?"

"Yeah. I have some reading to do. And if I get sleepy, I'll just take a nap. Will you pick up something for dinner?" The young girl asked.

"I probably won't return home before 7 p.m. or so. What did you have in mind?" The mother asked.

"Chicken sandwiches. Something like that. There is plenty of salad makings in the fridge, I can do that." \

"Well, I did shop for the basic foods we usually eat in the evening. I don't think you'll starve. After you rest awhile, see if you can work on that book report, Okay? Oh, and can you find all your laundry you need done and carry your bag down to the laundry room downstairs?

"Okay Mom." Shanna put her dishes in the sink, and went back into the bathroom.

Roselyn sighed. *At least she seems better. Right now, I'd better get ready for work. I'm going to have to clean off the driveway to get my car out.* However, since she had already dressed in 'working' clothes and only needed to pull on snow boots and a warm coat.

Chapter Four

When she reached the garage, the doors were both up and Ellie was running the snow blower to clear off the driveway.

The snow removal people had already plowed their street, but left the ditch packed with extra snow. Now Ellie had to clear the bottom area where the snow plow people had blown the snow in a trough. Ellie glanced up as her mother came outside.

Wisely Roselyn had dressed to shovel snow, not necessarily to go to work at the hospital. But it was a Saturday, and dress codes got casual. Both mother and daughter needed to dig cars out so they could drive down the road and get to the freeway. *Well, Roselyn thought. Let's get to it.*

It didn't take too long, working together, for mother and daughter to clear the driveway. Both then had to return inside at least to grab some 'indoor' shoes for their Saturday afternoon activities.

Roselyn was pleased to reach the hospital only a few minutes late. And when she walked down the hallway to her office, she found the area rather quiet. Several offices had not yet been opened for the day.

She hung up her coat, and immediately went to her message box for the latest information on her patients. Since lunch was over, she checked to see how her adult burn patient was doing. The latest report concerned the burn scrub, and the notes from the tech and nurse were positive.

Roselyn also want to see how the boy's mother was doing. She pulled on her white coat, and went up to the adult burn unit to check on her. She found Mari Barlow awake. As she walked into her room, the young woman opened her eyes.

"Do I know you?" Mari asked. She carefully eased over and propped up on one elbow. A grimace flashed across her face.

"Oh, don't move because of me." I'm Dr. Rosenbaum, and a therapist working with your son."

"He's better this morning, had his morning scrub, and then came and ate something with me. As far as I'm concerned, I'm not as bad as I was either. My smoke damage situation is getting better. And I'm breathing better, but I'll still on oxygen." She touched her nose.

"Extra oxygen is pretty common therapy. Everybody with covid symptoms are on oxygen therapy. "You'll probably go home with oxygen."

"The idea of going home hasn't jelled in my head yet."

"Don't worry about it. Just rest and think positive thoughts." Roselyn smiled. "Well, I have patients to see, and I'd better start my work. It's very good to see you awake and feeling better. I'll come around later to check on you."

Roselyn stood, straightened her jacket and walked back down stairs. Now for a visit to Benjamin. Again as the day before, he was curled up in the corner of the small room. This time he glanced up. And for a tiny moment a glance of recognition flitted across his face.

Dr. Rosenbaum walked in, pick up a chair and placed it near him, and sat down. "Good afternoon. How are you feeling this afternoon? Have you had any lunch or could you use a snack?" She waited for any reaction from the boy. She noticed a flicker, a tiny movement, and finally he eased slightly closer. "Good, you wait here, and I'll go find a snack that we can share."

She got up and walked to the door, and quietly left the room. Roselyn had arranged for a tray of healthy snacks. Small chicken sandwiches, a bowl of popcorn, an orange and an apple both arranged on a plate in slices. She also brought in two bottles of water.

The boy finally came close enough to see what lay on the food tray. For a long time, he seemed to study the contents of the tray. Finally, he picked up a kernel of the popcorn, sniffed it and then put it in his mouth. Chewed and swallowed, then reach for another one.

As Roselyn watched Benjamin eat popcorn, one kernel at the time, she finally allowed herself to think about the messy situation at her house. The upsetting situation Taylor had caused by leaving his wife, two daughters and a son, though he was thousands of miles away.

She suddenly thought about Eric. What would he think, how would he take to the idea of his father walking out on the family? What had he really done by leaving three children, and a wife for a much younger woman? For a moment Roselyn was mentally lost, not comprehending how her husband of 25 years could really turn his back on his family. She supposed that her religious background and strict upbringing had not prepared her for modern marital behavior. Oh, she had friends that had divorced. But that was a deviation to the rule, not by any means common.

Suddenly Benjamin came to her with a toy; A little cat with gray and white 'fur. He shoved it into her hands and glanced at her. "Kitty." He said.

Her attention focused on this little boy. "Yes, a kitty, Benjamin. Do you like kitties? Here, do you want to hold this kitty?" She offered it to him.

For a long moment he stared at the toy on her lap. Then he took it and held it close to his face. For a few minutes he walked around the room hanging on to the soft toy. Then he dropped it on the floor and stomped on it. "Dead!" He said. Then he returned to the corner and curled up on the floor.

Even though she had worked with other disturbed children, at that moment she felt shock. What had this child seen? Lived with? Had he been witness to, or subject to other shocks, sadness. Many children live with tragedy, cruelty, but because some had kind adults in their lives they do not suffer endlessly. Yet other children, like Benjamin are born more vulnerable. Especially like Benjamin suffering brain trauma.

Soon though, Roselyn had another child to meet, to learn of his or her particular trauma. And so on went her afternoon. It was after 7 p.m. when she could leave. Luckily it was a Saturday, and the traffic though busy was lighter. As she reached her house, she could see the garage door open and Taylor's car was parked in her normal spot. At that instant she was really angry.

For a long moment she thought of parking right behind him. Then sitting in her car, she knew she would have to come out and move it when *he* was ready to leave. So she parked half a foot from the end of his Mercedes and angled the car to be in front of the house.

When she walked into the house, she noticed that Shanna was standing in the living room talking to some strange girl sitting in the living room. She walked closer to get a good look at this strange girl. As Roselyn moved closer, she could see two things. This female was several years older than Shanna, and she looked familiar.

Roselyn walked into the living room and spoke. "Introduce me to your friend, Shanna."

Shanna reacted as if startled. "Oh Mom. You should remember Marlene Jenkins, Dad's receptionist." Shanna glanced at her mother, as if to say: *This is Dad's new little flame.*

Marlene suddenly looked down at the thick taupe carpet. Roselyn could easily see and almost feel the girl's embarrassment. The color rose in her cheeks above, her heavily applied pink rouge, and heavy mascara she had generously to her eye lashes.

Roselyn's first reaction was*; Honestly, Taylor, you can do better than this poor girl.* "Hello Marlene, you go ahead and chat with Shanna. I need to address a situation right now. Excuse me."

Roselyn strode upstairs, nearly breaking land speed records to get to the master bedroom. She stopped at the doorway and stood watching Taylor taking clothes from his closet. "Will you be able to get *all* your clothes into the apartment closet where you are now living? Oh, and don't forget your skis."

"Don't worry Roz, I'll soon return for the rest of my things in a day or two. Taylor's voice rose in slight irritation. Then more pleasantly he said. "Do you have any coffee? I've had a rough day. I sure could use some."

For a moment she just stared at him, but then shook her head. "Coffee, coming right up." She eased back down to the kitchen and began the coffee ritual. Then she checked the refrigerator. *What do you know? There is the remains of a coffee cake.* She pulled it out and some small plates from the cupboard. She set creamer, sugar, spoons, and napkins on the kitchen table. Next, she closed the shutters on the bay window. *I suppose the table is ready for Taylor and his latest 'squeeze'.* Roselyn walked out into the hallway and called. "Taylor, coffee's ready." Walking back into the kitchen she cut the remaining coffee cake into small servings and warmed it on a serving plate. After setting the food on the kitchen table, she searched the fridge for the remains of last nights' salad. Then she made a plate of salad with dressing and some croutons and sat down to eat it.

Below, the front door opened and Ellie came in. She slammed the front door closed, because of a fierce gust of wind.

Hearing the front door slam, Roselyn went out onto the walkway. She could see Ellie hang up her coat and wool scarf on the front hall coat tree. "Did you say there was a stiff wind blowing out there?"

Ellie, hands on hips gazed up at her mother. "Just a small tornado churning out there. When I exited the freeway, it was breezy, but not like we're in for a 'wind event'. And then I see Dad's car in your parking place." The girl started up to the kitchen. "Your car, I believe is okay. Because you parked tight, near the curb." Just then they both heard and felt the wind rattle the windows." The girl walked up to the kitchen level. "I don't know, about this wind. Maybe you'd better park in the third garage behind Eric's car."

"I'm not sure it will fit and allow the garage door to close." Ellie came in and poured a mug of coffee. She took a sip, and then another. "Give me your keys. I'll go check to see if I can move Eric's car half a foot closer into the garage."

"Okay." Roselyn walked into her office and grabbed her car keys from her purse. "Here. Be careful."

Ellie ran downstairs pulled, on and zipped up her parka. Sets of keys went in both pockets. She went down to the third garage, and started Eric's car. She estimated she had about a foot more space between Eric's car and the back wall. She climbed into Eric's car and let it run for a minute or two. Next, she stood in the opened garage and waited for a slowdown of the wind. Then she eased Eric's car forward. Next, she ran out and opened her mother's car and slid into the driver's seat. The wind buffeted the car, but then there was a tiny break in the wind's force. She backed out the car, and pulled into the garage way behind her brother's Toyota. Dropping it into low gear she inched the car into the garage. When she could almost hear the two automobiles inches from each other, she stopped. She carefully slid out and not walked, but fought her way to the two almost touching autos. Hanging on her mom's car, Ellie checked the line on the floor where the garage door would come down. There were only inches to spare.

Ellie walked around her, and then her father's car to the inside wall where the garage door controls were located. As she pushed the 'close door' mechanism she closed her eyes and said a little prayer. She heard the door close, but no other offending sound.

It worked! The two cars fit in together! Luckily, her car and her father's sports car fit into the garage with a foot or so left at the end of each, or she would be trapped in the third garage all night. All of a sudden, she was hungry, and the large freezer stood there full of dinners and pies to bake. Searching the nearly full cold box she chose a Chinese style frozen meal and carried it into the house. Whatever the rest of them chose to eat, she would eat this 'TV' supper.

Chapter Five

Ellie returned to the kitchen and it had suddenly become crowded in there. Sitting around the table were her father, his 'friend' Marlene and Shanna. Her mother stood by the coffeemaker and watched it brew another potful. She stared at everyone in the kitchen and said. "The first cup is going to be mine." She glanced at the Asian TV dinner Ellie had placed in the microwave. "Did you find that in the garage freezer?"

"I brought it in. I think there may be another one." The microwave beeped, and Ellie got up grabbed a plate from the dish cupboard and set her dinner on it.

"Okay. I'll go take a look." Roselyn went back out into the garage and soon returned with a TV dinner. She set it on the counter and read the directions. "Okay." she said almost to herself. She did as the box suggested. She set the dinner in the microwave and punched in the suggested cooking time. "I think I'll start with some tea rather than more coffee.." She began to heat water for a mug of tea. She glanced over at the kitchen table and realized that all the close chairs were taken up with her two daughters, Taylor and his 'for now' girlfriend.

"Hang on Mom." Shanna said. "I'll slide around closer to the windows and give you my chair." Shanna stood, put her hands on her hips and glared at her father and his girlfriend.

Taylor watched Shanna and then cleared his throat. "Marlene, are you finished with your coffee and cake? I believe it's time to leave."

The girl looked up with obvious discomfort. "Oh, you're right. We'd better go." Just at that second the wind gusted and Marlene was forced to put her hands on the table for balance and tipped over her nug with the remains of coffee. The brew splashed onto the placemat. Part of a set Ellie had put around the table. Immediately, the girl jumped up and stood against the wall with a look of almost terror on her face.

Roselyn's first thought was to go over and clean up the table, but she held back and let others at the table deal with the mishap. Ellie, who was sitting at the other end of the table, slowly stood, slid out and went to sink, ran water on the dish cloth, and then retrieved the tipped over mug, plate and placemat. "Set them in the sink." Roselyn said. She ran warm water on the dish cloth and handed it to Ellie.

By that time everyone was up, and had moved away from the table, Ellie noticed a coffee stain on Marlene's sweater. "Here." Ellie took Marlene's arm. "There's a bathroom on the lower level. I'll show you where it is."

Roselyn watched as Taylor stood and took his place setting, and placemat to the counter by the sink. "I think we really need to leave." Just then the house felt another buffeting of wind, and momentarily the power went off, but then a second or two later flashed back on. Below, in the lower-level bathroom a squeal was heard, and then Ellie said loudly. "It's just a power surge. See, it comes right back on."

At that exact time of the power outage, Taylor stood with an iron grip on the stair railing. Almost immediately, he called out. "Come on Marlene, let's go!" He stood on the stairs and watched Marlene and Ellie come out of the basement bathroom.

"I need my purse and coat." Marlene called up. "Please Taylor." Both young women then started back up to the main floor.

Taylor with coat in hand whirled around Marlene and wrapped her in the coat. Then he glanced up at Roselyn. "I'll return tomorrow or Monday for more of my belongings. Good evening, everyone." When he gazed outside and could not see his car, then he remembered he had driven into the garage. He hustled Marlene out into the garage and didn't bother helping her into the front passenger seat. As he backed out the wind, again buffeted his car. He sat frowning as he gained control of his Mercedes. Slowly he drove down the street.

Ellie who had watched her father drive away wondered how he now felt about this young woman he had brought into his life. Ellie was angry with her father, but not surprised. By marrying her mother, he had taken on a lifestyle that was a poor fit for how he really wanted to live. She had to admit that at the age of fifty-four, he was still lean and handsome. Attractive and attracted attention of many women. For years he had been, for the most part well-spoken. However, trying to fit even partially into LDS family and its strict lifestyle was a real stretch for him. She knew that he was proud of her brother Eric. Even though now he was spending two years on a Christian church mission. Her father was proud of his son's sacrifice, but probably didn't understand why the young man chose to volunteer to leave home to introduce strangers to this 'new American religion'.

Perhaps, if the opportunity came up, she would sit down with her father and try to explain why Eric had temporarily left college, sports, and girls to preach this rather peculiar religion. She supposed that if she really understood the Jewish religion, she would know why her father clung to the 'old ways'.

The wind eased and the house quieted down. Roselyn finished cleaning up the kitchen, and went to her 'work room' and started reading some files of her patients. But after half an hour she gave up and went to the master bedroom, and began pulling clothes from her closet. She tried on two outfits. The first a camel-colored straight knit dress and a brown wool jacket. The dress was large enough, but showed her weight gain, and did nothing to hide the extra pounds she had gained over the summer and fall. The jacket would have to remain unbuttoned, because it was 'snug' to say the least.

As she stood in front of the mirrored closet door, the extra pounds she had gained over the last few years could not be hidden. She blinked in dismay. How had this happened?! Tears came in her eyes. What had she been wearing during the Summer and Fall, what clothes? Then she began going through her closet. Full skirts, easy fit slacks, overblouses A-line skirts, and of course up until a month ago, sandals.

Now the weather called for jackets, corduroy or denim pants, boots, sweaters. Luckily, she had several cardigans, but most of her knit shirts were tight. Face it Roselyn. You've snacked you way out of your clothes? *No wonder Taylor complained. He's still a bastard for leaving her, but now she could see what he had been viewing for many months. What are you going to do about your overindulgence? Roz?*

Well, it's too late for an exercise session now. She sat down on the bed and pulled up the quilt. Minutes later she heard a knock at the door.

Then she heard. "Mom, are you going to wash my clothes I took downstairs?" The rather timid voice was Shanna.

Roselyn slid off the bed and opened the door. "Do you need some of your clothes washed for tomorrow?"

"Yeah, I need my black skirt, and vest washed. I can wear that white shirt we bought in Mexico last summer, you know, tomorrow, when we go to church."

"Sure, we can go wash your things right now. Are you sure you feel well enough to spend two hours in church?"

"I think I'm okay. So far what I ate tonight has stayed down."

"All right, let's go wash." Mother and daughter went down two flights of stairs to the laundry room and Roselyn started sorting Shanna's clothes. As she made two stacks, she mentioned why she did so. "Just to be safe, we don't' mix dark clothes with light colored items." Roselyn started to sort the bag of clothes. And now there were two piles of laundry on the floor, Roselyn picked up and put one pile in the washer. "Now we want to set the wash temperature pour the detergent in the washer." She demonstrated that move. "Now water temperature should be warm for this batch." She took Shanna's hand and moved it to the 'warm' setting. "Okay, now we let the washer do its job."

Shanna looked over at her mother. "That's pretty simple."

"Most of the time it is, and there are many things in a household that can be put in a washer. Knowing how to use the correct settings, - - - she touched the dials on the washer- - - - are very important. We'll come back when you need to dry the clothes."

"Mom why haven't you showed me how to do this before now?"

Roselyn was silent for a long moment. "Perhaps it is because all of these daily chores mothers do for their families identifies them as a mother. We feel that mothers must do those services for their children and husband to be worthy of the name 'mother'. When you think about it, it's rather ridiculous. We, I suppose, view ourselves as some kind of necessary individual in the family. And the more we are depended on, the more we see ourselves as a necessity, and part of the family. Strange definition for a mother, isn't it?"

Shanna stared at her mother. "From what I've heard about young people now getting married, it seems to be a more cooperative deal. She does what she needs to do, and he either helps her with tasks of some regular chores. Whichever one is better to handle the situation that needs to be handled. Like guys are better with cars than girls. As far as cell phones are concerned, she has hers and he has his."

"Oh, I get that since now most kids get a cell phone when they're about twelve." Shanna said. "We have to learn to use them. It's kind of like Algebra."

"All I can say is: Hurray for girls." Roselyn said. "As I look back on Taylor and my relationship, it was veery traditional. As least in today's definition of marital relationships. However, we each came from very different households, even though he was brought up in a traditional Jewish family and I had come from a normal Mormon family. At least I viewed it as such. When I was a teenager, I assumed that if a whole family came to church together every week, the people were all normal Mormons. I found that you should not assume that.

When your father and I moved into this house, and I began attending Sunday meetings and taking my children, I felt this 'ward' was full of normal LDS people. The more I began to 'work' and make friends with many of the women, I realized each family was different from every other. It made getting to know each woman more fun.

Since that time the LDS church has changed. They have shortened the time spent in Sunday meetings, and no longer have an active youth program, as they once did. I'm afraid the pandemic has really changed or cancelled the many youth programs that they once had. There is more pressure to teach the basic church tenets in the home. Well, enough of this. I'll let you come down here and check your clothes in the washer and put them in the dryer."

Chapter Six

Roselyn retreated to her den and tried to read a professional magazine. After two pages of an article, she realized that for the last five minutes or so, she had been sitting in front of her computer with her eyes closed. She stood up, went into the bathroom, brushed her teeth, and cleaned the makeup off her face. It was time to try for some sleep. She turned on the Ten o'clock news and much of the reporting informed the public of the high winds, and the damage they caused in certain areas of the Wasatch Front.

A few minutes later she struggled away from the comforts of her bed and checked on Shanna. The teenager was asleep. Next, she went downstairs and found Ellie on her cell phone with the TV on, laughing and chatting. Roselyn told her to go to bed. Still talking, the girl nodded and mouthed *okay,* Roselyn shrugged and went back upstairs, closed the shutters on the kitchen window, turned off the lights and returned to her bed.

She was surprised when the next thing she knew it was nearly 5 a.m. After a trip to the bathroom, she returned to bed. Gazing at her clock, she mentally decided she must awake at 8 a.m. And she did.

The next morning when the three females from the Rosenbaum family arrived at church no one asked any questions, other than how Eric was doing on his mission. Roselyn was on the church music council, and they had a short meeting after the morning services.

Ellie had driven the three of them to the ward building. So her mother sought her out and told her to take Shanna and go home. She, (Roselyn) would get a ride from one of the other women on the music committee. Sometime later, when Roselyn came home and walked into the kitchen, she could smell something mouth-watering.

"What did you find to eat?" Roselyn asked as she walked into the kitchen. She watched Ellie take a large pizza from the oven. "You bought a pizza?'

Apron clad Ellie stepped back. "We decided that we would have a larger meal in the early afternoon. It's because neither of us had much breakfast. So we went down to the City Crest Pizza place and bought one ready to bake. You had already made a salad for dinner last night, and there was lots of it left. So we are having a midday meal." She grinned.

"Well, I certainly will not argue with this situation. I'll go wash my hands."

While they were eating, Shanna spoke up. "If Dad wants to live with a young 'dumb' girl like Marlene, all I can say is 'whatever'. He's the 'loser' in this family not you."

Roselyn smiled at her daughter, kids nowadays seemed to be much more involved than she was at Shanna's age. But now Roselyn had paper work to do before she returned to the hospital on Monday. She decided to get on with it. A while later the phone rang, and since she was sitting next to it she answered. "Hello?"

"Good afternoon, am I speaking to Roselyn? This is Elaine Barstow."

"Oh, hi Elaine what's up.? Sorry, I sound like one of my daughters."

"That's okay. What I wondered is that in the musical Christmas story we chose to present on the Sunday before Christmas, there is a short Soprano or it can be an Alto solo in the musical story. It seems that in the narrative there is a woman on the hillside with some of the shepherds. She's one of the shepherd's wives I suppose, and she brought her goat. She goes down with the shepherds to worship the new little baby Jesus. The song tells of first being a new mother., Then the last verse mentions the birth of this special babe. And how special this new young mother is to have been chosen to be Christ's mother. It's just three short verses. But with more emphasis on women's roles in Christian churches, I thought we would add this little song."

"You want me to do this little solo? I haven't sung solo for many years."

"I've heard you sing before. You have a great alto voice. No one else has as strong a voice in that musical range than you do. I'll tell you what. If I bring the music over, will you take a look at it?"

Elaine couldn't see Roselyn frown. She wasn't frowning about being asked to sing. It was standing up in front of the whole large congregation being as fat as she was. She took a deep breath. "Okay, bring it over, and I'll take a look at it."

"Great I'll bring it over after I have some lunch. "

Roselyn went back to her paperwork. But she couldn't stop being somewhat upset at being asked to sing, and yet rather pleased about the whole situation, too. About an hour later, the phone rang and this time Ellie answered it.

Several minutes later Ellie came carrying the basement phone. She stood at the top of the stairs and yelled, "Mom, Eric wants to talk to you."

Roselyn came from her den onto the stairway with phone it hand. "Hi Eric, how's life in the South of the Border, mission field?"

"We're all doing pretty good. "I have two items I want to discuss. First L want to know the 'skinny' on why Dad walked out?"

"Now, since Ellie told you the 'news of the day' around here, do I have to editorialize it.?" His mother asked.

"Yeah. But I'm not surprised. And I'll tell you why. I was down town maybe two weeks before I left to come here, and saw his car parked near an overpriced down town bistro. I was with my friend Stratton, and we parked and wandered in. Nobody stopped us for I.D. Anyway, there he was in a back booth with some young 'honey'. Very cozy. I was ready to march back there and ask if he was now having psychiatric 'session' in this night club. I was really steamed."

Roselyn took a ragged breath then asked. "So what did you do?"

"Strat and I marched back there and stared down at him. Then I said. "When we saw you in here wondered if you would buy my friend and me a drink?"

Dad stayed cool and said we were too young unless we would settle for a couple of cokes.

I said. "No thanks Dad. with an emphasis on the word 'dad'. And then I said, 'catch you later'. And we left."

"When did this happen?" Roselyn asked, hardly able to breathe.

"I've been out here 19 months. It was maybe a month before I left."

"So what you are telling me is that he's been seeing other women for some time." Roselyn choked out.

"Yeah, something like that. I'm having a rough time figuring out why he's behaving this way. So the reason why I called is that Stratton's father is a divorce lawyer. He said you should know him, from when you and his dad were in college."

"Who is his father?" Roselyn asked.

"Come on Mom, Luke Landre. Didn't you guys sing together? Stratton told me that you and his dad and two other guys were in a band together."

For a moment Roselyn thought back to her college days. Why hadn't she connected Stratton Landre with Luke Landre? At least the name? She cleared her throat. "What's Stratton's father doing now?"

"He's an attorney. He's in a practice with David Casper. You should call him. I'll call Stratton, and ask him what his father is doing now. Anyway, I've a meeting with some people in the ward we're now assigned to. I'll call you later in the week. Take care of my crazy sisters. See ya soon. Good bye."

Roselyn sat there in slight shock. Finally, she set the phone down. Luke Landrey!? She hadn't thought about him for ages. She sat back in her chair and tried to remember the last time she had seen Luke. That's right, he came to the wedding when she had married Taylor. She heard a couple of years later that he had married a girl named Caroline. Roselyn had thought about him from time to time for the first years after she had married Taylor. Back when she first knew him, she thought he was really a just a quiet guy, but really talented musically. They would hang out at the Union Building in a quiet room and sometimes sing together. Then one winter night a couple of her friends called and asked she would like to go down town to a bar and hear Luke and a friend play and sing. They were hired to entertain that evening for a short time. They were going to sing and play guitar and piano.

The night turned out to be 'wicked' weather wise. At the time, Roselyn was driving a small Ford Pinto. Never the less, she managed to pick up two friends and make it to the bar without crashing or getting stuck. The three of them sneaked in and found a table. After buying expensive cokes and popcorn, the three of them just sat and waited. A few minutes later Luke and Travis took to the stage.

After not much interest from the few customers in the place, it seemed they were going give up and quit. Roselyn stood up and yelled. "Sing *Life in the Fast Lane."* He had sung that song many times, and a few times she had sung it with him.

He stood up put his hand over his eyes to shade them and gazed around. "Is that you out there, Roz?" Come on up, let's do it together." Jeff Squies started playing a couple of riffs of the song.

Sheri pushed on Roselyn. "Get up there!" She said in a loud voice.

"Jeri said. "She's over here." She stood and pointed at Roz.

Roselyn stood up and in her snow boots, stomped up to the stage. "Okay." She said to Jeff. "Give us an intro." And he did.

Luke started out with the first line of lyrics, and up picked the next line on his guitar. Then Luke sang the next line of the melody. Roselyn had to sing the next line and he backed that line up on guitar. Jeff played an interlude and next they sang the next line together. Then Luke sang another line. Jeff stood up, yelled to the audience and said. "Sing it with us." It turned out to be rousing and really fun. For a few minutes it seemed everyone in the bar had forgotten about the snowstorm outside and were enjoying themselves.

Luke launched into another old song that he knew, and he knew Roselyn had also sung it with him. Also, after that they had used up their allotted time. Someone put money in the Jute Box and a few people got up to dance.

The two guys joined the three girls, and soon the waitress brought over a big bowl of popcorn and more cokes. "How did you know we'd be down here?" Luke asked.

"One of your old buddies called me to tell me you guys were singing down here tonight. So.. the three of us thought we'd check out the 'word'." Roselyn said.

"Okay, so next time we'll include you guys. But I think we need to rehearse before we try extemp- - - - again. We were lucky Jeff remembered the song, in the right key."

A few minutes later Sheri glanced at her watch. "Hey guys, it's close to midnight. We don't want parents calling the police thinking we're stuck in the snow."

"Yes ladies and gentlemen' it's time to 'flee the scene'." Marcie said.

Reluctantly, the girls got up. "Better get on the road." The three females stood, and slowly walked to the door. Once the girls returned to their homes is was well past midnight, and they were not greeted by worried, or upset parents.

When Jeff arrived home, his younger brother had sneaked up and unlocked the kitchen door for him. Jeff managed to get downstairs and ready for bed without waking parents.

When Luke parked his car in the snow clogged driveway, he managed to come into the house through the kitchen. The house was quiet, because his father had an all-night shift at the power company, and his mother was lying on the sofa 'dead drunk'. He found a quilt to cover her.

Chapter Seven

On Monday morning Roselyn returned to the hospital and found that her young burn patient and his mother had been released from the hospital. The maternal grandmother had moved into the household, and would remain there until the mother was released from the bi-weekly appointments. However, she had another request to come to the maternity ward.

After a gulp or two of her coffee, she called and asked for a Dr. Willowby. A nurse answered the phone.

"This is Doctor R. Rosenbaum. I have a request on my desk to visit with a Dr. Willowby."

"Oh yes, Dr. Rosenbaum, Dr. Willowby wanted a consultation about a maternity patient, who had just given birth. Let me see if she is on the floor, or in a delivery room."

Roselyn heard the soft chatter of maternity wing. Then "Oh, here she is. Dr. Willowby, Dr. Rosenbaum is on the phone."

"Yes, Roselyn said. "You left a request for me to check on one of your patients?"

"You are a clinical psychologist? I have one of my patients that is either delusional or lying. Could you come down her and talk to her."

"I'm not busy right now. Are you able to explain to me your request?"

"I have one patient in labor, but she has an hour or two left before delivery. Now would be good."

"Okay. I'll be down very soon." Roselyn told the desk nurse where she was headed and to buzz her if necessary. Once on the maternity floor, she had Dr. Willowby buzzed. A few minutes later a trim young woman walked up to the desk.

"I'm Dr. Willowby." She gazed at Roselyn. "And you must be Dr. Rosenbaum."

Willowby put out her hand for Roselyn to shake. "I'm glad we have someone with your skills to help me with this dilemma."

"Okay explain to me the situation." Roselyn said. "Let's go sit in the lounge."

"Okay. I delivered a young teenage girl early this morning. She has no husband, and of course there is a boyfriend in the mix, plus her parents, and the boy's family. However, the supposed father of this child is Caucasian. The baby I delivered at 4:40 a.m this morning shows mixed race, probably black or officially negroid."

"She is now protesting loudly that we mixed up her supposed infant with another. That can't happen, or at least I made sure it didn't happen, because the second an infant comes out of the mother, he or she receives a wrist band, matching the one on the newly delivered mother plus the attending nurse is right there in the delivery room."

"Oh Boy!" Roselyn said. "How old is this girl?

"She's 17, and will be 18 in January."

For a brief moment, Roz thought of her 17-year-old daughter. "Have you told her there couldn't be a mix up?"

"Yes. But her parents will be up here to see her and the infant early this evening."

"Okay, let me talk to her. But first I want to see the baby. What was it? Girl of boy?" Roselyn said.

"A little girl. 6 pounds 13 ounces. And I think she's really cute." Dr. Willowby said.

"So, what course of action do you want me to take?" Roselyn asked. "By the way, I'm Roselyn Rosenbaum, and you're- - - - -?"

"Janet R. Willowby. I'm married to a Jefferson Willowby. Really an old-fashioned name, when you think about it."

"Very American." Roselyn said and grinned. I think, I'll go about speaking to this young girl from a scientific angle. What's her name again?"

Dr. Willowby picked up a chart. "Cynthia Chartruss." And she rattled off the girl's address.

"Hmm, that name sounds familiar. I should check on that." Roselyn said. "I believe I'll go see miss Cynthia right now." Roselyn walked into room No. 357, and found the girl half-asleep. She walked over pull up the blanket to cover her. The girl moved and opened her eyes.

"Who are you?' she said. What do you want?"

Are we going to have a little hostility now? "My name is Dr. Rosenbaum I came to speak with you about the baby girl born to you this morning." Rosen gazed down at this very young girl.

"They brought me the wrong baby. That little baby was black. She's not mine They got her mixed up." She frowned, pulled herself up to sit in a sitting position.

"Well, in all hospitals in this area, the protocol is to give the newborn a taped bracelet matching the mother's immediately. So it's very rare that babies get as you say, 'mixed up'." Roselyn lifted the girl's arm a touched the bracelet.

"You don't understand I can't have a black child! She fairly screamed. It's bad enough that I was pregnant in the first place."

"Nevertheless, in this hospital procedure has to be correct. So if you continue to protest that female infant is not yours, we must make sure that there truly has been a mix up, and we'll do it with DNA test. I'm sure you're familiar those tests."

"What if I don't want one." Cynthia scowled and folded her arms across her chest.

"As long as you are in this hospital, we have to follow the laws of the state of Utah. We have to make sure each infant either goes home with his or her mother, or is open for adoption. And believe me a healthy newborn will be adopted quickly. Did you have another young man in mind to be your baby's father?"

Cynthia settled down in the bed, grumbling as she did. "You'd really do a DNA test?"

"It's very important especially for an adopting couple to know the health of the newborn they would be lucky enough to adopt. Of course, since you are not an adult, and since you have parents, they will have to help you make these legally adult decisions. I'm sure DNA testing will be necessary."

Cynthia put the heel of her hand on her forehead. "*I was dumb enough to go to that party, and this is what got myself into". She mumbled.* "Oh, Ms. I mean Dr. Rosenbaum; my parents will be up here this afternoon. Will you still be here then? It's because they think that this pregnancy is because I had sex with Dillan Ross. I've had a few dates with him. I guess he's lucky 'cause he's 'off the hook' now."

"If they come in before 5 p.m. I should still be in the building. Just have the nurse call me. However, just to be safe, I'm ordering the DNA test. We need to understand that this Dilan individual is not the father of this infant. You suggested him? Perhaps I should be here when your parents come. Just to help everyone understand the situation you've now found yourself in."

Roselyn found Dr. Willowby in the break room and sat down next to her. "Hi I spoke with Cynthia, and ordered a DNA test for mother and baby. I explained the situation about adopting out her newborn. But since she is a minor it's up to her parents. She's less than ready to assume the responsibility for another human being than many adolescents that I have worked with. I suggested adoption, and she didn't react negatively."

"Thank you. I really hit the 'panic' button when she started yelling about mixed up infants."

"From talking to her, what I learned is that this pregnancy was the result of a party she and at least one other girl attended. The young man she most likely had sex with was of course mixed race. The result; a nearly seven-pound infant. She hinted there is another teen-age boy in the situation."

"So you plan to hang around? Thank you, Roselyn I have one child; a boy who is seven years old and is tended by my mother. The idea of having a teenager gives me thoughts of escaping to Canada."

"I believe Canadians 'do it' too." Roselyn laughed. "If you need me, I'll be in my office. She went back down to her office to catch up on some paper work. It was soon lunchtime and since she again did not eat much in the way of breakfast, and she was hungry.

After lunch Roselyn was called into a room of an older woman who had fallen off her front porch stairs. She had twisted and fallen sideways and broken her hip and also had a serious concussion. The hip surgery had been done two days ago. But the concussion had caused her to sink into a coma.

The attending physician met the woman's son and his wife in the patients' room. The doctor was young and what they called a talented 'bone' man. The couple were local people with two young children. Both of them worked full time, and did not have the room nor the ability to take care of this 78-year-old woman in their home. She however, lived in an older house close by her son's place.

Roselyn was called in to help the couple, and to suggest an alternative. She knew that she would be assigned to help them, so she looked up alternatives to care for this woman who probably would not recover much of her former physical or mental health. The big if was; would she recover much at all.

Roselyn had dealt with before with a situation like this before. The best alternative would be a 'day care' individual. Most likely it would be a middle-aged woman who had some training in daily care of an individual in a semi-conscious, and possibly later a bed-ridden state. It was much cheaper than a private care center. And the son of this woman and his wife could not afford that kind of complete, in-house care for this woman However social security could help. Roselyn met them in the mother's hospital room.

"This is Mr. and Mrs. Rodreiges. And the patient was the young man's mother, and she had been the care provider for this couple's two children. Both the children, Amilea, age seven and George age ten. They are in school now, but their school will be out for Christmas vacation for ten days." The young man said.

Roselyn shook the young man's hand. "It's good to meet you both. I'm afraid that your mother is very ill. And at the present time will need daily care of her own."

The young woman picked up the patients' hand. "She has been such a good sitter for us. We already found an afternoon care for the children while they are in school. But during the Christmas vacation, we'll have to check to see that the school may have daycare during the Holidays."

"Now we must find some care for you mother." Roselyn said. A senior living place will be too expensive. The best alternative is find a woman who will come in and stay with your mother, fix meals for her and keep her clean and comfortable."

The young woman sniffed and wiped her eyes. "It's so sad to see her like this. Possibly now we must find a baby sitter for the children during the Christmas Holidays, and someone who will take care of 'Mama Angie', too?"

I understand. Let's go down stairs into my office. I do have lists of women who might care for your mother. As far and Christmas vacation, do you know of a woman or a teenage girl who would possibly tend your children while you both work during the Christmas Holidays?"

The young mother turned to her husband. "What about the Cabrollas girl? She's in high school. She would probably like to earn some money?"

"That's a possibility." The young husband said. "Now we have to find someone for Mama." His face dropped into a sad frown.

"That is why I asked you two to come down here in my office." Roselyn went to her filing cabinet, and took out two thick files. "In these files are lists of women who do 'adult day care'. Look through them and first look for women who live close to you and knows your neighborhood. Also read about them, what they charge and why they chose to do this work. For example, some will not tend a man. Also special security, since your mother was retired and had worked for over 20 years, possibly will pay for a care giver for her."

The young couple left a few minutes later with a list of names, some fairly close to where the mother lived.

As Roselyn went on with her day yet at this moment, Taylor had just had a patient in his office who was a veteran, and suffering permanent mental damage caused by fighting in combat in Iraq. This was about the time that Taylor had also been in that country.

But soon Roselyn received a call from the maternity wing telling her that the parents of new mother Cynthia had arrived in the hospital. She immediately called the lab to see if the DNA test of mother and child had been done.

Chapter Eight

Taylor Rosenbaum sat in his office watching the late afternoon sun disappear and the darkness move in. It was another long cold night to drive home. But he wasn't going home, but back to the apartment he now shared with Marlene. The first few days were fun with her. So young and energetic, but to sit and even talk at breakfast with her had become a 'chore'. It was just so easy to share his day with Roselyn, to even chat with his girls. He missed his son, Eric. His ski partner, his hiking buddy. Why had his life changed so quickly in these last few days? Deep down inside he knew. And that thought reminded him of how his feelings about fidelity in marriage really began.

Flipping a long pencil in his hand, he remembered the first time he had taken another woman to bed while being married to Roselyn.

It was 9:40 p.m. and the ceiling fans were set on high speed, yet Taylor's shirt was damp with sweat. He sat in the dark office trying to wait for the operators to place this phone call from a small village in Iraq to Murray, Utah USA. It had become a long evening's process. The operator in Florida told him the call was ready to go through to a. Roselyn Rosenbaum located in Murray, Utah, USA. He nearly shouted.

"This is Roselyn Rosenbaum. Is that you Taylor! Where are you calling from? Uh, hi, I mean it's so good to hear from you. To hear your voice."

He smiled. "Yeah, it's old Taylor, here sweating into a greasy puddle."

'I'm getting a distinct clue that it's hot there in Iraq?" She laughed; her laugh was so musical.

"You could say that and no one would dispute your findings. How are you doing? How's Eric? Is he walking yet?"

"He's getting smarter everyday. Learning new words, and climbing on anything and everything he can get a good hold on. The sofa, the kitchen chairs. He can say Mum, and Gam. Something like that."

The reason I called you is to thank you I for the 'care package' you sent. The thought was nice, very nice. But sending food, junk food is a waste of time and money. However, since we're in an American Hospital here. The government flies in fresh nutritious food. We have guys that prepare it for us everyday. We don't need junk food. Thanks for thinking about us, me, I appreciate the thought. And I'm sure it wasn't cheap to mail."

"I won't do it again. I'm sorry." Roselyn sniffed. "Doctor Rosenbaum, Sir."

"I'm sorry I hurt your feelings. It's just unnecessary. He softened his tone. I really enjoyed the snapshots. It was really fun to see Eric, and how he's growing and your family. Keep them coming."

"How's your work?" She chose a more neutral topic.

"This damn war is really heating up We're starting to see more and more casualties. It's getting grim. Some of the war wounds are- - - -really a challenge. I'll probably be here at least another three months. Through the summer. They say around here that sometimes they get a rainy season. I don't know how all these tents will deal with heavy rain."

"From what I've read, I figured I won't see you until Fall, September or October, and I *do* miss you." she said.

"Good, save up lot's of lovin' for old Taylor."

She sighed, now he sounded like the old Taylor. She really did miss him. "It looks like I'll have to hang up. "Write soon, when you have time. Love you." She was gone. Roselyn held onto the phone for a long time, but finally set the receiver back into its cradle.

Taylor walked from the officer's quarters, across the compound to another building housing other medical personnel. The hospital and other buildings were army barracks type buildings, all placed on a foundation of short stilts. The living quarters were across the compound. It reminded Taylor of a brown railroad train all hooked together. The living quarters were across the grass, (If you could call it grass). Taylor entered that building and searched for room #10. He tried the door and found it open. Walking over to a small table by a single bed, he set down one of the packages Roselyn had sent to him. From there he eased to the window and stood as the small air conditioner hummed softly and blew cool air on him. He stood with his eyes closed, and lifted his shirt to feel the delightful air on his chest and back. From a door close to him he decided it had to be a bathroom, because he could hear water running. It sounded like a shower. Soon the water stopped, He waited a few minutes, but then knocked softly on the door. "Come out and have some junk food." He said.

A moment later a youngish blond woman stepped from the bathroom, walked to the table and searched the package. "Hmm, brownies, and they're still fairly fresh. Oh, some chocolate candy, but a bit soft. "Better put these in the fridge."

Taylor watched her walk down the hall, take the package and stuffed it in a small refrigerator. Lt. Edith Franklin then walked down the hall into the 'dayroom'. It resembled a small kitchen, with a long table and a refrigerator. She returned to room #10, picked up a brush on the table and began to brush through her 'cap' of blond curls. Next, she went into the bathroom and brushed her teeth. She only wore a short cotton tank top and a pair of white cotton briefs. The clothes hugged her small trim body.

Taylor stood behind her and stroked her back and shoulders. 'I like it when you don't put on a bra." He nuzzled her cheek and wrapped his arms around her. Then began to stroke her body from head to foot.

"You like your women wearing very little or not very much, or possibly nothing at all. Yeah, you like your women naked." She leaned against him.

"Hey, before we go on with this activity, I want to know where you got the goodies."

"Roselyn sent them to me. A sort of care package, I suppose. I received it just today."

"Well, that was 'sweet' of her." She laughed at her pun. "Are you going to tell your wife about me?" She stood in front of him and twisted against him.

"Ah no. You see Roz in of the Mormon faith and they don't believe in sex outside of marriage."

"Don't you think she'd somehow figure it out. You being such a virile man." She stood close to him and ran her hands up and down his body. Then she backed away and pulled on a pair of sweats.

"What are you doing? I came over to make love to you." He frowned down at his body, ready for sex.

"I want to go for a walk. So make it fast." She came up and slid down his pants. . Then she put her arms around his neck and wrapped her legs around his torso.

"I'm not good doing this standing up." While he pulled off his shorts, he gently lowered her down on the narrow bunk. As he entered her, he kissed her and the act was explosive and fast.

For a few minutes they lay in a tangle both breathing hard. Then she pulled away from him and grabbed some clothes off the chair and hurried to the bathroom. A few minutes later she came out of the bathroom and handed him a wet wash cloth. "Clean up, then we can go for a walk. It's better at night, cooler." She sat down on a chair and slid on some shoes. "After our walk, we can come back and do this properly, all night long."

Chapter Nine

Taylor, because he dropped the pencil he had been flipping up and down, was brought out of his reverie. "Yep, Edie was a great woman to become involved with back then. All of them at the military base were caught up in a nasty war situation.' He thought back. How long had he been in that field hospital in southern Iraq? Another three maybe four months. Edith Franklin had been transferred back to the 'States' soon after their affair. She was a marvelous nurse, and sex partner. He wondered where she was now? If she had married and had a family? He would learn about Edie sooner than he could even guess.

The three women in the Rosenbaum family carried on the Christmas traditions. Roz, Ellie and Shanna went out Christmas Tree shopping. This time for a 'real' tree. There was a large fresh tree lot down at the shopping area located close to the major cross street along the boulevard. It was a major street. The cross streets led up into what residents called the 'cove'. A few schools had been constructed east of the road. It ran south and eventually crossed the roads leading to both Big and Little Cottonwood Canyon roads going up both canyons. There were 'feeder roads coming up from the major road that came east from the valley below. These crossed roads that drove up into the 'cove' was where they lived. The neighborhood where they had seen their house and remodeled it was in an older area, but still had some prestige. People who had homes up against the east mountains in Salt Lake called it the 'cove' because of the shape of the mountain base. Many of the houses in the 'lower' cove were at least fifty years old. But very few were torn down. Rather, people bought them and just spent large amounts of money remodeling. Living up several hundred feet higher than the valley floor, meant cooler temperatures in the summer time and great views of most of the city. Plus, the average family living there were much closer to at least six or seven ski resorts than the average native of Salt Lake. For some families this meant a real plus.

Taylor, though his family was not native to Utah, soon the children in the family learned to ski. Many of the elementary schools where he had lived had a 'ski school'. One day a week from December to mid-March a bus load of children was taken to one or two of the local ski resorts for a chance to take ski lessons. It wasn't too expensive, and the bus would return the children to the school around 5:30-6:00 p.m that evening. Many of the children where Taylor's family lived had allowed their 10- to 12-year-olds to participate.

So Taylor's mother paid the fees from her household funds so that Taylor could go to ski school. It was one of the best things he had ever done. And he thanked her generously until she passed on, only two years before.

He found that living in Salt Lake area that skiing was very popular sport especially among the middle to upper middle-class families. It gave Taylor an 'in' with these people. For every ride on the ski lift 'up' you shared the bench with someone. Many times, it was a lawyer doctor, or some stockbroker. A great way to do a little business.

He even met Roselyn at a ski resort. At that time, he was enrolled in classes at the University of Utah. But it was rare that even with a heavy load of classes, an individual would have a free afternoon.

So one sunny February day he had the afternoon off. He took his skis with him to school that day, and after a quick lunch he drove his old car up Little Cottonwood Canyon and parked at the base where the road to the ski resort had been widened with parking on both sides. Since it was mid-week the parking lot, was not full, and from his car it was a ten-minute walk to the ground level ski lift.

The day was clear, with a light wind and as the sun began to 'slide' down in the western sky, Taylor wished he could 'bottle up' the whole experience and save it for a rainy, blustery day. Never before had he felt the euphoria, he felt that afternoon. It was just good to be alive. The sun was lowering and the 'light' was leaving. When he went to try for one more 'ride' on the ski lift, he found that the lift operator had put out his sign. LIFT CLOSED. And in smaller letters below; *OPEN TOMORROW* 9 A. M. He stood there crestfallen. Yet behind him he heard two feminine voices.

"What; Closed? Ah, we missed the last run?"

"I'm afraid we've already *had* the last run. Come on we'll have to get in another line to drive down the canyon. The sooner the better."

Taylor turned to view two females in their late teens, both attractive. One was blond and the other one darker haired and taller. "I was hoping for that last run, too." The taller one said.

Both girls nodded at Taylor and turned to ski down a hard snow path to the parking lot. Once they reached the wide parking area there many people who were opening car doors, stripping off skis and getting ready to drive down the steep canyon road to the two lane the wider roadway. One led to 94th South, which was a cross road to several smaller towns at the base of the canyon.

When Taylor reached his car, he found that the girls' car was parked two cars away. He managed to ease out of his skis, stow them on the roof of his car, but then glanced over at the girls. One of them was struggling to snap the skis onto the roof carrier. So he stomped over still wearing his ski boots to offer help.

When the dark-haired girl dropped a pole to the ground, he was there to scoop it up. "Here, let me help you." He picked up the pole, put it next to the second pole and worked to snap both sets of skis onto the roof carrier.

The fair-haired girl had been putting clothing and other items in the backseat area of their smaller car. She came around, smiled and said, "Thank you. It's seldom we have a 'knight' wearing navy blue ski clothes to help us." She stuck her right hand out. "I'm Roselyn Stroud, and you're- - - - -?"

"Oh, Hi. I'm Taylor Rosenbaum, it's very nice to meet you."

The second girl came over close to Roselyn. "And I'm Saundra Blakely." She put out her right hand. Offering it to Taylor.

"From which high school did you 'ditch' to come up here this afternoon?" Taylor asked with a grin.

The blond girl put her hands on her hips and flashed a frown. "How do you know we're in high school?" She asked.

Taylor touched the bumper sticker on the rear of the car. "East Valley High. It says right here on the bumper sticker mounted on your car."

"Okay, but the car belonged to my brother. Now I get to drive it." The dark-haired girl said.

"Where's your brother?" Taylor asked.

"Out of state, on a mission." She snapped. "Now I'm next in line for the use of this car."

"Does your family know you two are up skiing, and not in school?" Taylor asked.

"Of course. We had to go home to change. "Oh, I'm Roselyn. And she's Saundra." She stretched out her hand. And you said your name is Taylor?"

He nodded.

"Now we'd better get on the road. Nice to meet you, Taylor. See, I even remembered your name. Thanks for your help." Roselyn said and waved as Saundra backed out the car and drove down the parking lot to the line of cars easing down canyon road.

Now thirty some years later, Taylor sat in his office, flipping a pencil rather than getting ready for his next patient. He had to study his daily schedule for a moment to see who would be coming in next. Oh, it was a mother and a daughter both suffering with 'post pandemic fog' A new 'after ailment' of covid 19'.

Three people in this family had become ill with the virus all within two weeks of each other. The oldest patient, a grandmother, and next her daughter and then the granddaughter.

The women who were coming in were relatives. The mother was

married to the second son and then also their 15-year-old daughter. The mother was the one who seemed to have the worst case of 'brain fog".

It was fortunate that Taylor had received a grant from the federal government to study and work with patients they called 'long termers'; people with some strange symptoms from the contracting the covid/ variant; delta.

Taylor also was interested in some of these patients who had also had at least one shot of a vaccine, but still had a milder version of the covid 19. These he would study separately. Make it a study of his own.

Suddenly Taylor's office phone rang and when he picked it up. The call had originated in Mexico. He knew his son, Eric, was in Mexico serving an LDS mission. Taylor picked it up. "Hello?"

"Hello? Is this Dad; Taylor Rosenbaum?"

"Yes. Is this my son, Eric Rosenbaum?"

"I tried calling home, but no one seems to be there. The mission I'm in here in Central Mexico is closing temporarily. So two of us; Elder Nathan Johnson and I are being relocated to Colorado Springs, Colorado. Both of us only have close to five months left to serve."

"So the two of you are being sent back to the U.S.? Is there a problem in your area?"

"You might call it a problem. I can't really discuss it on the phone. Once we leave here and it will be this evening, I'll call you or Mom and give you the details.

I know that Christmas is less than a week away, but the Church is sending us back to the States. There's room for us in the Colorado Springs South mission. Oh, our ride is here to drive us to the airport. I'll talk to you tomorrow. Give everybody our love for them. Our car is here. Talk to you later."

Taylor was left standing by his desk, holding the phone. He felt a strange danger in the air. He'd better talk to Roselyn. He wondered if Eric managed to call, or at least leave a message at home.

Then Taylor heard the outer door open into his office. He walked out to greet his patient. There he gazed at both the mother and daughter.

"Come in and take a seat. Which one of you would like to talk to me first. Or would you prefer to have a session together?"

"Well?" The mother turned and frowned at her daughter. "I suppose I should let her talk to you first."

"Okay, Adelaide, is it? Come in and have a seat." Dr. Taylor Rosenbaum held the door open for the young girl to come into his office.

The teen age girl glanced around the office. "Should I lay on the lounge?" She nervously raked a hand through her long hair.

"There is also a comfortable chair near the desk. If you'd prefer you can sit there.?" Taylor spoke in his most professional manner.

Adelaide giggled, but then eased into the chair. "I've seen those movies where the patient has all these strange, you know, remembering important things while lying on a couch." She giggled self-consciously. But then she sat down in the chair. "I think this will be okay."

"Good. Taylor sat down behind his desk. "So how are you feeling today? Compare today, with how you felt, say two weeks ago." Taylor asked.

The girl frowned. "Okay, today I don't feel as bad as I did say two weeks ago. I actually tried to go to school Thursday and Friday of last week."

"How did that work out?" Taylor asked.

"The worst part was getting around school, and making it to class in the five minutes we have between classes. I got tired climbing stairs, like that." Adelaide seemed to stop and recall an incident. "But, I talked to my health teacher, Ms. Knolls. She said that being out of school for over two weeks, and being so sick, it will take a few days to get back my stamina."

"So how do you feel about her advice?" Dr. Rosenbaum asked.

"I think she was right. I sat and finished an assignment for her class yesterday. It's just that I forget about things. You know, like where I put things and forget about where I forget where I put them. I've never been a list maker, but I tried it and it kind of worked."

"I believe that you are recovering from a strange, new malady., and should use these ideas to get back to normal. Just make sure you return to your regular sleep patterns. That will help you ease into your normal activities."

"I can see that's a good idea. Adelaide stood up. "Thanks, I'll send in Mom now."

The mother was still having some symptoms of the pandemic illness. Taylor sent her to the lab to give them a sample of her blood. After he looked at the results, he possibly would prescribe a calming drug to help her. From what she expressed, her forgetting was causing more anxiety than what she had forgotten to do. He suggested carrying a notebook with her, and as she noticed something that needed her attention to write herself a note.

He tried to help her understand that everyone who had come in contact with the virus had a slightly different reaction to it. She seemed to feel better and wanted to drive home before it became dark.

Soon it was past 6 p.m. and very dark and cold outside. Then he realized that there were less than two weeks before Christmas. Enjoying Christmas with Marlene just didn't excite him.

Chapter Ten

When Roselyn reached the house only Shanna was home. Roselyn dropped her things in her den and went into Shanna's room. Her younger daughter was curled up in the favorite blanket, asleep.

Roselyn thought that she could take a short nap before fixing some supper. But the ringing telephone chased that idea from her mind. She grabbed the one in the kitchen. "Hello?"

"Mom, this is Eric."

"Oh, Hi Eric. How are things in sunny Mexico?"

"That's what I called you about. In about ten minutes or less, I'll be climbing aboard a plane bound for El Paso, Texas and then on to Colorado."

"Colorado! The mission is transferring you to Colorado?"

"Yes, those are the facts, Ma'am. Thank the good Lord. We've got some internal problems down here. "We'll change planes in El Paso, then fly to Colorado Springs. That will be the city of my new assignment."

"Okay, I'm getting the subliminal message that you'll explain more once you're stateside." Roselyn said.

"Correct on that thought. I'll call you later. Oh, I already talked to Dad. I called his office. "Okay, now they're waving. Time to get aboard. It's a nearly a four-hour flight. Talk to you later."

The commuter plane was a 737. Somewhere in Eric's mind he remembered that Locked of Boeing had quit constructing this particular air craft. Yet here he and Elder Johnson were finding their seats to fly back to the States. Oh well, he wouldn't worry about this change. Even though he would miss some of the good people that he had learned to love and taught about the Book Mormon and its revelations.

Luckily, the weather was overcast and it began to rain halfway into their flight, but the not too windy. The plane just kept flying. He settled down in his seat and soon fell asleep. It seemed these past few weeks he was always tired.

He awoke when the plane changed altitude. He could also feel the change and the reduced speed. They finally landed on a runway, and the pilot then announced that they would taxi in close to a large building.

They exited the plane into a tunnel of sorts. Most planes 'deplane' into a soft cover walkway into the various airports. When they reached the actual building a young woman carrying a sign greeted them. On the sign were their names.

They walked up to her. "You want us to follow you, ma'am?" Elder Johnson asked.

"Yes, get in the traveling cart". She walked across the way to a moving cart and driver. "First, we have to pick up your luggage. Belt yourselves in." She climbed into the driver's seat and they set out for a ride through the huge building.

Elder Johnson touched Eric's shoulder. "We could have used one of these in (Mexican City)."

In less than ten minutes they arrived at Gate 27, and an electronic sign flashed FLIGHT 72 Colorado Springs, Denver. The driver of the cart walked up to the boarding Steward and announced: Passengers Johnson and Rosenbaum." The steward waved in the direction of the two young men. "Climb aboard." He gestured to Eric and Nathan.

The two young men climbed aboard a larger mode of transportation than they had flown into Texas.

A young steward led them to two seats in the rear of the plane. He took their carry-on bags and quickly slipped them in the overhead. Then he walked up to the front of the plane. "Seat belts fastened?" He glanced around. 'Good.' Then he hurried into the cockpit. With in a very short time, the plane began to taxi down the runway.

A few minutes later he announced information about their flight.

"In two hours, thirty minutes we will be landing at Colorado Springs, International. Please wear seatbelts, during the flight, because we will be encountering the western edge of a winter storm."

Eric and his companion settled back into their seats, and soon both had fallen asleep.

The sounds of the plane's engine changed and woke Eric. Then he could feel the airplane begin to descend. Next the steward came on the intercom and announced. "We will be landing at Colorado Springs regional airfield in ten minutes. Everyone must vacate the airplane. If you have connections to cities in the Midwest, or eastern cities in the U.S., check your tickets to find your next flight provider."

Once on the ground, Eric and Nathan pulled out their cell phones and Eric called the local LDS mission home. The call was answered after four rings. "Bishop Anderson here, to whom am I speaking?"

"This is Eric Rosenbaum and Nathan Johnson, transfers from The Mexico Central Mission."

"Yes, Elder Rosenbaum, this is a high councilman Thomas Weiman, I'm on my way to pick up you two, I'll be there is fifteen minutes. Make your way to the Exit number two."

A few minutes later they could see their baggage coming down a circular baggage carel. They walked in that direction. Once they had their bags they found a baggage trolley, and piled it up, and walked slowly to the central exit or EXIT TWO.

Eric ducked outside and came back with snowflakes on his jacket. He automatically brushed at them. "Boy, it's been a long time since we've seen snow."

For a moment Elder Nathan, studied his companion. "What a surprise: winter!"

"Well, it is December 19th." Eric said. He continued to stand and gaze through heavy glass doors. 'Hey, here comes an SUV." Under the outside lights the automobile's color was an obvious: bright blue.

The car stopped and honked. Eric stepped closer. and watched the rear hatch rise up. The driver got out of the big SUV.

"Hey Elder, put your gear in the back." I'm from the Colorado South Stake." The man climbed out of his car. Nathan could see the automobile hatch go up, and began to drag his belongings out the door close to rear hatch of the car.

Soon the luggage and the two young men were in the SUV and the driver shook hands with Eric and reached back to Nathan. "I'll bet it's not often you guys get picked at close to 3:00 a.m. in the morning. I'm Herb Anderson, from the Stake High Council. I'm taking you two to a missionary house."

"No, not too often." Eric laughed. Thank you for coming for us."

"Okay. I'm supposed to be transporting one Eric Rosenbaum, and a second young man; Nathan Johnson. Am I correct?"

"Yes sir. You're right on." Nathan answered.

"Okay, good; got the right young men." We should be there in 20 minutes. The older man turned the car radio to a soft rock station and drove toward the freeway. Twenty minutes later he exited freeway and drove a few blocks into a middle-class neighborhood. About three or four blocks later Eric could see the spires of a church. It was the typical architecture of an LDS Ward Building.

Herb drove into a double driveway close to a large two-story house. The lights were on in the rear of the house, and as the car stopped near a side door, they could lights burning inside through rear windows.

Both young men and the driver exited and as the side door opened, the driver went in and held the door open for Eric and Nathan to bring in their gear. They walked into a large kitchen- family room and against the south wall they could see a wide stairway.

A middle–aged woman wearing sweats gestured to them and pointed at them to follow her upstairs. Once upstairs, she waved them to follow her. She led them into an average sized bedroom. There were two beds, two chests of drawers, and a desk. There was curved walk-in wall closet. As they followed her upstairs she said. "This will be your room. Also, across the hall is a bathroom."

She turned to watch the two missionaries carry or lug their

belongings up the stairs. Once they were up, she waved entrance to the room. "Since it is nearly 4 a.m. we won't expect you two to be up at the usual 6:30 a.m. However please be as quiet as you can getting into bed. I'm the mission home hostess, and we'll give you two a half-day off. We'll expect you two down for lunch about 1:00 p.m."

"Excuse me. ma'am. What is your name?" Eric asked.

"Oh, so sorry. I'm Sister Walquist. Please just get ready for some sleep as quickly and quietly as possible. Do you now have all your belongings upstairs?"

"No, a couple more bags." Both young men galloped back down and dragged up their last bags.

The hostess stood and watched them as they took their bags into the room. "Well, goodnight. See you two midmorning." She turned and walked down the stairs.

For a moment, Eric stood and watched her leave and lights in the kitchen and hallway go out. Then he went into the room and dragged his suitcase and set it on the bed. He took out a shirt and a pair of slacks, socks and underwear, closed the suitcase and set it at the rear of one of the beds. He opened the closet and found good suit hangers for his warm jacket, and suit.

Nathan opened the door. "The bathroom is a good one and there are fresh towels." Nathan had visited the bathroom, and soon returned.

"Good to know." Eric said and grabbed his shaving kit from his suitcase. When he returned, Nathan was in bed and left only the closet light on. Quickly he undressed, hung up his clothes and slid into the second bed. It was long enough for his six-foot frame and comfortable. His last thought before fatigue won, was what a crazy day and night this had been. And he wondered what tomorrow would bring.

Chapter Eleven

An evening three days later, Taylor dropped by the house to pick up some files from his office located in the front of the Rosenbaum family home. He again parked his car in the garage. When he went into the house, he noticed it was rather quiet. Then as he stood in the entrance way, he could hear the television downstairs in the basement level.

Better yet he picked the scent of beef and garlic. And entering the kitchen and checking the refrigerator, he noticed a leftover pasta beef casserole. He knew what a good cook his wife was, and there was a fair bit of it left. He hadn't yet returned to the apartment he shared with Marlene, nor was he eager to do so. He had not had any dinner so he took out the casserole, He also found some salad, and two left over bread sticks.

He made a plate of food and sat down at the kitchen table to eat. Then his younger daughter, Shanna came bouncing up from the lower level and walked into the kitchen.

"Well, Hi Dad. Did you come over for some leftovers?"

"No, I came to pick up some papers from my office files. However, my nose led me to the kitchen. How are you doing? How's school?" Did you help your mother with this beef casserole? Even warmed up it's quite good. Did you help Roz put it together?" By the way, where is your mother this evening?"

"Mom is over at church rehearsing for the Christmas program. She's singing a solo."

"Interesting. Your mother does have a fine singing voice. However, I came to ask about Eric. Have you heard from him since Saturday evening?" I received a phone call from him saying that he was leaving Mexico. He was being transferred from Central Mexico to Colorado. Do you have any details as to why? Or if he arrived safely to the city of Colorado Springs? I believe he said that's where he was to be transferred."

For a moment Shanna wanted to be flippant with her father, because he walked out on them. But he *was* concerned about her brother. She decided to tell him what she knew. "Dad, do you want some coffee with your dinner? I could make you some instant."

For a moment he stared at his glass filled with ice water. "Sure, make me some coffee. That would be nice."

He watched Shanna as she put on the tea kettle, and then set a mug on the counter. She reached into the pantry and pulled out a jar of instant coffee, and a glass jar of sugar. She set the sugar and a teaspoon on the table next to him.

While the water came to a boil, his beautiful young daughter fixed herself a glass of ice water, and set it at the opposite end of the table. When the teakettle whistled, she jumped up turned off the stove, and poured water into the coffee mug. *How old is she now? That's right her birthday is in April. She'll be eighteen; His almost grown and younger daughter. When she graduates from high school, what are her plans? Or rather, which college does she plan to attend?*

For a long moment, he had a feeling of profound sadness and it gripped him. It was a better situation for his children when he lived here.

For a few minutes they chatted about her schooling, but then the garage door leading inside the level of the house opened and he heard Ellie's voice. "Hey Dad's car is in the garage, where- - - - - -? She came upstairs and into the kitchen. For a moment she just stood and stared at him. "Came home for dinner, huh Dad?"

But then some silent signal came from Shanna, and Ellie glanced at the casserole dish. "Maybe I'll have something to eat, too." She shrugged off her coat and put it in the dining room and draped it on a chair. Returning to the kitchen, she pulled out a plate and a water glass. Then spooned some of the casserole onto the plate and set it in the microwave. While the food heated, she filled her glass with ice and cold water. When the microwave pinged, she took the food and water and set it on the end of the table, sat down and began to eat.

"Did you have an evening class?" Taylor asked and glanced at his watch.

"Yeah, contemporary American Lit. There is a list of books we're supposed to read. Most of them are, I guess, are American classics. Some of them have an 'okay' story, but some are terribly boring."

She took a bite of her dinner, and a sip of her water.

She stared at her father and expected some kind of rebuke, but he just nodded. "I suppose the literary department wants you to understand what it was like to live in America 50 or 60 years ago. I know you find it all boring, but what happened in the past does shape the future." Taylor glanced down at his empty plate, picked up his mug of coffee and took another swallow. "I'd better drive back to the apartment before I fall asleep. Tell your Mom, I enjoyed the food." He kissed the top of Shanna's head and touched Ellie on her sleeve. "Good evening, you two." He went downstairs to the garage, and soon the roar of his car, A.M engine could be heard.

The week flew by but Christmas Eve morning finally dawned. Since it was a Saturday, and the last shopping day before Christmas Day, Ellie climbed from her bed at the ungodly hour of 7 a.m. to get ready for work. She knew it would be busy at the department store where she worked.

As she drove to work, she thought about this particular Holiday Season. It had been better, from the year before. More people came into the store rather than phoning or e-mailing an order. The U.S. was in the second year of the covid 19 pandemic. More people were out shopping, and the major shopping mall where she works was busier. But still not like the frantic shopping that went on before covid-19. came to the world. At any rate she would be busy, and still had gifts to wrap when she arrived home.

By evening the three Rosenbaum females were sitting down to

dinner, and only Shanna had all her gifts under their tree. Tomorrow, their Sunday church service was at 10:30 a.m. and the choir was in charge of the Christmas Service. It was then that Roselyn would sing a solo.

The three females managed to make it through the disruption of their household, with both Eric and Taylor absent from the usual Christmas Day. Eric, however would be allowed to call and speak to them. The three females had that to look forward to.

In Colorado Springs, Edith Franklin Fletcher was driving home from a fourteen-hour shift at the local military base hospital; Camp Carson. She had worked there on and off for the past eighteen years.

When she returned home from her military service in Iraq, she was sent to Camp Carson, the military hospital located in Colorado Springs, Colorado. She had almost a year to serve in that base hospital, and she also realized she was pregnant.

When she contacted her military superior, she was surprised at their mild reprimand. They still needed her service as a nurse at the Camp Carson hospital. And because she was still considered in 'uniform', the U. S. Government paid for her delivery. Day Care was available at the base, and so after one month leave, she returned to work, leaving her newborn son there, in the hospital nursery while she worked.

One day she met Captain Fletcher while picking up her son, Jonah. By then he was six months old. One fact that stayed with her everyday as she picked him up from the nursery and took him home, was how much he resembled his half-brother toddler's pictures his father Taylor Rosenbaum had showed Edith. Her son resembled Eric Rosenbaum more and more each day.

Now it was Christmas morning, twenty years after Jonah had been born. His half brother, Eric would perhaps be in his early twenties, about twenty-two years old. Tired after her long shift at the base hospital, Edith was driving home this Christmas morning. She drove past an LDS Church on her way home from that shift at the Basel hospital.

People were milling around at the entrance to the building and on the walkways surrounding it. Now she remembered that *it was*

Christmas Day, and a Sunday. One of their services must have just ended. The traffic slowed almost to a stop, and she there staring at the people milling around the front entrance to the building.

Suddenly glancing at the people, she noticed the tall young man. He stood on the sidewalk chatting with an older man and woman. What struck her was that he so reminded her of Taylor, her old love, and the father of her son. She thought of her own son, now close to twenty years old.

She sat there almost spellbound, but a honk from a car behind her snapped her back to reality. She stepped on the gas and her car lurched, but she slammed on the brakes, and managed to drive on at a normal speed.

A few blocks later she reached her house and her children were lounged on the sofa watching a football game. "How was your shift, Mom?" Her daughter, Megan asked. Her voice raised over the roar of the crowd. The football game was being played in a large stadium in some city where an NFL game would be played.

Edith walked near the sofa where her two children sat watching the game. "Who's playing?" she asked.

"The Broncos and the Lions. Detroit is ahead." Megan answered.

"Good, I'm glad you two found something to do. Right now, I'm going upstairs and take a nap. By the way what did you two manage to eat for lunch?" She asked and smiled, as she hung up her winter jacket in the front hall closet.

'We ate the leftover pizza." Megan said. "We're actually bad enough to feed ourselves." She went back to sipping at a drink.

Edith nodded and walked upstairs. Once in the bedroom, she stripped off her uniform and took a shower.

The shower refreshed and relaxed her. But in her thoughts began swirling around as to how she could see that young man again. Had he moved to Colorado Springs because of a job? Was he married? Why was he here? But then she yawned, and eyes felt like sandpaper. Even as she climbed into her bed, she began to put together a scene in her head. He could be a missionary for the LDS Church.

She had a patient in the hospital, a while back. He was a young soldier from Idaho and had contracted covid 19. Even though he had had a second shot recently. He had not been really ill, but the army wanted him in the hospital because of a fever. He talked to her about his religion. And she did not let on how much she knew about his Mormon faith.

She found herself sitting on the edge of the bed with her eyes closed. She pulled on a night gown and a pair of warm socks, closed the shutters and slid into bed. She would think on that young man she saw outside the church, later. Before she slept, she said a little prayer for her dear departed husband, Herbert Fletcher. She had met him when she was first assigned to the military hospital at Camp Carson near Colorado Springs.

As she lay in bed, she recalled her situation when she had first returned from Iraq.

Chapter Twelve

Once her pregnancy became evident, she was given easier duty. They were short on nurses, and her health was good. She chose not to quit the military. She really had nowhere else to go. When her baby was born, a healthy boy, she had a six-weeks forced vacation. She used the time to find out that Taylor had returned to Salt Lake City, Utah.

One day about two months after her baby son was born, she was on duty when patient on crutches crashed into a food cart. He was a wounded soldier and was trying out a new pair. He was sitting on the floor, and had used the crutches to scoot over against the wall.

Edith knew she would not be able to pick him up, so she called for an orderly. Between the two of them they managed to get the fallen man into a wheel chair, and took him back to his room. Then helped him into bed.

"Sorry, I was just trying out these crutches." He said as they helped him back into bed. I'm just tired of lying in bed and wanted to explore the area a bit."

Nurse Franklin helped him to sit up. "Would you like some water? Or I might be able to find you a bottle of coke, or more coffee."

He shook his head. "I guess I'm just so damned bored. I'm tired of TV, and I just can't move around the way I would like to." He scowled down at his hands.

"How about a book? I mean some mystery story. Do you have a favorite author? There are some really good novels in the library here. I could go find one for you. Do you have a favorite mystery writer?" Nurse Franklin asked.

"I never read too much growing up. Unless it was an automobile hand book on how to fix an engine or drive train."

Are you a big fiction reader?" he asked. "Or are you a fan of those sexy romantic novels?"

"I read all those romance novels while in high school. Now mystery novels are more fun to read. You sure you don't want me to go find one for you?"

"Well, okay. Find one you really liked. Maybe I'll take a look at it"

A half hour later she returned with a John Grissom novel. When she walked into his room, she found him asleep. She left the soft cover novel on his nightstand, and went back to her duties.

Two days later he was transferred to the rehab wing and she didn't see him again for a long while.

She had a good apartment in the housing area of Camp Carson, but soon she would have to find something in the City of Colorado Springs. Since a military base was part of the town, many soldiers with families were allowed to rent private housing. It seemed as if anyone owning a structure with four walls, and a roof put out a sign that the Army had allowed this place to be rented by someone in the military. This house or an apartment was 'Okay'.

One day, she had picked her son, and had gone shopping at the PX on base. While standing line to check-out Jonah became fussy, and Edith picked him up from his carrier and began to bounce him on her shoulder. The woman standing in line behind her began talking to and waving at her baby.

"Do you live on the military base here?" The older woman asked. "Oh, my name is Doreen Goff. And you are? - - - - -

"I'm Edith Franklin, yes, for now, but I'm going to have to vacate my place. It is large enough for a small family, and since it's just Jonah and me……, I need to find something smaller and at least partially furnished."

"That's interesting. Because my husband and I bought a medium sized house here in the city. And he's been called up to go to the middle east for a year. I'm not looking forward to being alone in the house while he's be gone. This house is up in Shay Canyon. Not way up in the newer area, but up there far enough, that the nights are cooler. It has a basement apartment, partially furnished. Maybe you would be interested in it? Would you'd like to take a look at it?"

"Would having a baby downstairs bother you?" Edith asked.

"Heavens no. We had a young couple in there. Baby and all. The young man mustered out and they moved back to Moab, Utah. When would you like to come and see the place?"

"Well, I might be able to take a look tomorrow. What is the address?' Edith asked.

"From the street that runs south from downtown, you drive up 47th Avenue past the McDonalds and turn south. It's 4870 Concord Drive on the west side of the street. It has a rock front trim on a beige house with a double garage in front."

"Tomorrow, I'm off at 3:00 p.m. I'll drive up from the hospital. It will be about 4:00 p.m. Is that okay?" Edith asked.

"Yes, that would be fine."

The next afternoon, Edith and a sleeping Jonah drove up on the west side of Colorado Springs and easily found the house. Edith briefly left Jonah in the car while she rang the doorbell. The owner Ms. Goff, opened the door and waved Edith in.

"Oh, I left my baby in the car< I'll go get him." Once she had the baby in his carrier, she followed Ms. Goff to the front of the house down six stairs to the basement level of the house. A door opened into the lower level. The six stairs led down under the front porch of the house. It opened into the front room of an apartment.

"This is good to have a separate entrance into the apartment." Edith commented. The door opened into the front room. A desk and chair were located against the east wall near the door. A few feet from the living area, through an archway, there was another room. The archway led into a fairly large bedroom.

"When the people who built this house finished the basement, they decided to separate this area from the more living area with the arch. Mainly because of the small size of this living space. This way the rooms have better air circulation. I believe a college age girl lived here last year." Ms. Goff said.

In the room was an older bedroom set. A double sized bed with an arched head board of some dark wood. There was the usual basement window on the south wall. Against that wall was a dresser with a mirror and matching chest of drawers. On the west wall was a wall closet. There was also one nightstand on the right side of the bed.

As Edith walked into the room, she could not help but touch the bed. The mattress seemed firm. There was room for a small crib on north side of the room.

Back into the living room, a short sofa sat against the north wall under a window. Across from the sofa was a red fake leather swivel chair. Next to that there was a small table and two chairs. TV stand hugged that wall with a 19-inch TV opposite the sofa.

A few feet away was a bar and behind that was small kitchen. The sink was under another window, and next to that a fairly long counter and a four-burner gas stove. The bar had open shelves opposite the stove and shelves built over the sink and stove. At the end of the bar against the north wall, there was a small refrigerator. The bathroom was next to the kitchen wall, it contained a small shower, toilet, and a small counter top with a built-in sink. There were small shelves and a bottom drawer built in behind the open bathroom door. The whole floor was covered with beige tiles, but there was an attractive rug in the walking area of the living room.

Edith was mildly surprised that such a small space could seem so livable and comfortable.

Mrs. Goff sat down on the sofa and smiled. "So how do like the place?" she asked.

Edith's eyes widened. "I'm amazed that it seems so comfortable. The bathroom's tight, but I can manage. I'll have bathe Jonah in the kitchen sink. But's that's no problem. What are you asking for rent, and would I have to sign a lease?"

"I charged the young couple living here before $200. per month. And if you're here when it turns cold, an extra $25 a month for the heat and the light bill and the TV. Right now, I have ordered a ceiling fan for the living room, but last summer the young couple did okay with a box fan. Because the basement stays pretty cool in the summer, it won't cost you much now. Winter comes, and as you know it gets pretty cold in Colorado. I'll have to charge you about ten dollars more for the heating bill. I keep my house at 72 F in the daytime and 68F at night."

This is still cheaper than living in the government housing. 'The place sounds reasonable for me. Where is the closest Laundromat?"

"Oh girl, I have a washer and dryer. I know you'll have uniforms to keep fresh, and baby clothes to wash. You will need to buy your own detergent and now I'll show you where the washer and dryer are."

Ms. Goff led Edith to a back door, part of the basement under the sun porch at the west of the house. Again, it was part of the basement, and there was a furnace room and a washer and drying. Next to that a sorting table. and two laundry baskets. On the north side of the room was a stairway was constructed leading upstairs.

"As you can see the main floor of the house is right up these stairs so you'll sometime hear me going up and down. Oh, there's cupboards over here against the wall of your place. This is where you can store your detergent."

Edith gazed around. "The design of this place is amazing. So I can take these stairs and go out in the back yard?"

"Well, I didn't design it, we just bought it. But you're right the design is really unique."

As Edith drove on home on that Christmas morning, she recalled that little apartment that she, Jonah and Herb lived in twenty years ago. While she lived there, she got to know Herb. When Herb Fletcher had been released from the hospital, Edith lost track of him for a few weeks.

For two weeks after he was released, she was busy moving into the 'on the economy' housing. But one evening he called her. They chatted and made small talk. Then he asked if he could take her out to dinner. The move on his part surprised her.

"My big problem is day or evening care for my infant son. Also, I have moved off base. I've found a cosy little place up Shay Canyon."

"Well, if I take you out for supper you'd have to drive anyway. We would have to work the whole situation out. But let me try, and if I find a solution, is it okay if I call you back?"

She was smiling the whole time she talked to him. And as she remembered, the bottom line was: He called back, and they began to date. They managed to have an interesting courtship, and married six months later.

Chapter Thirteen

As Edith drove home, that day after Christmas morning, she mentally tucked away those old memories. Now her goal was to meet that young man she had seen in front of the LDS Church. He had to be Taylor's son. When she and Taylor were working at that military base hospital in Iraq, she remembered he spoke of that little boy. Back then he wasn't even two yours old; just a toddler.

Over twenty years ago she had been so carefree, clueless, really. When she realized she was pregnant, she was terrified for a few days. Then she thought about what an amazing doctor Taylor was and how talented he was. Hopefully some of those genes would be passed on to her child.

Being in the military sheltered her somewhat. And when the baby she carried was born, he was a strong eight pounds and five ounces. a bright beautiful child.

When she married Herb, he treated her son as he belonged to both of them and was also his child. With Herb's help, the boy grew up strong along with a marvelous foundation of love and trust. Then three years later Edie had another baby, a girl. They named her Teresa, after Herb's mother.

When she thought of Herb, her chest still hurt, she missed him so much. But he pursued his life-long desire be the best mechanic. It was what he did before he joined the army, and was a very valuable soldier. Once he left the military, he worked hard to be the best technician for anything that flew. He studied and became a top military mechanic.

After all, luck had been hers when she met him, he was in the hospital, because he had fractured his right leg. He had fallen from the rear of a bomber. The pilot had not realized that he and another mechanic were still in the rear of the plane, and began to ease the plane onto the runway.

Fortunately. the other mechanic just suffered bumps and bruises and a slight concussion. But the poor pilot received quite the reprimand for revving up the engines of that monster plane with the rear doors still open.

As Edith walked into the house, she noticed that the driveway and walks had been shoveled. Jonah had been at work late the evening before, but he must have come home and cleared the walks and driveway. He was a great kid, actually she had to start thinking of him as an adult. All six feet and one inch of him, and twenty years old. He had been willing to work on the driveway. Adding to the fact that he was now in his third year at Colorado State, College and managed to keep a B average.

As she drove into the familiar driveway and garage, she remembered that this house wasn't more than two blocks from that apartment she had rented twenty years ago. The same place where she had invited Herb to have dinner with her and her infant son almost twenty years ago. She thought about that normal sized double bed she and Herbert made love in for the first time.

"If we're going to carry on this romance, we'll have to do it in a king-sized bed." He growled.

The whole situation sent her into gales of laughter. Luckily, they had moved Jonah and his crib into the hallway near the bathroom door. Still in his baby sleep, he stayed serene.

Three months later Herb began to house-hunt. And found this older but suitable family home.

One glance let her know that her two children, Jonah, and Teresa seemed quite comfortable on the sofa with a spread of snacks on the coffee table in front of them. The roar from the TV hinted that an NFL football game was in progress.

"Hi Mom. Teresa called out. "You want some snacks? We've got chip and dip, sodas, and some chili. I opened a can."

"Maybe later." Edith came around and watched the screen for a minute or two. "Who's playing?"

"The Bears and the Forty-Niners and the west coast is winning." Jonah answered.

"I'm going upstairs for a nap. Maybe I'll wake up for the next game that will be on TV this evening. What did you decide you wanted for supper?"

"I decided we should have Tacos. They are easy, and Ms. Mendosa brought over a plate of yummy cookies, and fudge. We can eat that later."

"Do you have to work tomorrow?" Edith asked her daughter.

"I don't have to be there until 2:30 p.m. and I'll have to stay until 9:00 p.m. But my big, brave brother here- - - - - She punched Jonahs' arm. "Said he'd drive me to work."

"Okay, since the house still seems to be firm on its foundation, I'm going upstairs and sleep. See you two later." Edith walked upstairs, to her bedroom and bath. She stripped and stepped into the shower. A while later, as she stood combing thru her short curly hair and even after turning 51 years old there were only a few gray hairs mixed in with the blonde.

Again, she thought of the young man she had seen earlier. How could she meet him? And then she remembered her neighbor.: I *"ll call Juanita Mendosa, she belongs to the Mormon Church.*

Monday morning, as she was making breakfast, Edith picked up the phone and called her neighbor, Juanita. "Hi, this is Edie, how was your Christmas? I'm calling to thank you for the Christmas treats you brought over."

"Oh, good morning, Edie. I'm glad you enjoyed the cookies. Rita wanted to do the 'neighborhood treat' thing. It was really her idea. You and I know how crazy Christmas can be, especially when we both work full time."

"What I really called about is a tall young man I saw standing out in front your church yesterday morning. He looks really familiar. How can I invite him to my house?"

"Oh, I'll bet you're talking about a missionary transfer that just arrived here from Central Mexico. He and his companion were relocated in supposedly, to Colorado Springs from Mexico. There's got to be an interesting story behind this rather strange move of these missionaries. His name- - - - She called out "Rita, what are the names of those two new missionary transfers. Would you come and talk to Edie?"

Less than a minute later the young girl came to the phone. "Hi, Edie. You want to know about those two missionaries that just came in?" The tall, cute one is Elder Rosenbaum and the shorter one is Elder Johnson. Rosenbaum is from Salt Lake and his companion is from some little town in Utah. You want to meet them? That's easy. I'll go over to church tomorrow grab you some 'pass-a-long' cards. You just fill them out and I'll take them to church with me Sunday and give them to the missionaries. Well, I've got to be at work pretty soon. Talk to ya later, Bye."

As Edie stared at the phone in her hand, her heart beat a little faster. *I knew it. He is Taylor's son. I just have to meet him, and ask him about his parents, and how his father is doing. But how am I going to explain to him how I knew his Dad?*

Since it was Christmas week, the new elders from the LDS church would either be more busy than usual or perhaps not? She would just have to 'wing' it. Late Tuesday afternoon she again drove by the LDS ward building and noticed several cars in the parking lot. She took the chance, parked her car and got out. It had snowed an inch or two, and the parking lot was slippery. But she was careful and picked her way to the side door where she could possibly get in the building. She found it was open and she could hear the yelling from the gymnasium, a large area also used for parties and other activities. Another name for it was a cultural hall. Sure enough, there was a 'pick-up' basketball game going on.

She stood for a minute or two. Long enough to pick out that tall, young man on the floor involved in the basketball game. She watched the play, as well as the young guy she had seen on Christmas Day. And now she knew he was Eric Rosenbaum.

He seemed quite familiar with the game, and she watched as he scored with a 'lay-up'. She just couldn't stand and watch the game any longer, so she turned and walked up a long hallway to the front of the building. There were stands with cards and other writing materials. Soon she found a stack of 'pass along cards' and grabbed a few. As she walked carefully to her car, she hoped the bishop, or whoever was in charge of missionaries would send the 'new ones' to her house.

Three days later when she returned from a shift at the hospital, there was a phone message from two missionaries; Elder Russ Barnes and Elder Eric Rosenbaum. They would like to set an appointment for a visit to her home.

Edie wanted to make sure that her son Jonah would be home, too. So at dinner that evening she casually discussed that fact that she had filled out a 'pass along' card to meet them.

"Mom." Teresa said. "Are you really getting interested in the LDS Church?"

"Not so much the Church, but some of the missionaries. So I sort of invited them over. At least two of them. You know they come in pairs." She laughed. "When I was in Iraq, I met one or two medical people from Utah that were of that faith. They were good people. Kind, good natured, and hard working. Nearly all of the ones I knew were really patriotic."

Two days later, Edith made an appointment with the two Elders from the LDS Church. A few minutes before they were to arrive for a visit. Jonah finally arrived home and went upstairs to take a shower.

Teresa had a late activity at school, and had not come home yet. Jonah had come downstairs to the kitchen and was searching for an afternoon snack. Just then the doorbell rang, and Edith hurried to answer it. As she opened the door, she was a bit breathless. "Please come in." She invited them into the living room. When she finally could see Elder Rosenbaum, she had a 'flashback' going back twenty years. It seemed as if the younger version of Dr. Rosenbaum had just come into the room.

"Please have a seat, I'll go see if my child- - - - - are- - - - -," She turned to see Jonah standing with a cookie in his hand staring at Eric.

Jonah stood speechless for a long moment. "Mom who are these guys?"

"We're Elders from the LDS Church, we came to tell you about the Restored Gospel of Jesus Christ." Elder Barnes said.

The young missionary turned and stared at Jonah. He then turned and gazed at his 'new' companion. He looked first and Jonah standing in the doorway with a glass of milk and cookie in his hand. In his other hand he bit on a cookie.

Jonah quickly set the milk back on the kitchen counter, and walked a step or two in Eric's direction. "Have we- - - - do we know- - - - -?"

Elder Barnes stared at both the two young men, too. "Hey, are you guys cousins or something?"

Eric recovered more quickly. He walked toward Jonah, put out his hand and said, "I'm Eric Rosenbaum and you're- - - -?"

"My legal name is Jonah Fletcher." But then he scowled at his mother. "I now think she has some explaining to do."

Chapter Fourteen

"Okay." Edith said. "I'm not sure this is the time to explain how I know about you, Elder Rosenbaum, or of my and Jonah's connection to your family. It actually began over twenty years ago in Iraq." She leaned toward Eric while sitting a chair. "I was there in a military field hospital, and your father was a surgeon at that time and in the army's medical corp, as was I serving as a nurse."

You, Eric Rosenbaum was just a little boy, and your mother had sent pictures of you to your father and he showed them to me. So, at that time, I knew your father quite well. Mainly, I worked in the same field hospital in Southern Iraq. I was a surgical nurse at the time."

"Hey guys, it looks like we're going to be here for a while. Come in and get comfortable. Jonah said, and waved his hand at the sofa and love seat in the living room.

"Okay, just to get you up to date. My Mom, over here, came home from Iraq 'with child'. Me." Jonah said. "So I'm guessing, knowing my, or rather our father's/track record' He *knew* her in the 'Biblical' sense. My mom married Herbert Fletcher about the time I was six months old. And possibly about that time dad returned to Salt Lake, and my sister, Ellie Ann, about ten months later become part of the reunion."

Edith turned to her son. "I had no idea - - - - -?"

"Mother, dear you have no idea what Teresa and I discuss. Oh, by the way Teresa is my seventeen-year-old sister, going on thirty-five."

"Well, I just 'joined the club'. I have a seventeen-year-old sister, too. Eric said. "Oh, before we go on with this conversation, I must make sure none of this leaves the house. Elder Barnes do you understand about the privacy of this conversation?"

Barnes glanced at Eric and Jonah and then dropped his head. Then gazed up at Eric. "I understand perfectly."

"Okay, now we can discuss this somewhat unusual situation." Eric said. He walked to Jonah and pulled him up from his chair. "Nice to meet you brother." Then he gave him a big hug.

They both turned to Edith. "You orchestrated this meeting. Why?" Eric asked.

She studied both of them for a long moment. "Because both of you needed to know that you each had a half-brother. A fine, strong brother."

"My Dad, Herb was the best guy anyone could have for a parent. What's this Taylor, guy like?" Jonah asked. He leaned over and touched Eric's arm.

"First of all, he's okay, and is Jewish. I never could really understand how my parents 'hooked up.' But they did. He just has a hard time 'keeping his pants on' especially when he in close proximity of an attractive woman. Right now, my parents are 'split'. From what I understand from my sisters, 'take' on the whole thing. My father walked out on my mother, because she worked very hard and earned an advanced degree in clinical psychology. She works with mainly children who are traumatized, usually, in a hospital setting. His main complaint about my mother is that she gained some weight while involved in her studies."

"So what you are sharing with us is that Taylor is a selfish jerk." Jonah said.

Edith raised her eyebrows and said. "So Taylor has turned from a fine doctor into a real prick."

"Oh, I think he's still a good therapist. I guess he's having a mid-life melt-down. My older sister said he is living with some inept 26-year-old secretary. And the latest word is that he's growing tired of her too. However, he is paying for my church mission." Eric said with a half smile.

"Okay, thinking back twenty plus years ago. He was a fine doctor, but he complained constantly. However, he did show me pictures of you, Eric," Edith said. "He was very proud of you. So to clear up the situation. When I first saw you, you reminded me of your father. And look like him. Also, when I learned your last name, I just had to meet you."

Jonah sat in a leather chair that swiveled, and he took advantage of the chair and swung back and forth. "Hey Eric, I know this sounds strange, but I'm glad Mom hunted you down. It's good to know you and of our connection, to each other."

Eric reached over and slapped Jonah's knee. "It's always good to find a little brother you didn't know you had."

Edith got up and left the room for an instant. She returned with her cell phone. "Let's get some pictures. Come over here, both of you and let me take some."

"I have to take some, too." Teresa said and quickly left the room, returning with her phone.

So for the next half hour or so, the main activity in the room was picture taking. Finally, Teresa said. "Mom, come over here and let's get some of you between the brothers."

"Oh, I don't need to be in the pictures." She frowned.

"Okay then take one of me in the center with the two 'bros' on each side." Teresa teased.

"Hey that's a good idea. My sisters would enjoy seeing a picture of Jonah's little sister. You are about the same age of my sister, Shanna. If I send these to her and Ellie with a request for their pics." Eric laughed. "Then you'll get to meet the whole family".

"What about your Mom?" Jonah asked. "I'd love to see pics of your mother."

"That's right. The only pictures I ever saw of your Mom was when you were just a toddler, Eric." Edith said.

"I could ask for a recent picture. The sisters may have to be sneaky to get one. But I'll ask." Eric said.

"Well, since you two are here. I have pumpkin pie with whipped cream." Edith said. "Let's move this conference to the kitchen." She stood and wiggled her finger at the young people in her living room.

"Mom makes great pie." Jonah said as he put his hand on Eric's shoulder. They all moved to the kitchen.

That night as Edith settled into bed, her mind went back to Taylor. What a handsome 'devil' he was. Remembering back 20 plus years was of war wounded men and hours and hours of surgery. As she studied her reflection in the mirror, she closed her eyes and for a long moment she recalled the long hours she stood next to Taylor in a crude surgical area blocked off with canvas walls making them into movable rooms. So primitive, but they did save lives. *War truly was hell.* She thought of those three young men sitting in her home a few hours ago. She hoped and prayed that they would never experience any kind of war. But wars went on endlessly, because of evil men wanting to tear other countries apart.

That evening as Eric and his companion knelt to have their evening prayers, he came to the conclusion that the Lord had somehow directed Edith to recognize him, because he did resemble his father. And also, he was able to meet her son. Now he knew that somehow knowing his half-brother was an important piece of information in all their lives. He thought about phoning his sisters first. Yet his mother needed to know about Jonah Fletcher, too.

NO. His sisters needed to be informed before Mom. What day was it tomorrow? It was a Friday. Ellie would probably be at work. And he had a missionary meeting with the local mission presidency at 10.00 a.m. He raised his wrist near the window behind his bed and glanced at his watch. It was 11:35 p.m. He'd call tomorrow morning right after breakfast.

He settled down in his narrow, but comfortable bed. He closed his eyes, and soon fell asleep.

While Ellie was in the hall bathroom, she heard the phone ring in the kitchen. She ran down the hallway to her Mom's den and scooped it up. "Hello?" She was slightly winded. The first sound she heard before she coughed, was- - - -

"Hi, who did I wake up?" Eric said.

"Eric? Hi back. You managed to get me, Ellie." She cleared her throat. "What's going on?" Anything special?"

"Yeah, pretty important. Do you have time to chat?" He answered.

"I'm supposed to be at work in an hour. Is your news world-shaking?" She said, half seriously.

"Pretty world shaking." Eric cleared his throat. "Is Mom up yet? What about Shanna?"

"Before you say anything else. Does this important message involve Mom or Dad?" She asked.

"Indirectly it involves all of us, but directly, it involves our 'dear' father. Yesterday, I met a new relative of ours. A half brother."

"You mean our 'dear' father was married before?!" Ellie said, words dripping with sarcasm.

"Not married. This happened when he was in the military. During the Iraq war. Remember, he was over there as a non-combatant. I was nearly two, and he had to serve for about 18 months."

"So he served more than just those needing medical and surgical attention. This happened before I was born, right? What else is new?" She sighed.

"The guy I met. His name is Jonah Fletcher. His mother saw me and my companion, another missionary for the LDS church, Elder Barnes. And what's weird is this guy, Jonah, we look like each other. My companion and I met this young man yesterday at his mother's house."

"So, how old is this 'half-bro?" Ellie asked.

"He's less than a year younger than I am. I remember Mom and Dad talking about when he served a medical mission in Iraq. Jonah's Mom was a surgical nurse over there at the same time Dad was there."

"Good ole' dad. Up to his old tricks, only they were fairly pretty new back then." She scoffed. "What else is new in the lives of the Rosenbaum family?"

"I met both his Mom and Jonah. I've been thinking about this mostly all night. Do you think we should tell Mom?"

"Now? Today? Naah." Ellie took a long breath. "If you choose to do so. make friends with him and his mom. Is she married now? Does this Jonah, guy use his step father's name?"

"Yes. It's Jonah Fletcher. And his stepfather is dead. Jonah spoke of his father as a great guy."

"Well, chalk up this family as one in the 'lucky' column." She stopped talking for a brief moment and took a breath. "I'm not saying we're not doing okay. Just that if one really 'looks around', the ideal American family is suffering more than ever. Well, I must move along this morning. I'm glad you called. I love talking to you. Take care and keep us 'in the loop'."

"Before you go. I'm glad I could talk to you, too. Keep me in your prayers, and I'll keep you in mine. Bye, for now." He broke the connection.

"So Dad's infidelities go back more than 20 years. Why am I not surprised." She mumbled and returned to the bathroom.

Maybe later she would scramble some eggs before her mom left for the hospital. *She decided that, now four of us or possibly now five counting Jonah's little sister, needed to take care of a couple of mothers.*

The New Year came and began its trek across the world. Biggest problem: Inflation all over the country. Plus, the remaining dregs of the covid virus was still inflicting its finality on the lives of some people. Yet, people were tired of 'hunkering down" And began to plan trips, shop and certainly in some areas were moving, buying, and leasing houses.

Certainly, where the Rosenbaum lived up an older, but exclusive area, there was always remodeling going on. Just driving to the university and back, she was reminded because, she would see new apartments, and new housing being constructed.

Idaho and Utah were the number one and two states with an influx of population in the country and nothing was slowing it down.

On Ellie's way home from classes at the university, she stopped at a Christian Church on a main road connecting to her house up on the hill. It was a Saturday in January and hinted of snow. For some reason she parked and walked into the chapel. It had the usual Christian motif in structure. No one was about, so she went into one of rear pews and sat down. It was quiet and deserted. Some how she felt comfortable in this building and began to pray. Something she seldom did while at home.

Chapter Fifteen

About two weeks later Eric received a rather sad phone call from a friend, also on a mission. It was from Stratton Landre. His father was an old friend of his mother's.

"Hi Stratton, what's up. How's your mission going along?"

"I'm being sent home. My Mom's real sick. I don't know exactly what the medical problem is. But the word is that she's ill and in the hospital."

"What hospital? My mom works at the university hospital. If your mom is in that one, my Mom could check on her. What's her full name and age. Tell me and I'll call my mother and have her check on your mother."

"Your mom could do that?" Stratton asked.

"There are ways. A hospital is like a little community. At least that's the way my mom sometimes described it."

"Okay, her official name is Caroline Hughes Landre. And she's 52 years old. Does that help?"

"I'll call my mother tonight or tomorrow. Then whatever she finds out I'll call you back. When are scheduled to fly home?"

"About four days. I'm waiting for a replacement, or a transfer of two new guys. I'll call you back or you call me, whatever comes first. Man, we can certainly thank cell phones. The missions can't restrict missionaries from phoning home the way they used to."

"That's a new wrinkle in our favor. But, we need to stay in control. No phoning old girl friends." Eric laughed. "I'll let you know what I find out."

It was late that evening, when Eric called his mother's cell phone.

Roselyn heard it ringing in her office, and raced upstairs to grab it. "Hello?

"Hi, Mom? Did the correct individual answer the phone?"

"Eric? Glad I made it upstairs to my phone. I'm going to have to carry it around in a pocket. How are you doing? What's going on?"

"Glad I called you. Do you remember my friend, Stratton Landre?"

"Is that Luke Landre's son? If it is, yes, I remember him. Isn't he on a mission, too?" "Where is he now?" Roz asked.

"The reason why I called is that since he only has less than two months to finish his mission, they are sending him home in a few days."

"Why is he being sent home early?"

"His mother is real sick in the hospital. I wondered if you could find out her situation? Her name is Caroline Hughes Landre, and she's 52."

"If she's up at University Hospital, I may be able to find out why she's a patient up there. If she's in the main hospital in Murray, maybe not. Why won't his Dad tell him the details?"

"I think it's up to the mission president. Just like they've never given me or my companion the details of why they moved us from Mexico to Colorado Springs over three weeks ago."

'I suppose the missions have their reasons." Roz said. Then she paused. "Okay, I'll see what I can find out, and get back to you. Have a good night, and a profitable tomorrow. Love you. Bye."

Roselyn set down the phone. *Wow, one never knows. Hmm, should I call Luke? I haven't seen him in years. It wouldn't be good to ask questions. I'd better find what I can on my own. Use a bit of subtrafuse.*

The next day Roselyn had a normal 9:00 a.m. to 4:00 p.m. shift. There were always sick children, teenagers, and even some adults who had problems and needed her attention.

When she arrived at the hospital she went to her office and there were the usual messages about who she needed to visit. Her first patient was a teenage boy who had been shot, accidently. Or was it an accident? His name was Rayvon Richards, age thirteen. The information sheet mentioned a family member's involvement. An older brother took the weapon from the house and met up with friends and went to a party. *(that usually leads to a powder keg)*.

From the police report, the brother met two friends and three of them planned to crash the party. Rayvon heard them talking and decided to follow them into the house. The situation at the party became volatile. There was an argument, but the younger brother's arrival seemed to cause even more of a fight. The father of the girl hosting the party then came home, saw the cars around his house and walked in. He immediately broke up the party sending all the kids home. Outside the boys argued and the younger brother trying to grab the gun was shot.

The father called the police and the older brother, and the shooter went to jail. Because of the involvement of seven girls and nine boys, the school they attended hastily came up with new policy that went into effect. None of the teenagers involved could attend school on Monday. They could not come back until the school district had the police report. Whether or not this was legal would have to be decided by the school board. It could possibly go to the county police. And later to court. So now Roselyn needed to speak to the younger brother who had gone to the party to save his older brother from trouble. And became the victim. Roselyn's job was to help the younger brother to not only process what happened, to him, but understand that he could have avoided the situation. He could have chosen not to go to the party. She needed to help him see that his behavior caused serious problems to his family, and perhaps even to his older brother.

Later on, she found the list of patients that were severely ill. After reading it she found Caroline Landre's name as a patient in the cancer ward. During her lunch break, Roselyn went up to that ward and located Caroline's room, and she found Caroline asleep, Roselyn decided not to bother her.

But posted in the 'break room' on that floor was an information chart and she located Caroline's treatment schedule.

Roselyn could possibly need to have a discussion with her physician, but from the schedule, it seemed that Ms. Landre had a blood cancer. *Oh boy! Roselyn thought, very serious.*

As Roselyn walked downstairs to her office, she felt a great sadness. Caroline was only 52, and her own birthday anniversary was coming up in March. This woman's medical problems were not hers, but she was of the same generation. People in their fifties now could possibly live into their mid- eighties. However, there are many factors that caused an individual to pass on much earlier. Because the individual is subject to a disease like cancer. Lifestyle, family inheritance and several other influences.

Just before she left to go home, Roselyn went back up to the cancer wing and as she walked to Caroline's room the door abruptly opened and out walked Luke Landre.

He stopped midstride, looked down at Roselyn and said, "My god Roz what are you doing here?"

"I work here. I am a licensed clinical therapist. I came up here to see how your wife, Caroline Landre is doing. If perhaps I could help her understand her illness." She put her hand on her hip and gazed up at him.

He stepped back and surveyed her with critical exactness. "Okay, have you been in to talk to Caroline yet?"

"No not yet. I came up a few hours ago and she was asleep."

"So when did you go back to the university for an advanced degree?"

"About three-perhaps nearly four years ago. I know from what I read and heard that you are a practicing attorney." She gazed up at him. *For being in his fifties he looks pretty good.*

"Do you need to go somewhere right now?" He waved his hand at a bench located across the hallway.

"No, I'm through for the day. That is unless I receive an emergency page." She pulled her cell phone from her pocket.

He took her arm and guided her to the bench. "For a fifty plus year old, you're looking pretty good. Sit here and tell me about your family."

"Well, for starters I married Taylor Rosenbaum. We have

three children. A boy first; Eric. Right now, he's on a mission in Colorado Springs."

"Of course, Stratton and your son are good friends. I believe they had a class together at the university. Any girls in the family?" Luke said and a ghost of a smile creased his face.

"Yes, there are two girls in the Rosenbaum family; EllieAnn is twenty and Shanna is seventeen. Ellie attends the university, and Shanna is a senior in high school. Do you have any girls?"

"Yes. Two years or so after Stratton, we had twin girls. They'll be twenty next birthday. I have to let you know that it was a *real* circus around our house for a year or two, and probably is still going on," He grinned and shook his head. "That's why I'm still in shock over Caroline's illness."

Roselyn laughed. "I'm so sorry about you wife's illness. But I do remember those crazy years, with three little kids to deal with. The only good thing is that babies are usually born to young parents."

"Yes, that is a blessing. Well, I've a conference call with one of my clients in about an hour." He stood and offered his hand to help her off the bench. "I'm still processing Caroline's illness. Do you know anything about how the medical people will proceed with her treatment?"

"No. I'm not an MD, just a therapist. Even under these circumstances, it was good to see you a again. Take care." Roselyn walked to the elevator, and pressed the 'down' button.

While driving home Roselyn was thankful, that so far, her health was pretty good, except for the extra pounds she carried around. She realized that it was not quite dark right now at 5 p.m. has it had been two weeks ago. She supposed that was a fact that made her feel a little better. Now she needed to decide how much she should tell Eric about Caroline's illness. As a medical therapist she needed to protect the patient, as well as her family.

January moved on to February, and for a few days there was bright sunshine, though still very cold. But the weather prognosticators could not forget about winter. One Tuesday morning the 'weather' let everyone know in the cove that '*winter'* was still in charge'. The day was overcast, and cold winds blew from the south.

When Roselyn went into the office area on her floor with her lunch tray, a gust of wind rattled the double paned windows. She managed to hold on to the tray and not spill her carafe of tea. "Wow, what was that?" She said as she set her tray down.

A new nurse stood up, took Roselyn's tray, and set it down on the table. "It started to gust strong winds about a half hour ago. So we turned on the TV for the weather report. It looks like we are in for a big storm. Hi, I'm Suze Mcfee. We, my husband and I just moved here from Pomona, CA. Is it always so cold and windy in Northern Utah?"

"We can have cold wet winters, or not so much. Last winter we had one really snowy month, and another fairly stormy one. We are in a drought situation here. A good, wet winter would help." Roselyn said, and put out her hand. "Good to meet you."

The wind kept up and about mid-afternoon it began to snow. Less than a half-hour later an announcement came over the loud speaker. "Due to the approaching storm, the management has suggested that all non- medical personnel should leave for their homes soon. We have enough room here for certain individuals to stay overnight, but it would be better if those non-medical people leave as soon as possible. According to the national weather service, we are expecting a heavy storm, here in the east mountain ranges of Northern Utah. It has been predicted that it will move south during the night. Those living in northern and central Utah need to leave soon."

Chapter Sixteen

Roselyn went back to her office and gathered up some work she had to do. Before she slipped on her coat, she changed from her shoes to boots, made sure she had gloves, and left the desk light on. She walked from her office to the elevator down to the parking garage.

Driving home was good and bad. There was heavy traffic, but because of the traffic the cars going south and east had already begun to drive over the fallen snow that began over a half-hour ago. So, driving home was less hazardous than negotiating fresh snow. To add to the chaos, there were always those cars and light trucks that were not as stable in bad weather as others.

Luckily, the snowplows had just made a trail up into the cove. Roselyn decided she would not get on her phone while driving. Visibility was also a factor, because of the lashing snow, dark clouds and the wind. As she turned west on the last street leading home she swerved and nearly hit a parked car in front of a house three doors east. She was forced to back away from the sloping curb. A neighbor, out shoveling noticed her problem and came and knocked on the passenger window.

"I'll shovel around the front of your car. Help you with more traction."

"Okay. I won't move." She watched him shovel. Then after a few minutes, he again knocked on her window and waved. First sliding the car in low gear, she inched the car in reverse and managed to back into more of the center of the street. Slowly she made it to the front of her garage and eased a right turn in toward her parking spot.

Both her daughters were out shoveling, and Ellie knocked on her window, stomped into the garage and lifted the door and directed her mother in.

Once Roselyn was out of her car and stood in the open garage, she yelled at her daughters. "You two are fantastic. Thanks a bunch."

"When there are only women to do the work, we plan and then execute." Ellie said. "Glad you made it home. Come in and make the soup. I started to dice up the vegetables, and the chicken is already in the pot. I think we're about done out here anyway." She stomped off the snow from her boots, and walked into the house. She kicked off her boots, and eased down the stairs to her bedroom. Moments later she returned wearing slippers. "I've worked up and appetite. Let's get that soup done."

Roselyn did much the same. Leaving her boots in the front hallway and went up to her bedroom and grabbed a pair of comfortable slippers. Washing her hands then she began to finish the vegetables and put them into the big pot with the chicken.

When Shanna came into the kitchen, Roselyn said. "You come and watch the soup. Just bring it to a simmer. "I'm going to make some biscuits."

Less than an hour later the three Rosenbaum females sat down to freshly baked biscuits, hot chicken, vegetable soup and a beverage of choice.

After cleaning up the kitchen, Shanna went into the living room and turned on the TV. "Mom. She yelled; The TV is out. A message scrolls across the screen about *loss of picture.*

Roselyn went into the living room. "Hmmm, I thought that we had 'storm proof 'cable TV. Sorry girl, I'd better check on the furnace. TV, we can live without. Heat not so much." She searched a kitchen drawer for a flashlight, and marched downstairs to the furnace room. She checked the furnace, the blower, the thermostat. Everything seemed to be in order. Then she came back upstairs.

Shanna sat in the living room and had a book in her lap. "I guess I could get into this book."

"Are you reading it for a class at school?" Roselyn asked.

"Yes. It's for our psychology class. It's about modern psychology. Modern being the 20th Century. It's about Sigmund Freund. He supposedly invented psychoanalyzing people. Find out their inner turmoil and 'stuff' like that."

Roselyn laughed. "You should call your father. That's what he does for a living."

"Is that what he really does? He used to talk about a 'session' with certain people. I thought he was a 'head" doctor?"

Ellie dropped into a chair, laughing. "From what I understand, he became a medical doctor first and then learned to psychoanalyze. ''Learn about their inner fears, desires, their mental 'traps'." She said in a deep theatrical voice.

Roselyn shook her head. "Not quite that dramatic, Elle Ann." Her mother said.

"Hey, that's what you should do, Go call him right now. He'd probably get you enough information about who he sees, and what they tell him for a whole term paper." She jumped up and ran to the kitchen for the phone.

"Hey, I don't want to talk to him right now. I need to read this book." Shanna said.

But Ellie returned holding the phone and talking. "That's right, Dad. She needs to read about the life of Sigmund Freund. Yeah, it's for her psychology class."

"Well, he was the 'father of psychoanalysis. Tell her to look him up on the computer. There is probably a wealth of information about him. Tell her to call me if she has any trouble. While I have you on the phone, what is the weather like up there right now."

"We had to shovel the driveway so that Mom could park in the garage. If you really want to know, I'll go down and look out the front door. Hang on." Ellie walked down the stairs to the front entrance. She opened the door and eased out on the oval shaped porch. "Wow, there's about five inches of snow on the front door mat. The TV is out, but we still have the radio and the internet. We're fine."

He cleared his throat. "If the front doormat has that much snow, what about the storm coming down off the kitchen balcony?"

Ellie trudged back up the stairs. "I have to put the phone down so, I can get out on the balcony. "Here." she handed the phone to Shanna. "Talk to Dad while I check out the snow level on the deck." Ellie pulled out the brace that lay across the window track. She pushed the door open and stepped out. "Oh my gosh, there's at least a half a foot of snow out here."

"Be careful. Do you even have any shoes on?" Roselyn asked as she stood and watched her daughter open the sliding door.

"I have flip flops with rubber soles. Besides I'm not going out any farther." She gave the sliding door a mighty shove and dropped the long pole in the door track.

Shanna put the phone to her ear. "Ellie says there's at least six inches of new snow on the deck. But the snow is blowing in from the north-west."

"How do you know where the storm is coming from?" Taylor asked.

"It's on the internet, type in channel three." Shanna said. "You can even get it on your phone."

"Thanks for the information, daughter. I'll call you tomorrow." Taylor set the phone down, and walked to the front door and looked out. No one was in the hallway. Living in this small apartment with Marlene. . . . was bad enough. But he really missed his office at home. He needed to move back home, but would Roz even let him back in? He'd end up sleeping in the basement on the old sofa bed. He picked up the phone. "Well, you 'guys' take it easy. I'll check on you tomorrow."

Taylor shut down his cell phone, and dropped onto the sofa, and put his feet on the old scarred coffee table. He glanced around the small living room, with the kitchen bar separating the living area from the kitchen area. The building this apartment was in was only two years old. But it *was* an apartment, not his spacious three level house. He had not seen Roz for three months; Besides the fact that he had alienated his daughters and probably his son, too.

Was living with this pretty young '*thing*' worth losing his family?" Right now, he wasn't so sure. Well sitting here wasn't getting any work done, and he had reports to do. He moved over to the small desk he had been using. Right now, he dearly missed his desk in his '*home office* However he had work to do, and he'd better get some of it done.

The wind slacked off, but the storm came down in steady 'sheets' of white. With no TV, and only the weather reports on cell phones, the three females each moved into their bedrooms or in Roselyn's case, reports to do. But soon the girls came from their bedrooms. and put on their night clothes. Less than an hour later Roselyn did the same. The house became quiet.

The nearly silent windless snowstorm dropped quiet sheets of snow, and the weather took over the Wasatch Front. Sometime as dawn approached the storm moved south and slightly west. It now became the problem for Utah County where BYU University was located and began its assault on another large city and college campus.

The Intermountain West, and on south to the western Utah had been dealing with a drought for many years. They were also receiving heavy precipitation in a form of a rain-snow mix. Perhaps some of the fervent prayers that had been offered up had been heard and higher powers responded.

With the blessings of a heavy storm came modern complications, wet snowy roads, more than normal traffic accidents. Yet people had been warned, and several truck stops were fllled with many truckers stopping for the night. Where shelter was available the parking lots of many towns began to fill with cargo trucks, and other long haul drivers seeking shelter.

Since it was a weekday morning, Shanna woke at her usual time to get ready for high school.

When she walked into the kitchen, she noticed her mother standing at the front door gazing through the glass storm door. She could see that the storm was over, and the winter sun was fighting to shine through the remaining clouds. "How much snow is on the lawn?" Shanna asked.

Her mother began to laugh. "I think we're buried in here. Please go get the yard stick we were using last night." Roselyn asked.

Shanna quickly returned to the front door. "I have boots on. Let me go out and measure."

The mother watched her younger daughter step out on the porch. Then she had to lift her feet to get out on the lawn. She took two steps and then plunged the yard stick into the snow-covered lawn. She stepped back into her footprints and laughed. She lifted the yardstick. And carefully stepped back on the little porch, then up to the front door, holding high the top of the stick.

"How much snow?" Yelled her mother.

"The stick went in 18 plus inches, actually 18 and a half." Holding it carefully, she opened the glass door and stepped inside and stood on the entrance mat. "Look Mom. Go get a marker. We have to make a mark. So, no one can dispute reality."

Chapter Seventeen

Some five hours later the first snow plow came by and began clearing a narrow strip leaving hard packed snow in the middle of the street. The only place the snow could go was into a huge pile at the dead end of their street. (It really couldn't be called street, maybe a lane.) And a snow clogged one across the end of their street. Since the sun was bright, people up and down their street began coming outside, and began to clear off walkways and driveways.

The only place that the snow could go was on every lawn in front of every house of every street in the cove. To even drive down to the grocery store, was an adventure. And that was if you had a four-wheel drive. At least everyone on the street had electricity and the gas lines were buried deep so the residents had heat. Even though the Rosenbaum house had underground utilities, just not any TV. The three Rosenbaum females had plenty of school work to do. Or in the case of Roselyn, she had case files to update. But by mid-afternoon, a type of 'locked in' boredom set in. Probably the one positive about this 'super storm' is that it happened in the third week of February. Which meant longer days of light, more sunshine.

And cell phones functioned just fine. About five p.m. Shanna stomped into the kitchen and began a search in the pantry for a bottle of cola A few minutes later she climbed up to the bedroom level and stood in the doorway of Roselyn's den and asked. "Is there any more cola? And what are we going to have for dinner?"

Roselyn glanced up from her paperwork and said, "Isn't there any more in the pantry?"

"Nope."

"Did you go downstairs and search the food storage room?"

"You mean I'm going to have to go down there and look for a simple coke in that 'icebox'?"

With a half smile on her face, the mother said. "Your next choice is to get on your skate board and 'ride down' to SIMS Market. Of course, then you would be forced to carry both your skateboard *and* the beverage of choice up the hill and down our street to reach your home."

Ellie came upstairs and could hear her mother's answer to Shanna's question. She touched Shanna's shoulder and said, "Well, once you get down to the retail area, you could walk over to the pizza parlor and get a drink in a paper cup, 'to go'."

Shanna grumped in disgust. "You two think being locked up in this snow-covered house is fun?!"

"No one said anything about this giant snow storm being fun." Ellie said grinning. "At least we have heat, lights, and cell phones that work. Once you get back to school, you and your friends can trade 'locked up in the 'snow cave' stories." Ellie laughed.

"I'll bet there are many, hundreds of families living in and around this valley that don't have underground utilities, with power outages, and even frozen pipes." Roselyn said.

"Frozen pipes! Come on, it's February." Shanna said.

Just then the phone rang, and Ellie grabbed the phone from the kitchen bar. "Hello?"

"Hi, I heard you guys have a record-breaking snowstorm snarling up traffic and causing zillions traffic accidents." Eric said.

"Hi Eric, where did you hear that?" Ellie said.

"TV. We've been watching for a time. How are you guys doing?"

"Officially, we have 18.5 inches of snow on the front lawn." We measured it with a yard stick. So, nobody is going anywhere." Ellie said. "At least the sun is out, and the city came and plowed a little trail down the street. We're fine. Just no TV." Do you have any hint of it coming storm over there?"

"Yes, the dregs of your storm is supposed to pick up moisture and intensify hitting our area tomorrow." Eric said.

"What we've heard is that your airport is closed until possibly tomorrow. And I guess the highways are a mess with a zillion traffic accidents, and road closures. I just had to call and check on you 'guys'." Eric laughed.

"We're fine. This is the time when food storage comes in handy. But of course, not everyone has the means to have a good supply of canned goods as we have." Ellie said, "Maybe Mom will decide to teach Shanna and me to make bread." She laughed.

"You know, maybe I'll give Dad a call. See how's doing in the little apartment with 'what's her name?"

"I think her name is Marlene. And she's maybe 26. What was he thinking? What *was he thinking?"*

"I don't think he had his 'head 'in the game." laughed Eric. "More like his hormones."

"Oh, and lots of flattery. *Oh Dr. Rosenbaum, you're so brilliant, and handsome and virile!* Ellie said and squealed in laughter. "You know maybe now is the time to let him know that he has a son in Colorado Springs."

"I have thought much about that little secret. The only reason I haven't told Dad about Jonah, is that I respect Mrs. Fletcher, and don't want to hurt her. However, I may just give Jonah a call and see what his feelings are about meeting his biological father."

"By the way has your friend Stratton left his mission to come home? Mom said something about how ill Mrs. Landre is."

"I've been really busy the past few days. I'll give him a call. I'll let you know if we get some of your storm. Take lots of pictures and send them over. I'd like to see you in our 'snow hut' that used to be a house. I'd better get off the phone. Take care. Love you Mom and girls.."

Eric sat back away from the small desk in the 'training' room located in the mission center where he now lived. He had less than three months to serve. So far it had been a successful almost two years. But what was going on at home sometimes pulled him away from finding people to teach the LDS gospel. Even though he and his companion had been transferred from Central Mexico to a quiet suburb of Colorado Springs, he missed the more relaxed atmosphere of Mexico. Yet he found the quiet area here in Colorado Springs pleasant, but definitely colder. He opened his Bible to the Sunday School lesson the adults were studying. If we went out on a 'teaching' call he would at least be able to talk to investigators about the Old Testament.

After dinner, he had the assigned chore of cleaning up and loading the dish washer. There was always trash to take out. As he carried the trash outside, he felt the change in the weather. The deep cold had changed to a warmer breeze, and it was definitely windy, and he also felt a higher humidity. He smiled, they were going to get some snow, too. He loved snow, mainly because what you could do with and in it. Top of the list was skiing. You couldn't find better skiing than what Northern Utah offered. He decided it would be a great experience to be in Colorado during a good heavy, snowstorm.

After dinner the missionaries had a meeting with one of the local bishops. He gave out lists of possible families to visit and introduce them to the LDS religion. One of the families were the Fletchers' The mother had filled out a 'Pass along' cards. She was inviting them to her house Friday afternoon. Today was Tuesday. He decided that he and his companion better study and prepare to meet with that family again.

The weather did change and they did receive a good heavy snowstorm, but nothing to give the huge storm in Northern Utah any competition. The day of the snowstorm, their mission president sent the missionaries out to clear walks and shovel driveways of people living in and around the neighborhood.

When he gave them their 'clearing' assignment he said. "This is a 'good neighbor' assignment. When or if the home owner asks what you are doing, just tell them they are helping clear out the neighborhood, but also tell them who you are and what religion you represent."

So, the young missionaries went out with shovels and brooms in hand to clear the snow away from the homes near the LDS Ward

House. First, they rang doorbells and asked permission to clear the snow away from walkways and driveways.

Most of the home owners were surprised and delighted. One man asked Elder Barnes if he would have to attend their Sunday Service.

"Oh, no sir, we are just volunteering to do snow removal. Just a gesture to help you get your walks cleaned, and your and driveway more easily accessed. However, we are inviting you to come to our Sacrament Service at 11 a.m. this Sunday. And nearly every Sunday in the future."

The older man came out on the porch. "Well now, I'm surprised and like your idea of service. Go ahead and clear away the snow. But ring the doorbell when you finish."

Chapter Eighteen

Once Eric and Markus Barnes had finished clearing away the snow, they did ring the doorbell. An older woman wearing an apron over her jeans and sweater invited them in.

"Please come in and have a snack." She asked. The two young men glanced at each other, but Eric nodded, and the woman opened the storm door and invited them in. "It's warm in here, so take off your coats and leave them on the 'coat tree' in the hallway."

They did as she asked and followed her into the kitchen. She waved at two chairs near the oval table and they sat down.

"Either of you dislike hot cocoa?" she asked.

Eric shook his head. "No, ma'am. Markus smiled. "No ma'am!"

"By the way, I'm Beth Killian, and I am most impressed that you two would offer to do snow shoveling. Were you sent to do this around the neighborhood by one of your leaders to do this service? And do you both live in the tan brick house near your church building?"

"Yes and yes." Markus Barnes said.

"Well, this is a most interesting way to invite people to learn more about your religion. This is my way of thanking you for your hard work." She turned back to her counter took a mug from the microwave and set it along with a plate and spoon in front of Markus, and another mug from the microwave near Eric. She also set a plate of chocolate cookies more in the center of the table. She then set another mug in the microwave and warmed it. She set that mug on the table and sat down near it. She took a sip from her mug and turned to the young men. "So tell me about where you each are from and how you became a missionary for your church."

Eric stirred the hot chocolate in his mug and took a sip. It was hot, rich and delicious. "This cocoa is really good." Then he took another swallow.

"From what I've read and heard your religion, is based in Utah. Correct?"

"Yes. LDS Church Headquarters is based in Salt Lake City, Utah. Oh before I go on. "I'm Elder Eric Rosenbaum from Salt Lake and- - - - -"

"I'm Markus Barnes from Cedar Breaks, in Southern, Utah. "My town is closer to the southern border next to Arizona."

"The Mormon Church started in Utah, didn't it?" Mrs. Killian said.

"No, actually it began in the Midwest, Missouri and Illinois." Eric said.

"Interesting. I'll have to Google it." Ms. Killian said. She glanced around the table. "It seems that you young men have finished your snack. Would like another Cookie?"

"Oh, no ma'am. We'd better get along we may find another house to shovel." Eric answered. He stood up, walked toward the front door and reached for his coat. "Come on Barnes, we'd better go." Searching his coat pocket, he took some cards from his inside coat pocket. "These are 'pass along' cards. These give you information about the LDS Church and when the Sunday meetings are held. Thank you for the treat." He moved to the front door.

The two missionaries left the house and walked back to their mission home. They felt a stiff breeze. Markus glanced up at the sky. "It's starting to cloud up. Maybe it's going to snow again."

"It's still winter. It can snow buckets. Let's get on back to the 'house'." Eric said.

When they walked in, their 'house' mother asked them to come in through the kitchen and leave their wet shoes or boots in the entry way to the kitchen area. "How many houses did you shovel out?"

"Two. The last one had a triple driveway and a large lot. However, the lady of the house invited us in and we gave her 'pass along' cards. Elder Barnes answered.

"Well, you two have done fine service, today. Go upstairs and relax. Dinner will be at 5.30." Sister Ross said.

Eric took the second turn for the bathroom in the hallway upstairs. When he came out and returned to their room, Markus was asleep. He kicked off his shoes and lay down on his bed. He was physically tired, but the idea of Jonah Fletcher meeting their biological father nagged at him. Before he called his Dad, he decided he would ask what Jonah thought about the idea.

Down the hall was a room which could be another missionary bedroom, but was used as a small meeting room at the present time. While walking to the empty room, Eric grabbed his cell phone and called the Fletcher residence. As luck would have it, Jonah answered the phone.

"Greetings on this snowy day." Jonah answered.

"Greetings yourself, this is Eric Rosenbaum."

"Hey, big bro how's today unfolding?" Jonah said. "Have you been outside?"

"Oh yeah." Eric said. "'Been out shoveling driveways and walks. It seems that Colorado Springs got its' very own blizzard. "Didn't have to borrow any from Northern Utah."

"Interesting. I just finished our driveway a while ago. Mainly so Mom can get her car in the garage. She has a shift that doesn't finish until Midnight. Luckily, it quit snowing a few hours ago."

"The reason why I called is that I'd like to know how you feel about me calling our mutual father and telling him about you. Your existence, I mean." Eric asked.

"I've been thinking about good old Taylor myself. The older I get, and kind of understand male testosterone." He laughed self–consciencely. "I can sort of see why a man with a wife and child, even though they are several thousand miles away, would be interested in a pretty woman close by and available." Jonah said and cleared his throat.

"I understand what you're saying. Eric said. "I also think it's the way he was raised, as a non-Christian. Maybe I'm making up excuses for him, but he does have his way of seeing the world. I think he'd really be proud of you. I know he is of me, and my sisters."

"Okay, why don't you tell him, but also let him know of my hardworking Mom and the great stepdad I had." Jonah let go a long breath.

"Okay. I just had to get your permission. And we have to keep up our relationship. I'll be released from my mission a less than three months. Then I'll return to Salt Lake and college. It may be, however a few days before I can't hide out and will call him. Luckily, we all have cell phones. Before there were cell phones, missionaries could only call home on special occasions. Now things are really different. But still, no calling some girl a missionary left home, and he keeps on checking on her."

"Kind of like being in the military and 'boot' camp." Jonah laughed. "Let me know how your phone call to 'our' father goes."

"I'll let you know how this 'revealing experience' goes." Talk to you in a few."

Nearly two days passed before Eric had a successful phone visit with his father. The missionaries had 'zone area' meetings in the evening before Eric managed to talk to Jonah. And he and Marcus had two new families to visit that day. The first family they met with were in their area. However, the father was more interested in why the LDS Church was so wealthy rather than the religion itself. However, the missionaries did leave a Book of Mormon with the lady of the house.

The next evening Eric managed to go into the 'study' and call his father. When Taylor finally answered his cell phone, he was still in his office downtown. "Dr. Taylor Rosenbaum, how can I be of help to you?"

"Hi Dad, how are you doing?" Eric tried to sound at least 'friendly'.

"Eric! Is this really my son still serving a mission in Colorado Springs? How are you holding up, so far?"

"I've been 'holding up' here in Colorado Springs for over two months. How are you doing? I know you're not living at home anymore." Eric tried to keep any emotion out of his voice. *Just a friendly tone.* He said to himself.

"So how much longer are you going to be working in that area?" Taylor asked.

"About three months. I should be released sometime in May. It depends on a replacement. When a new guy comes in." He cleared his throat. "The reason why I called - - - - *Why am I so damned tense.*

"Well, it doesn't matter why you called. It's just so good to hear your voice." Taylor spoke with some emotion.

"Okay, there is a major reason why I called. I met a woman around Christmas Time. She asked to meet me. Her name is Edith Fletcher."

"Edie Franklin? Married name Fletcher?!" Taylor could hardly talk. Just hearing her name brought a myriad of emotions to his mind, as well as his breathing. He touched his chest. He coughed. "How did you meet her?"

"She saw me and wanted to meet me. Apparently, I reminded her of you."

Taylor worked hard to speak calmly. "She's living in Colorado Springs? Is a- - - - is she married?"

Eric could hear the emotion in his father's voice. *Wow, he must have really had a 'thing' for her.* "She works as a nurse at Camp Carson Hospital. She's a widow. But what is really interesting, is that she sought me out. She said I reminded her of you."

"A- - - - how and when did she meet you?" The father asked.

"On Christmas Day, and I was standing outside the Ward House, and she happened to drive by. So my companion and I met at her house about a week later. But what is even more interesting is that she has a 20-year-old son, and he and I really resemble each other. His name is Jonah Fletcher. We are about the same height, and have similar body structure. Ms. Fletcher had Jonah and I stand in front of a big mirror hanging over the fireplace in their living room. Then she grabbed her cell phone and began snapping pictures. Then I took some of her and Jonah together. I'm about two years and three months older than he is. I'll send you some pictures from my cell phone to yours." Eric said and tried to keep up an innocent tone of voice.

"You say he's close to 21-year-old?!" Taylor didn't say anything else for several seconds. Though Eric could hear a hitch in his breathing. Then very softly he muttered. "Oh, my God!"

"Yeah Dad. I have a half- brother. And we're both pretty excited about it."

For a long moment there was silence on the phone line. Then the mission president walked into the room where Eric sat speaking to his father.

"There you are Elder Rosenbaum. Put that phone away and come into the living room. We're having a meeting about all the snow shoveling you young men have done yesterday. Come." He walked over and patted his shoulder. Eric stood up. "Right now, let's go."

"Sorry Dad gotta go. Talk to you later."

"Well at least you were speaking to you father. That's good." President Linden waited a beat and watched as Eric shut down the phone and come to his feet.

Chapter Nineteen

The meeting of the fourteen missionaries and President Linden went on until about 9:00 p.m. He praised the young men for their hard work and pleasant demeanor while doing the snow shoveling. Also, the mission home had received several phone calls from the neighbors in praise for the young men's shoveling work. Then President Linden passed out several 'pass along cards' to the pairs of missionaries to call on these people.

Eric was barely 'tuned in' to the president's instructions and assignments. Finally, the young men were invited into the dining room for cake and milk.

President soon sent them up for an hour's study and bed by 10:00.

Eric had a hard time getting to sleep, and kept thinking about his father and what *he* was thinking.

In Salt Lake, Taylor stood staring out the window of his office, and hashing over his conversation with Eric. All his thoughts went to both his son he just learned he had and the boy's mother. He began to remember the young Edith of 21 years ago. Her beauty, her skill as a medical provider, and what a great lover she was. Eric said she was a widow. If she had been married soon after, she left Iraq, she could have other children.

The phone rang, startling Taylor from his thoughts. "Hello?"

Taylor, are you coming home for dinner?" Marlene asked. "It's after 8:00 p.m."

"Ah, I've been busy. I had an important phone call." He snapped.

"I know how busy you are, Darling. I bought a roast chicken. And I know how much you like chicken and mashed potatoes. It's all waiting for you."

"Go ahead and eat. I'll be there as soon as I finish up some things, here."

"Okay, but I'd rather eat with you." she sighed.

"I'll leave in a few minutes. Goodbye," He dropped the phone in its cradle. Then he stood up and began to pace. *How can I find more information about Edie, Edith Fletcher.* "Eric said she worked in the Camp Carson medical facility. I'll google it." As he paced, he realized he was talking to himself.

Before he 'engaged' his computer, he dropped into his chair and stared at the computer screen. *So what are you going to do with this information when you find it? Do you want to call her, meet with her, see her son? He stared at the files on his desk, jumped up and began to file them.*

Twenty minutes later he stared at his clean desk. *Now what?* He reached for a clean file and began to type two names on his computer: **Edith Franklin and Jonah Fletcher.** He printed them and began a new folder. Next, he looked up their address in Colorado Springs. Then he sat back and stared at the file for a long time.

Suddenly, he jumped up and grabbed his coat, and headed for the door. He left his office, and went to his car. Luckily it was in the underground parking garage, dry, but very cold. As he drove the five miles to the apartment building where he lived with Marlene, again he could smile at being able to park in an underground lot. At least he had been smart enough to pick an apartment building where there was sheltered parking.

When he walked into the apartment, he found Marlene curled up on the sofa watching TV. She glanced up at him and smiled. "It will only take me a few minutes to warm up your dinner."

"Oh, I can fix a plate. You go ahead and finish viewing your program." He turned to the small coat closet in the front hall an hung up his coat. Then hung his suit coat on a chair in the kitchen. Rolled up his shirt sleeves, and began to pull containers from the refrigerator. Soon he had a plate of food ready for the microwave. He grabbed a glass of water and sat down at the table. After a few bites, he found himself sitting with a plate of food in front of him staring at the wall. His mind was several thousand miles away, and over twenty years in the past. Why hadn't Edie told him she was pregnant? *Why hadn't Edie told him she was pregnant? Perhaps she didn't know yet? Or was it because she knew he had a wife and child at home?* What would have been the outcome back then?

Mindlessly, he ate the food on his plate and set the dishes in the sink. He heard the beginnings of the ten-0-clock news and he joined Marlene on the sofa. Some of what the newscasters said registered in his mind, some did not. Abruptly, he jumped up, went to the bedroom, stripped, went into the bathroom and took a shower.

Standing in the bedroom he slipped into underwear, jeans and a sweatshirt. He walked back into the kitchen, took some pills with water. Suddenly he said. "You'd better come to bed. I'm going to rise early tomorrow morning, so I may wake you."

"Okay darling, right away." She touched his back and walked into the bathroom with a nightgown in her hands.

A few minutes later he took off his pants and sweatshirt, and climbed into bed. He gave her a brief hug, turned out the lights checked the apartment and returned to bed. A few minutes later he heard Marlene's soft breathing of early sleep. But Taylor lay there wide awake.

For at least an hour, Taylor silently hashed around all this new knowledge of a son he previously didn't know existed and of course new knowledge about his mother. His first memories were of Edith. Now he had to admit that he had been in love with her and still was. Then he thought about Roz. He just had to see Roz again and talk to her. Did he still love her? Did she love him?" What was his status with her and his children?

When he woke after the few hours of sleep he finally managed to relax into, a decision that finally jelled in his head. Marlene was no longer a factor in his life. He had enjoyed her these few months, but there was not the basis for of a long-term relationship between them.

He would take her out to a good place for dinner, and then explain to her their relationship was over.

The next afternoon he called the family house where Roz and the girls lived. "Good afternoon." He said, when Shanna answered the phone. ""Is your mother there?"

"Dad, is this you Dad?" You actually want to speak to someone in this house?"

His first reaction was a retort, or of telling her of his displeasure at being spoken to in that manner. But he held his tongue. "Is this my beautiful blond haired seventeen your old daughter?"

"Yeah, this is Shanna. Do you want Mom, 'cause she isn't home right now?"

"Not necessarily. How are you doing? How much snow did you find on your doorstep that snowy morning a few days ago?"

"You know what? We measured out on the lawn. 18 and a half inches." There was a hint of excitement in her voice.

"How was the house? Did it stay warm? Were you all okay?" He asked.

"Oh, we were all just fine, but no TV for a couple of days. Ellie said there was too much snow on the roof where the TV signal comes in. But like Mom said, it's late February, and the sun melts the snow faster.

"Let's return to your mom. Shouldn't she be home by now?" Taylor asked.

"Yeah, she should be here now, but if she has a new patient that's got a problem then- - - - - - -?"

At the hospital Roselyn rushed upstairs to the cancer floor. She came at the urging of Caroline Landre's doctor. She had been given a new drug and she had gone into convulsions, and was on full oxygen. Her physician had called her husband, Luke Landre, but he hadn't arrived yet.

Roselyn rushed in and was told by the nurse to come around the bed and hold Caroline's hand. As she stood there, she watched Caroline's convulsion ease, and Caroline finally opened her eyes, and could take a calming breath. "Oh, Roz." She choked, and closed her eyes., then lifted her head a little.

"Stay flat. It will help you to breathe. Good. Lie still." Roselyn said.

As Caroline's breathing eased, Roz put her hands on Caroline's shoulder. Someone in the room put a chair behind Roselyn. She sat and stroked Caroline's arm. "Relax, that's right, let the air come in naturally."

Roselyn sat and stroked and talked. Then watched Caroline as she relaxed and closed her eyes. A few minutes later Luke came in. He stood at the doorway for a moment and watched Roz and his wife. Roz had begun singing very softly to Caroline. He recognized the melody but could not recall the name of the song. She sang softly in that lovely alto voice he had heard so many times years before. Suddenly he knew that he loved both these women, and he felt doubly rich.

Roz glanced up, but held his gaze. "Come over here Luke and take my place. I think she can go to sleep."

"No, you stay. Let me go talk to her doctor."

Chapter Twenty

Roselyn stepped away from the bed and stood quietly and watched Luke give his wife a gentle hug. Her eyes fluttered open and a tiny smile creased her face. She touched his arm, but then her hand fell away, and she closed her eyes.

He wrapped her hand in his until he felt her hand drop away. He glanced up at the doctor and he gave a small shake of his head. Luke watched his wife relax and her breathing slowed. As soon as he could he stood and followed the physician out into the hallway.

Dr. Holloway stood waiting for Luke. "I'm sorry Mr. Landre, it won't be long now. She has weakened quite a bit just in the last two days. Luckily, she isn't feeling much pain now."

Luke stared at the floor. "For some time, I've been well aware of how ill she is. I was just hoping my son would arrive here as soon as he did. He's been on a mission in Missouri. He was supposed to fly in this evening, but as frustrating situations are going on all over the country, his flight was cancelled. Right now, my sister is waiting for his new flight to touch down at Salt Lake International." Luke spread his arms in a defeated gesture.

The Doctor nodded. "I understand. Your two daughters came in earlier. and Dr. Rosenbaum spoke with them. Roselyn is such a great help to me and other medics when we struggle with these critical patients and their families. She is so marvelous talking and having discussions with family members rather than the doctors trying in lay mans' terms and suggesting ways of dealing with the loss of a loved one."

"I appreciate your caring attitude. But you're only human. If you need to check on another patient, or critical situation, I understand."

Luke said. "I'll just go over here and rest a while."

A half hour later the elevator stopped at that floor, and as the doors opened and off came Stratton Landre and his Aunt Janet, Luke's sister. They both spotted Luke sitting on the bench with his eyes closed.

"Dad!" Stratton rushed over to his father and pulled him up into a hug. "So good to see you! How's Mom?"

"Stratton, so good you made it. Your Mom is very critical. Let me see If I can get you in there." He pointed at the hospital room door. "Just a minute." He walked in and realized that Roz was still sitting next to Caroline.

"Roz, Stratton just made it here. He just flew in. Janet picked him up from the airport."

Roselyn glanced down at the dying woman. "I believe she's comatose. But I'm sure he can come in." She stood and walked to the door. "If you need me, I'll be in the 'break room. on this floor." She stood and walked out the door.

Stratton dropped into the empty chair and picked up his mother's hand. *She's lost so much weight, even her hand is thinner. But he held it until his larger warmer hand warmed hers. She's too young to die. Parents shouldn't die until all their children are gone from the house and married. Or at least out on their own.* He thought of his father. What is he going to do without her? What about his younger sisters? Even though they both attend college, they still live at home. As he sat there, he couldn't imagine going home without his mother being there.

His eyes began to tear. He dragged some tissues from his coat pocket and wiped his cheeks and nose. Then he realized he still wore his heavy coat. He slid his mother's frail hand under the blanket and stood and took off his coat. Walking from the hospital room, he went out into the hallway and found his father, with a doctor sitting on the stone bench talking with his Dad.

Luke jumped up and put his arm around Stratton. "This is our son, Stratton, Stratton, this is Caroline's physician, Dr. Holloway."

Stratton reached down and shook the doctor's hand, as he glanced into the man's face, he noticed how the tired the poor doctor seemed, he noticed the fatigue in the man posture. *Cancer, everyone involved suffers.* "Very good to meet you. I'm sure you've done everything possible to heal my Mom."

The physician stared up at the young man, and a tired smile creased his face. "Depending on the specific patient, we try for a good outcome. Thank you, we all try our best. Your father told me you are just home from your mission to Missouri?"

"Yup, haven't had time to wipe the Missouri dust from my shoes. Actually, it was more snow than dust. But good people there. But Mom's pretty weak, isn't she?"

"I'm afraid so. Sad to say, she's pretty close to the end." The doctor wiped his face with a towel.

Luke glanced at his son. He was impressed. *The kid has really grown up.*

"I'd like to go home. I've been up since about 4 a.m. Utah time, and haven't eaten since. . . . . .I don't know when. The weather isn't going to get any better. There's a bus out there I can take to get home." He paced a small circle in front of the bench where Luke sat.

Luke sighed. "You're right. The two sitting here is not going to cure your Mom's illness. The doctors have done what they were trained to do, and fate has won out." He turned to the MD. "Are there any options left to help Caroline?"

The exhausted man shook his head. 'We've 'pulled out' all the stops."

"Okay. You go on home." Luke indicated to the MD. "Get some rest. Tomorrow will arrive whether you are here or not. I'm sure you can leave some instructions." He turned to Stratton "Let's at least go home and search the fridge." Luke said. He stood, put a hand on Stratton's shoulder and turned back to the doctor. "Call if there are any changes. He offered his hand to the MD. "You go home, too."

"At least getting some sleep sounds like a welcome idea." He walked back to the critical desk and issued some instructions. Then he watched as father and son took a last brief trip into the hospital room and then came out. As he walked down the hallway, they got into the elevator.

The MD turned down the hallway and issued instructions at the desk and to a nurse sitting there with a secretary. "Please check on Caroline Landre in a half hour or so. I'm going upstairs for a shower and I'm going to lie down in the men's sleeping area. Call me if there is any change." The doctor walked slowly down the hallway to another elevator.

Nurse Milligan turned to the desk supervisor; Corinne Johnson "These terminal patients are rough. But they happen. When Ms. Landre came in she was so ill, but always polite and kind. Cancer is such a *bastard!*

"Yes, it is. Luckily, we don't have the critically ill covid patients we had eighteen months ago. Thank the Lord for that. We get enough accident and even sometimes worse, abused women and gunshot victims." She threw her hands up. "Why go on. Let's face it, we are in the *worst of times.* That's what we got for electing a senile old man for our president."

Roselyn walked by heading for her office downstairs. She stopped. "I'm going home. I'll see you tomorrow or when we have another shift on the same day. Take it easy going home."

Chapter Twenty One

Caroline slowly became aware of the bed she lay in. It seemed to be early in the morning, because there was more light in the room. Had she really seen her son, Stratton, or was that a dream? She remembered that Luke had requested from the Church that he be released from his mission in Missouri a month early.

Again she thought, did she really seen him or had it been just a wish? Because it took too much energy to keep her eyes open, so she closed them. In her dreams she saw a long dark tunnel. Now her eyes were closed. But now in her dreams she had been staring at a long dark tunnel. Now that tunnel promised peace, and freedom from pain. But yet, she didn't feel she should flow into that tunnel.

She glanced around the room. She was still lying in a hospital bed. She was still so tired, and she closed her eyes, and her pain was gone. She still breathed, but to was taking a lot of focus to do even that. Then she saw a beautiful woman come close to her and hold out her hand.

"Come Caroline, it's time leave this difficult place you find yourself in. We can find a peaceful level of existence. It's your time to rise to a more peaceful realm." She took Caroline's hand and lifted her up. As Caroline stood next to the woman, she stared down at the gown the woman wore. Now her hospital gown was gone, and she now was wearing a white gown much like the woman wore.

The room now had brightened and the day seemed to be full of sunshine. It was so good to not feel any pain. She touched the gown she now wore. It was beautiful and she was pleased to wear a white gown. The 'being' now touched Caroline's bald head, and all the hair she had lost from her illness was again covering her head. It felt like her normal head of hair. It felt clean and thick.

Now Caroline turned to the woman and said, "I know I'm dying. What will happen to my family, husband and children without me?"

"For a time, they will mourn your passing. Bur brighter days are ahead for all of them. You have been a faithful woman, a mother and a wife but you are also a daughter of God. You have also been a faithful companion to your husband. Now there is heavenly work for you to do. Many lost souls wait for your tender care. There are many little children, lost and alone because of men's cruelty, and some women's selfishness. They are waiting for your help. Countless numbers. Let us go, because it is your time and you are needed." The woman took Caroline's hand.

Caroline took one last look at the white and gray room she had been in and the bed her form still lay in bed wearing a hospital gown. The angel held her hand and they rose up, and away from the large hospital building into the early morning sky.

The land line phone rang at 6:10 a.m. in the Landre household. Luke, who had finally fallen asleep less than five hours before, reached it on the third ring. Hello, Luke here?"

"This is Dr. Holloway, Luke. Caroline 'passed' just before 6 a.m. this morning."

"Thanks for calling. What should we do as a family, now?"

"We need a mortuary company to come and take the- - -- - - her as soon as- - - - possible."

"Thank you for the call and all you have done for our family. I'll give the funeral home a call right now." Luke sighed, rubbed a hand through his thinning hair. He walked to the chair where he had dropped his clothes the night before and pulled out his phone from a pocket of his sweat pants. He dialed the phone number and it rang a least four or five times. But a taped machine message played in his ear with the instructions to call back between 8:00 a.m. and 5:00 p.m. He sighed, set the receiver down on its cradle and stood staring out through the bedroom window.

Should I get up and make a pot of coffee, or go back to bed? He turned and shuffled into the bathroom and from there back to his bed.

Soon after eight that morning, Luke awoke and called Whitcomb Mortuary and told the woman who answered of his wife's passing.

The woman answering did have a soft, pleasing voice, and informed him that their organization would immediately go and pick up his deceased wife and transfer her back to their place of business. She suggested he make an appointment for this afternoon or tomorrow to arrange for a funeral service.

As he stumbled back to bed, he remembered that he had already spoken to a Mr. Brice and they had discussed a possible date. As he recalled their conversation, they discussed Tuesday of the next week. They had given him a brochure with a list of tasks he needed to implement. First: decide on a date for the last rites, and contact the cemetery. He knew the funeral director would help him with the best time during the day. Second; he also knew they must design a program with people singing, friends speaking. All those who would give the first and last prayers. Also, he would need prayers for those traveling to the cemetery. Since funeral would be next Tuesday, he had five days to plan the funeral service. Luke quickly dressed in exercise clothes, plus a pair of sweat pants and settled into his office.

The Landre household began to wake. First his girls; Cauline and Crista. .. He could hear them chattering back and forth. One of them found Stratton's jacket on the coat tree in the front hall. They both stormed his office. "Did Stratton make it home?" Crista asked. "We found his coat in the front hallway." Stratton actually made it home?!"

"Yes, he's down stairs in his room, but he was exhausted so let him sleep." Luke cautioned.

"Okay, "Rachel said. "Did we hear a call from the hospital? Mom died, didn't she?"

Luke glanced down at his sweats and nodded. "The hospital informed us that she 'passed' on early this morning."

One of the girls swiped at tears on her face. "We knew it would be soon. I guess I could go to class this afternoon. But since we're up, what would like for breakfast besides coffee? Whatever you would want to eat we'll fix it."

"Do we have any bacon?" The father asked. "I know we have eggs."

"Okay, scrambled eggs, bacon, and we bought some muffins. Do you want an orange? I mean, I'll actually cut it up for you."

"Let me shower first. I should go into my offices later this morning." Luke said.

"I'll go clean up too." I should go to class beginning at 1:15 p.m. Crista turned and galloped up the stairs.

After breakfast Luke left for his office. He needed to 'nail down' this funeral and make sure nothing in his calendar would interfere.

As he sat in his office, he began to write down who he should ask to speak, what music they would be singing. Then he remembered when he and Roselyn had sung at one of their friend's funeral. The guy had been killed in the Middle East and body had been shipped home. This guy's parents had been devastated. But his family had not been really active church goers. So he and Roz decided on singing a familiar Christian hymn. *Abide with me, tis Eventide.*

He sat at his desk and wondered if he dares ask her to sing with him now? He knew her husband had walked out on the family a few months ago. He wasn't sure how she would respond if he asked her. *Luke why are you even thinking about asking her. But he knew why. He also knew that he had been in love with her way back when they were singing together in rock the group. And last night in the hospital, he felt that surge of emotion toward her again.*

He needed to plan the rest of the funeral. So he grabbed a mug of coffee and went back to his office.

Taylor Rosenbaum sat in his downtown office and began to take notes on the session he had just finished with a patient who had just left his office. Once he had written his impressions and suggestions on what they should talk about next time, he found himself swinging back and forth in his expensive leather chair, flipping a pencil through his fingers.

He needed to move out of the apartment he shared with Marlene. The romance was over, if there really had been one? As he now thought about his reaction. His behavior was more of an adolescent reaction to Roselyn's receiving the PhD, from the university. This put her on an equal intellectual level with him. Why did that make him uncomfortable?

Her weight gain had been half century mark, a reaction to all the time she had spent preparing for her 'exam' and clinical work she had done. He also understood that at her age; early fifties, was a common time for people to gain weight once they reached that age.. He caught a glimpse of all the hospital work she did. One day he noticed her getting into an elevator for the fifth floor. He realized she had been heading to the cancer wing. She must have a patient or a family meeting with someone on that floor. No matter which, that was a tough assignment. It was so final.

Taylor managed to reach a realtor and asked about where he could rent a furnished apartment or condo for a month or perhaps longer.

"Dr. Rosenbaum there is a pleasant long or short stay hotel east on 2nd. avenue. "I'll give you a call with the exact address." Ronald Hophstead suggested. He rattled off the phone number. "Before you make any decisions, drive up there and take a look. Let me know what you decide. There are other options."

Taylor called, and later that afternoon and made an appointment to find and review two different apartments. Once he found the place, he realized it was an older mansion that had been converted into about six apartments. A rather interesting change from the usual walk-in commercial rental. A prospective renter must make an appointment. So Taylor drove up there, found parking behind the building, and walked inside. Once inside the building, there were directions to an office. The man behind the desk came around and shook his hand.

"I'm Hozi Frazer. Good to make your acquaintance, Dr. Rosenbaum. What kind of and how much room are you interested in?" Basically, we have two different apartment types here."

"Something where there is room for me to sleep, as well as work." Taylor answered. "Oh, and a possible kitchen area."

"I'll show you our two different situations. Oh and please call me Hozi." He led Taylor out to the lobby and to an elevator.

Taylor followed him one floor and was led down to a pleasant hallway. The walls were papered in a subtle, but rather traditional wallpaper. Hozi stopped in front of door 224. With a key, opened it.

The room was somewhat darkened. However, the first thing Hozi did was hit a switch near the entrance. And the room was flooded with indirect light. They actually stepped into an entrance hall with a door to the right. Hozi opened the door to a coat closet. Another door across to the left housed a small vacuum and shelves for cleaning products.

"Interesting." Taylor said. "Does the tenant do his own cleaning?"

"Oh no. But everyone has a mishap now and then. This is for a quick cleanup." He smiled.

"Interesting." Taylor nodded. Okay let's see the rest of this place." Taylor laughed.

"As you can see this is the main living space." There were two sofas, two easy chairs, a TV and a coffee table. "Over here is a mini kitchen. Along with a four-burner stove, refrigerator, counter and a round table with four chairs."

Taylor walked over to take a look at the area. and checked out viewed a small four burner gas stove, a rather slender fridge and a microwave. It was mounted above the kitchen's small counter. Cupboards held a set of dishes, and in one lower storage area, Taylor could see a set of pots and pans. He turned back to Hozi. "This seems quite complete."

"Good, I'm glad you approve. Now we go into the bedroom. Just one, but with a choice. Either you can use the king-sized bed or if you want more room or we can change it for two queen beds. You also have a walk-in closet." He indicated toward a door.

Taylor walked into a fair-sized closet with over- head shelves and three mounted single hangers for heavier coats or robes. He nodded and followed Hozi to another open area but with a pocket sliding door to close it off. In there was a fair-sized desk, an upholstered chair and a filing cabinet; Along with a small side table. This could be an area to use as an office. There was also a small sofa on one wall.

Taylor walked over to the south wall where there was a window. He pulled back shears and stood gazing at a southern view of the city. He could glimpse at both sunshine and clouds. He turned to Hozi, "What kind of parking is available?"

"Come follow me. It's in the lower level." They walked from the apartment to the elevator and Hozi pushed a bottom plate marked *level one.*

Chapter Twenty Two

When Luke phoned the Rosenbaum household, he was greeted with a cheerful voicemail: N*ot one Rosenbaum can pick up the phone right now. Please call back later. Or leave a message.* This message was in a pleasant female voice.

Frowning, Luke set his cell phone down on his desk. Okay, everyone is either at school or at work. He'd try Roz later, perhaps at the hospital. Did he even have her cell phone number?" He decided to wait and see if Stratton knew her cell number? He glanced at the possible funeral program he had scribbled down. Who else could he call to ask to be on the program? Ah, yes; The Bruckner girls. They sang in church every now and then. He could at least speak to the girls' mother.

A few minutes later his phone rang. "Hello?"

Luke, this is Roselyn Rosenbaum. I just learned that your wife 'passed on' early this morning. I'm so sorry for- - - -well I could say your loss. But that sounds so formal. I'm sure you're devastated."

"Thanks for calling me." He took a deep breath. "However, she had been quite ill for several months. The last radiation treatment, we knew it was not helping- - - - - - I mean, you as a para-medical individual- - - - and would understand. I'm sorry, to be rambling on," He cleared his throat. 'While I have you on the phone, could I ask a huge favor?"

"What do you need, just tell me?" If I'm capable, I'll do it."

"Remember when you and I sang at Tanner funeral?"

"Wasn't that for the Travis and the request of the Tanner family?"

"Yes. Well, I think that song would be a good fit in Caroline's funeral program. Would you sing it with me again?"

She could hear his rapid breathing. Then she took a deep breath. “Well yes, of course. We’d need to rehearse a time or two. When is the service?”

“Right now, my bishop and I decided on next Thursday. Is that a problem?” Just saying those words, he felt his chest relax, but somehow, he slid a pen from his desk and dropped it on the floor. “Oops.” He breathed out.

“Are you okay?” She asked.

“No, I mean yes. I just dropped my pen.” He gave out a strangled laugh.

“She sighed, but then laughed. “Can you find it.? You probably have at least 20 pens in your desk drawers. Find another writing tool.”

Then another laugh came out. “Yes ma’am. Right away, Ma’am.” His laugh was met with a giggle.

“Oh my gosh, we sound like teenagers on the phone. I hope none of your kids are listening to us.” But another little giggle came out.

“Okay, then will you sing with me?” He asked.

“Of course. When do you want to go through the song?” Roz turned to her calendar hanging on the wall. “What does your Sunday evening look like? That hymn has to be in the Church Song Book. Have you written out the funeral program?”

“So far a first draft. I just started working on it this morning.” Now she sounds like a wife. Well, isn’t she?

“Okay, if Sunday evening works. Do you want me to come over there?” He asked.

“If the weather stays dry?” She replied. “Last week we had over fifteen inches of snow from the ‘epic’ storm. At least that is what the weather man on Channel 15 called it. We still have piles of the white stuff on the lawns, but the roads are clear.”

“Good to know. I’ll call you if we have any changes. Thanks. Talk to you later.” He set down the phone.

Taylor had a consult at the Murray Hospital. A psychologist on staff asked him to speak to a patient who was in for a hysterectomy.

The surgery went well, but the woman was sometimes hysterical and other times having trouble with reality. When she awoke from the surgery, she at first, was silent, refusing to speak to her physician. She just *knew* he had removed part of her brain; The section that controlled her *femininity*. She told the nurses she was destined to be a young boy now. And grow up to be stunted man. No one would recognize her.

When they asked her why she thought that would happen. She told them her father who had only girls in the family, and had put a curse on her when she was twelve years old. Now she could do all the things boys did.

When her daughter came to see the woman, named Lila. She told her daughter her name was now Lincoln. Also, she said that when she was 'old enough' she would join the army.

Later that afternoon, Taylor visited the patient. "Good afternoon, Ms. Phillips he introduced himself. I'm Dr. Rosenbaum I've come to see how you are feeling since your surgery."

"I still hurt some, but as I grow up my surgical area will heal. When I get to my full height, then I'll be all healed. In a few months I'll be old enough to join the army."

Taylor carried her paper work. "I'm sorry, on your paperwork I have here. It gives your age at 62. Much too old to join the army."

"No, you don't understand in the surgery I had, it took out my aging gene. Now for a few years, I'm going grow young, and I'll grow into a young man. Soon old enough to join the army. When they took out my female parts, they put in man parts." She eased back into the pillows.

"What about your husband, and your daughters? Are you not going to want to be with them?"

"Look, Mr. doctor, did you say Rosenbaum? I've done enough cleaning and cooking and tending grand kids to last two life times. I'm going to be young and have adventures. How better than join the army. They used to say; *Join the Army and See the World. Why not!* Someday, when I grow up, I'm going to do that."

"I understand that sounds like a great adventure. But in order to do that you must pass a physical." Taylor said.

"Well, I won't be able to do that right away. I *know* that. I'll just have to go home and grow up for a while."

"When you return home, what will be your chores?" Taylor asked.

"My gosh, I just had surgery. I'll need to rest awhile. When I get better, I'll need to go to school."

'What school will you attend?" Taylor asked in a questioning voice.

"I won't have to go to school. One of my girls will come over and home school me. She will just have to go over and pick up the school work." Lots of children are home schooled. And then when we are finished with the lessons for the day, she can clean up and make dinner.

"That's interesting. Does she have a family to care for?" Won't she need to go home can take care of her family?"

"Well, yes. but her husband makes good money, and they can hire a baby sitter."

Taylor shook his head and smiled. "While you are being home-schooled, what grade do you think you'll need to study? What grade do you think you'll qualify for?" Taylor asked.

"I guess I'll have to take a test. It will be interesting which grade I can be in." The woman changed positions. "I'm tired and need a nap. If you want to talk to me more, just come back later. Okay?"

"I'll check on that. Well, it has been very interesting to speak with you. Continue to heal. Oh, what shall I call you?"

"When I was growing up, my name was Julie Fraser, and I married a Minson You can call me Fraser. You can forget Julie. That's a girl's name. Did you say your name was Dr. Rosenbaum? Do you have a first name?"

"Yes. It's Taylor." He patted her hand.

"Bye Taylor. Good to talk to you. Explain to my family about me. Please."

As Taylor walked down the hallway he had to smile. One of easier consults he had in a long time.. Ms. Minson was lucid, though delusional. Already he could understand why she chose to be an adolescent boy.

Now he really needed to meet the rest of the family.

When he called Ms. Minson's surgeon, he explained what he learned from the husband.

"The guy is "old school" you know, women run the household, and are not allowed to have much more than an opinion about the world. Her two daughters are more up to date in their thinking and behavior. I would appreciate a report on your conversation with Ms. Minson. The surgery was one of the more extensive than I expected. She needs to rest before she goes back to her usual routine. I'm thinking a week or two for her in a care center would be good. I'll explain to her husband she will not heal quickly if she goes straight home."

"What about the daughters?" Taylor asked.

"They'll tell their father that Mom needs special care for a few weeks. Thanks for your appraisal." Dr. Richards hung up.

Now Taylor had the disagreeable task of driving to the apartment where he and Marlene had been living. As he drove to the apartment building and on down into the underground parking. As he glanced around and realized that this parking facility was the most positive thing about this place.

As he locked the door of his car, and headed for the elevator. He stopped for a moment. How should he approach the situation? He needed to move his belongings out first. There was enough daylight to drive up to his new rental before it became really dark. That's what he would do. Move his personal things, first.

When he walked into the apartment he was greeted with the sound of the TV. At least Roz seldom watched TV, and never around the dinner hour.

"Oh, Taylor I'm glad I didn't fix dinner before you came home. You're working long hours today?"

"Yes, I had a hospital appraisal to make." He went straight to the bedroom and pulled out his large suitcase and began filling it with is clothes that were not on hangers. Next, he pulled out his shaving kit, and began to fill it with his personal bathroom items.

Marlene followed him into the bedroom and watched him pack. "Are you going on a trip?"

"Not exactly. I'll talk with you in a few minutes." He continued to pack, and then took the bulging suitcase and shaving kit out into the hallway and pressed the elevator button. Once he arrived down in the parking facility, he walked straight to his car and put those clothes and toiletries in the trunk. He returned and immediately cleaned out his desk and the small bookcase in this 'office' room. Then he carried them out to the elevator and down to his car. When he returned to the apartment she was standing in the entrance with her hands on her hips.

"Where are you going?" She asked. Her voice full of anger, and also, he decided. Fear.

"I've found a more suitable apartment." He said as he grabbed an armload of jackets and slacks.

This time she pulled several shirts and more slacks from the closet and followed him down to his car. He opened to the rear seat and laid the hanging clothes across the back seat.

"It's too cold down here to discuss this issue. I need to leave. I'll return tomorrow to explain this move. Go back upstairs. I'll see you tomorrow." He slid into this car and backed out. He waved at her and drove away.

Chapter Twenty Three

Twenty minutes later he drove into the underground parking of his new residence. There had been some traffic, but the once he reached his apartment the city noise was muted. He was glad he had shopped at a small market for something to eat for supper. He needed the energy to empty his car.

When Roselyn came home the next evening there was a message from Luke on her private line. She called his office line and left a message. The past two days had been exhausting. Not only Caroline's death, but also a thirteen your old girl had come into the hospital with a severe concussion. They did surgery to stabilize her skull, but when Roz left, she had sunk into a deep coma.

Everyone working in the children's unit was concerned, because her father was involved in high end commercial computers. He designed and installed them in med-range businesses. The family didn't lack for 'brain' power in the wife or the other children. The injured girl had been attending a private academy for children with autism. This girl had had all the advantages available.

As the attendant on duty came in to check on the teenage girl's IV, she found the girl's mother had fallen asleep. "Ms. Fredrikson are you planning to stay? We can bring in a temporary bed for you. You would be more comfortable. If you are going to stay much longer, you could go down to the cafeteria for a sandwich and a beverage."

"No, I must have fallen asleep. I have a teenager still at home, and a husband to look after. Thank you for your attention and care for Eleise. Usually, she couldn't stay in bed unless someone tied her down. But now- - - - - - -? Well.." She stood up and smoothed down her soft green cashmere sweater and walked to the door.. "I'd better go home and see to the rest of the family. And find some dinner for them; Even though they are quite able to care for themselves." She tilted her head and smiled.

The attendant held the door and marveled at this woman who had been the hospital for several hours, but looked as if she had just arrived. As she walked, she smoothed her blond hair and gracefully carried her hip length beige coat. *Which nurse Sandra, knew cost at least $500. On sale.*

The staff of the children's wing continued to do what the doctors suggested but the high fever continued in the teenage girl's body. The pediatrician, a Doctor Tyler, brought in as a consult; along with Dr Roselyn Rosenbaum. The feverish girl again was examined and her temperature had gone down a degree, but she still had a higher-than-normal temperature. They dripped in meds, antibiotics, fluids, which routinely came out as urine.

After nearly eight days in the hospital, a night nurse, J. Reamer, came into check on Eleise, and found her lying in bed. Eyes open, staring at the window. One of the nurses had raised the blind on the window about half way.

"Eleise." She asked. "Are you gazing at the window?" She touched the girl and found her dripping with sweat, but much cooler.

"Take off." The girl said. She pulled at the damp hospital gown.

"Let's do a sponge bath, and get a new night gown. Okay?"

"Okay. The teenager answered.

"I'll be right back."

After the sponge bath, and a bottle of water, Eleise settled in her bed with pillows helping her to sit up. Her stomach growled. "Hungry now. Lunch?" She asked the nurse.

"It's way past lunchtime, actually we're closer to breakfast. See the clock on the wall it reads 4:23 a.m."

The girl frowned. "Egg McMuffin time?" She said.

Nurse Reamer, blinked in surprise. "You like Egg Mc Muffins?"

"No, Jamie does. Gives me bites." A hit of a grin creased her face.

"Jamie is your brother?" Nurse Reamer asked.

Eleise nodded. Then she put her hand up high. "Big."

"I'll go see I we can find you an egg sandwich. You want milk?"

"Okay, cold."

As Nurse Reamer left the room, she shook her head in amazement. She actually had a conversation with that girl. Usually she screamed, and turned her face away. She had even slid a carton of milk on the floor from a food tray. Screaming "No want!" Of course, now her fever was nearly gone, and she must feel better.

At six a.m. Taylor awoke in his new bed in his downtown apartment. Not because the bed was uncomfortable, nor the sounds of early morning traffic woke him. He had to return to the Sugarhouse apartment, he had been sharing with Marlene for nearly three months. He needed to end the relationship as quietly and thoroughly as possible. He grabbed a robe from the hanger in his closet and went into the room he used as an office. He took out a sheet of paper and began to type.

Dear Marlene

"The time we have spent together in this apartment has been a pleasant diversion for me. We grew to be good friends as we enjoyed being lovers. During this time, we also learned that our differences in age and experience has become a major conflict. Since I spend over half of the time in my office down town, it would be much better if I lived closer to my offices. I have found a place in an older area in the Avenues. Really, too far from where you must travel to work each day.

I have also found the difference in our ages and experience has become a hurdle in building a lasting relationship. The lease on the Sugarhouse apartment will be up in two weeks. It is your choice to stay there, however I will no longer pay the rent. If you want to continue to live there you could invite in a roommate, or move back with the friends you lived with before we moved in together. Give your situation a clear thoughtful evaluation.

We had an exciting time together. But as with all experiences we take on in life, it is time for this one to end. I wish you well. You are an attractive, kind, ambitious girl. You will eventually find another man who you will find interesting. Think through this experience we've had together, and use what you have learned from it.

A friend always, Taylor

He left the note on the kitchen counter and an envelope with a fifty-dollar bill by the coffee canister on the kitchen counter. He checked all the closets and drawers for any of his belongings that might still be in the apartment. He also left his key to the door near the note. Then he closed the door and locked it from the inside. As he rode down the elevator to the parking garage, he felt greatly relieved, and had to smile. He must remember to call Eric tonight or tomorrow. He should be released from his mission in about two months. He would check with Eric to see if he had a definite date that he would be released from his mission. He had the thought about going over there and picking him up.

When Roselyn arrived home that evening, she had a phone call from Luke. Could she come over to his ward house to rehearse the song they were to sing at Caroline's funeral?

That evening, Ellie Ann announced to her mother that she and Shanna had decided to attend the funeral.

"That's okay. Just remember it is on a school day for both of you." Roselyn said.

"We know, but the Landre girls are our friends, too. Besides we haven't heard you sing since the Christmas program. I don't understand why you haven't done more singing. You have a great voice, Mom." Ellie said.

"I suppose that once I went to work at the hospital, I was so busy getting into my duties there, I was too busy to worry about singing."

"I also think it was because, you were still doing, as you said lots of work on your advanced degree, and- - - - -- - - -you had neglected yourself." Ellie said.

"You mean I sat too much and ate too much." I put on over fifteen pounds. But with Taylor gone, I quit cooking so much rich food. Are you two missing all those high calorie meals?" she asked.

"Heck no. I don't need all those extra calories, and Shanna can snack if she gets the urge. By the way, how many pounds have you lost?" Ellie teased.

"About seventeen pounds. One thing I have learned, once you cut back on eating all those rich foods, and eat smaller portions, you don't miss all the extras." The mother said. "While we're on the subject, I'd better search the closet and start trying on some outfit to wear at Caroline's funeral."

The first item of clothing she dragged from the walk-in closet was the velvet jacket she was going to wear to the dinner party, the evening Taylor walked out on her. *Boy, he doesn't realize what a favor he did for me by leaving that evening.* The jacket fit perfectly. But it was too much of a winter item to wear now. She must search for something lighter and more in keeping with the season; Spring! She kept up her search, and finally found an unlined navy linen jacket and a dark blue print skirt. She pulled those items out and tried them on. The jacket had no buttons and a wide collar, and deep cut sleeves. The skirt was of a dark print with a gold thread running through it. Luckily it had wide elastic at the waist. No zipper or buttons. Now all she needed was a beige or off-white cap sleeve 'shell'. That she would need to purchase. Shopping mall, here we come! And she'd better go tomorrow on her way home from the hospital.

That evening Luke called the Rosenbaum house, and Shanna answered. "Good evening may I speak to Roselyn."

"Hang a minute, she's upstairs. Mom, phone for you." Shanna called out.

"Hello? This is Ms. Rosenbaum."

"Hi." Luke cleared his throat. *This reminds me of being nineteen again and calling a girl for a date.* "Is it possible for you to come over to our ward house and rehearse the song we're going to sing at the funeral?"

"I can do that. Ah, what time? I was just about to go make salad for dinner." *Oh my gosh why, I am I telling him that?* "Ah, what is the address of your meeting house?"

"It's on 20th East and just north of 84th.south. It's on the west side of the street. About 7 p.m.?"

"She studied the clock on her desk. "It's a little past 5 p.m. right now. Okay, I'll see you then. Bye. *Why the church? Of course, the sound system. We need to try out the settings.* For a long moment she sat there and remembered when the band played in a bar, or larger building. The guys always checked the sound system. She smiled. Thinking back, old *Sitting there recalling old memories.*

Stratton finally emerged from his room. He had slept late and when he awoke the house was quiet. That's right, his sisters had classes at the community college, and his father had gone into his offices. Even though his mother had passed, life still moved on. He went through his clothes and found some old jeans and a sweat shirt to put on. After a shower, he was starving and went upstairs to find something to eat. There he found a well-stocked fridge. After a couple of scrambled eggs, toast, an orange and milk, he decided he could face the world. As he was fixing his own breakfast, which he had been doing for several months in the mission field, yet at that moment, he missed his mother more than ever; Because she would have made breakfast for him.

Chapter Twenty Four

The next evening, Roselyn drove her car to the church building where the funeral service would be held. She walked into the chapel area and the lights were on over the front where speakers' raised area was. She called out. "Hello, anybody here?" She watched as Luke and another man came out from a doorway near the back.

"Oh, hi Roz. Great, you found the building. We were just checking the sound system." He turned to the younger man next to him. "This is Tom Redding. He's the stake leader, in charge of this building's electrical system."

Tom waved at Roselyn and walked down to where she was standing. "Luke tells me that when you two were in college you 'guys' used to sing in a musical group." And you two sang all those eighties songs. We were just checking the sound systems. This building is new enough that the systems are pretty good." He grinned at her.

"That's why I'm here. To see if we can still get our voices to 'gell', and to be heard clearly."

Tom went to the piano and set a hymn book on the music stand. Then he sat down and played a quick introduction to the hymn that Luke had chosen to sing at the service.

"Are you going to accompany us?' She asked.

From the rear of the chapel, they all turned to a man's voice coming from the darkened area at the back of the room. He was a tall man and came striding quickly down the aisle to them. He seemed strong, muscular, and also close to her and Luke's age. Suddenly she recognized him. "Sam!" She yelled "What are you doing here?"

"I heard a rumor that you and Luke here were going to sing

together. I came so see if either one of you could still carry a tune." He grinned and carried a sheet music folder and set it on the piano music holder. Shrugging out of his jacket, he stood near the keyboard and pounded out a string of music exercises up and down the keys. Then he finished with a flourish.

Tom stood up and stepped away from the keyboard, smiling. 'It looks like you don't need me anymore, Luke. Call me if you make any changes to the funeral program."

Roselyn came up to the grand piano and leaned her elbows on the side near the keyboard and watched him 'warm up' by running chords and piano exercises up and down the keyboard. Then he played a typical voice warm up.

"Okay. As I recall Roz, you sing in this register. Sing with me." And he played the usual singer's warm up in an alto key.

As he played, and Roselyn sang, the warm up exercise. He said "Okay, good. Now it's you turn, Luke, my man."

Luke came and stood across from keyboard where Roselyn stood. Sam played the same exercises he had played for Roselyn, but is a lower key.

Luke sang the exercise. Then Luke handed Sam a hymn book. "Hey, Sam my man, now just play the hymn. We're not trying out for the Utah Opera Chorus."

"Okay, okay, just having a little fun." Sam pulled a piece of sheet music from the folder, stood it on the music stand and sat it up on the music holder and played an Introduction.

Standing on either side of the keyboard, Luke and Roselyn sang in the old harmony they were so used to doing 23 years before. Next, they sang the first verse of the hymn.

"Not had." Sam said, and made some notations on the sheet music. Then he played the song again, phrasing certain lines of the song. "Now sing the second verse."

After they had sung that verse, Sam sat back and in a serious tone, said. "I came to do what I could to ease your pain and loss, Luke. I remember speaking to you at the symphony a few months ago, and you mentioned that Caroline, your wife was quite ill. When I heard she had 'passed on' I decided to see what I could to help you to pay her a tribute. That's why I came tonight to help as much as I'm able."

Suddenly they turned as another man came strolling down the aisle to the front of the chapel. "Great, we're all here. Hey there Roz, good to see you."

Roselyn turned and ran up the aisle. She hugged the big man. "Good to see you're still alive after how many years has it been, at least ten?"

"That's right. You and your husband came to church when we had Grant's blessing. Yeah, my baby boy is growing up. He'll be eleven in a couple of months."

"Do you still have those knobs on your hands from holding drumsticks, Roger?" Sam asked with a grin.

"I still play from time to time. I went on tour to St. George and 'Vegas with Paul Whittier and his group. I came to see how you 'guys' were holding up, Luke, but it seems now the whole gang is here. Good to see all of you. Are we planning the music for the funeral?"

"Yes. Roz and Luke are going to sing. And I just decided to play a musical interlude." Sam answered.

"Have you set a date for the last rites and internment?" Roger asked.

"It will be March 25th, at noon." Luke answered, frowned and stared at the floor.

None of the people up front noticed when Stratton slipped into the back pew. *So this is the rock group my Dad sang with in college. This last guy played the drums. I'm glad Dad can connect with these people again. Boy' I'd love to hear them play and sing and not just church hymns either.* Just then Stratton's phone rang, and he shut it down quickly. He glanced at his screen. The call had been from Eric. Stratton hustled from the back of the chapel and walked out into the hallway.

There standing in the hallway. He returned his friend's call. "Hey, I couldn't 'pick-up' a few minutes ago, because I'm in our ward building and your Mom, my Dad and two of their friends are up front practicing music for the funeral. These two guys came, old friends of your dad and my mom. Remember, the four of them played in a rock group together. You know, when they were all in college."

"I've heard about the band my Mom sang in. I'm glad they can all connect again. When is the funeral service being held?" Eric asked. "And- - - -when did you get home?"

"I've only been here less than three days. I barely made it to the hospital before Mom died. But she was pretty wasted from the cancer. Hey, they're singing together. I need to go listen. They're singing some old Beatles song. I'll get back to you tomorrow." Stratton closed his phone.

The next morning Taylor went into the hospital room of the Harris girl suffering from a high prolonged fever, as well as exhibiting autism. On her chart it mentioned that her fever had broken and her temperature that morning had been in the normal range. She had also eaten breakfast before five a.m. that morning.

He walked into the girl's room. "Good morning, Eleise. How are you feeling this morning? I'm Dr. Taylor." He walked over to her bed and gazed down at her.

With no expression on her face, she stared at him for a long moment. Then her attention seemed to shift back to the TV and the cartoon character.

He pulled up a chair and sat down next to her. "Do you like this TV program?"

Now her attention shifted to him. She gazed at him for a long moment. "You, ea Daddy?" She asked.

Her question surprised him, and he smiled. "Yes, I'm a father. Do you have a Dad?" *Interesting, she's trying to categorize me.*

"My Daddy, home un very busy." Her attention shifted back to the TV.

"I read on your chart that you have been sick in the hospital a long time. Who comes to see you?"

"My Mommy, un my bruver." Now, she glanced at him. "He dis big." She put her hand way up in the air.

Just then the room door opened and an aid came in. "Oh excuse me. I came in to see if Eleise needed a trip to the bathroom. And I brought you a book to look at, Eleise."

The teen age girl slid out of the bed before the aid could reach her. "I go to bafroom." she said. She took the aide's hand and they went into the restroom.

Taylor could hear the toilet flush, and then water running. Less than a minute later, Eleise and the aid, with the name tag of Mary Lee came out of the bathroom and Mary helped Eleise back into bed.

Once the girl was settled back into bed, the aid went to the door. "See you later Eleise." She left the quietly.

"Look." Taylor said. Mary brought you a book to read. I'll read it to you if you like?"

The young girl straightened the covers and leaned back into the pillows. "You read now."

Taylor opened the 8x10 inch children's storybook. It was called **Ballard of the two-toned Bunny.** On the cover was an artist's design of a black and white rabbit. Before Taylor could read more than three pages, the Eleise interrupted him.

"He's sad." She pulled on the corner of the book. 'Why?"

Taylor, somewhat astonished, gave Eleise a measured gaze. "I think this story of the bunny is that he is different from other bunnies. Do you think this bunny is different from other bunnies? How do you think this bunny is different?" What tells you he is different from some others?"

While Eleise studied the picture, Taylor sat quietly and studied her.

"Is this bunny so different?" He asked. How is he different?"

She studied the page, and with her finger traced *Ballard's coat which was both black and white.*

"Dis bunny is both black un white." Is dat bad?"

"What do you think?" He asked the girl."

She continued to trace the bunny's coat with her finger. She shook her head. "No, he just different. 'Dere's many different kids and big people." Then she flashed a smile. "He likes coke *and* milk." She giggled.

Eleise lay back against the pillows. “Sleepy, no more read. Want water.”

Taylor went out and brought back a bottle of cold water and opened it for her.

“Okay, good.” She took a long swallow and handed back the bottle. Then she smiled and closed her eyes.

“Apparently, I’ve been dismissed.” Taylor shook his head, and set the water bottle on her tray. “Have a good nap. I’ll talk with you later.” *There’s more to that girl than meets the eye.*

Chapter Twenty Five

The next morning Taylor went back to see Eleise and found her mother in the room with her. "Oh excuse me. I'm Doctor Rosenbaum. I have been asked to call on you daughter."

"Yes. I'm glad to meet you. Eleise' doctor called us this morning and told us we could take her home. Her fever has returned to normal, and we will take her home today. Then have a nurse come in tomorrow. Possibly for a day or two a least. And you had a session with her yesterday?"

"Not exactly a session. I would like to speak with her again. She is an intriguing girl. I think another chat with her would be fruitful. I can meet her again, here or you could bring her to my office downtown."

"L could bring back here, or down town tomorrow. Eleise is the youngest of three children. The others are all in school now. What time would you like to see her?"

"Excuse me." Taylor pulled out his phone from his pocket. "Let me check my schedule." He pulled an app on his phone. "How about 3:00 p.m.?"

"That would work. My other children both ride the school bus home. Oh by the way, I'm Laura Engram." She put her hand out and shook Taylor's' hand.

"Well, I'll leave you to get ready to take her home. See you tomorrow. If you give me your phone, if you give me your number, I'll type in the office address. Good to meet you. See you tomorrow." He turned to the teenager resting up a pile of pillows "See you tomorrow." He gazed into her eyes, then walked to the door, waved and left.

About the same time Taylor opened the door to his new apartment and let himself in. Marlene opened the door to the Sugarhouse apartment/ she thought about the note from Taylor a few days earlier. Even though she carried a sack of groceries, she was well aware she had only eight days left to live in this rather pleasant apartment. Even with Taylor gone, moved out, she still liked living here. It was convenient, close to shopping and groceries. Since she had lived with Taylor for nearly five months, she had saved money, and she loved the underground parking. She would just have to find a roommate.

Right now, she would call a girl or two. She thought of one in the same building where she worked. What could be more convenient!

Soon the day of the funeral dawned. And Luke sat down with his list of items that needed to happen to make a smooth transition to the cemetery and return to the church building where the women and a few men attending his church were planning a simple luncheon for those who had attended the funeral. In the large area in a normal LDS building there was usually a large recreation area, and about the size of a basketball court. Here, they set up tables, because each building included a moderate sized kitchen. The large floor also was used for dances. A good sound system usually was also included when the building was constructed.

On this particular April Day it was raining. Not a heavy storm, just a stormy day. Those attending the funeral could be seen running from their cars toward the building; Those who planned on staying dry, carried umbrellas. As they came into the building a young man suggested they set jackets and umbrellas and perhaps coats in a large coat rack area located in the front of the building. Before the funeral began the closed coffin was wheeled to the front of the chapel just below the front seating and pulpit.

After an opening prayer, Caroline's younger sister read her biography. and a short history of her life; Marriage to Luke and birth of her three children. After her talk, a musical number from a trio that Caroline had belonged to. Next speaker gave a short talk. Then a 'remembrance' spoken by another friend. After that Roselyn and Luke sang together.

As Stratton sat and listened to his father and his good friends' mother sing together. He remembered that they, when in college, had sung so beautifully together and probably had been in love with each other. *What had happened between them to break them up? Watching them sing together now, he suddenly knew, that they loved each other again..* He smiled thinking of the future; Having Eric as a step brother wasn't such a bad idea.

But the culmination of the funeral was to listen to their friend, Sam Eldridge play, what he called *All that's beautiful and true; Caroline.* The man was amazing. Even now, Stratton, in his head, could hear the four of them playing and singing some soft rock ballad. He'd call Eric. Better yet, he would get a copy of the singing and Sam's mini-masterpiece. Stratton was amazed how talented they were, and how professional. How would it be to have parents out on the road, or even in a nightclub performing?

The burial, because the rain, took less time than actually planned. And they all went back to the church for some lunch. In a fairly heavy rainstorm, Roselyn hurried home from the church to check on her girls.

She wasn't hungry, but she checked on food in fridge and pantry. If either one was hungry any time this evening. she could suggest some foods that were in the fridge or pantry that they could put together some supper.

Roselyn had been wired, and now she was pushing almost to exhaustion level, so she changed clothes, and dropped on her sofa in her office and pulled up the old comforter.

About two hours later she opened her eyes and Ellie was standing over her. "How was the funeral?" she asked.

"Oh, hi. Sorry, I fell asleep." Roselyn said.

"I'm sure you are tired. Are you hungry, because I brought home a pizza? Come on downstairs. Shanna is fixing a salad."

Roselyn sat up. "Okay I'll be down in a few minutes." She went to the bathroom and rinsed her face then ran a comb through her hair. She eased down the stairs. Both girls were sitting at the table.

"There's a plate and the salad over here. What do you want to drink?" Shanna asked. "There's part of a bottle of coke here on the table."

"Okay, let me grab the salad dressing." Roselyn sat down and made a salad and took a slice of pizza from the box. "This looks good. Thank you for ordering the pizza."

"No problem." Ellie answered. 'I heard the funeral was a musical 'spectacular'." She grinned at her mother.

"I could say the music was a notch better than an ordinary funeral." Roselyn smiled.

"So you and Mr. Landre, back when you were in college, sang in an 80's rock group. And along with him a guy named Roger, the drummer and a Sam Eldridge, on keyboards Any thoughts of starting up the band again, Mom?" Shanna laughed.

"No. But I'll let you two 'ladies' know if it's decided to go out on the road, again." Roselyn sat back and tilted her head.

Getting off the 4th floor elevator of the Sugar House apartment building were Marlene, and an intake nurse employed at the medical department of the university hospital. This girl's name was Giselle Macy, and her present roommate was getting married in two weeks. She had to move from their apartment within a week.

Giselle had talked to Marlene and decided to come see the Sugar House apartment. The sugarhouse location was closer to the hospital than her present apartment. She liked the idea of an underground parking garage. And she also liked having one and a half bathrooms. The only problem was the king-sized bed rather than two twins or two queens in the room used as a major bedroom. Two queens would be a 'tight fit' if they shared the larger bedroom. The second bedroom was probably normally used for a child or an office. The two of them could use it as a den.

Finally, they called the manager for a discussion on the subject. Mr. and Mrs. Victor were the managers of the south building where the apartment was located.

When the two young women sat down with the managers, they

explained their problem.

Mrs. Victor smiled and said, “Managing this south wing of this apartment complex actually is quite a complicated job. However, we also have many resources that smaller buildings don’t have. Now you two are planning to move in together in Apt. 435 south. Is that correct?”

“Yes Ma’am.”

“I think it would be better to sit down at the table here.” She ushered both women to sit down at the kitchen table. Mrs. Victor opened a large log book, and glanced in Marlene’s direction. “Since you lived in the apartment 535 South, you’ve had a king-sized bed in the bedroom. Now you’re changing roommates.” She put her hand across the table to Giselle. “Welcome to Sugar House, South. Downstairs in one of our storage rooms and we have some furniture there not being used at the present time. Let’s go down and check if anything down there catches your attention.” She stood up. “Herb, she called. “We’re going down to the storage area. Which one of these keys fits the bedroom section?” She walked into their office and held up a set of keys.

He stood up and walked to his wife. Took the set of keys from her hand and pulled out two. “Use these to get in the padlock.” He nodded at the two nurses and said, “Pick the pieces easiest to clean.”

Once downstairs, Mrs. Victor led them to the far west corner and walked up to a ‘cage’ full of bedroom furniture. She opened the padlock and slid open the ten-foot-high cage door.

Marlene was surprised at the organization in the ‘cage’. There were rows of bed pieces and sections and other pieces. There were sets of king mattresses, springs, pieces, queen sections and lines of twin backs and stacks of mattresses and frames. Some twin headboards were wood in two colors and others were fake leather in the colors of crème or gray.

“I like this padded bed back. What do you think, Marlene?” Giselle said.

Marlene came over to touch the bed back. “It would be easy to clean. No wooden railings to dust. Okay, do you like the gray shade or the crème?”

"I like the crème, better. Shall we choose a pair of crème headboards?". They walked to some headboards that were stacked and were wrapped in large plastic covers.

"Now lets' pick some good firm, mattresses and springs." Giselle said.

So the girls began searching the storage area, and in a few minutes had begun to choose two sets of twin beds. Also, Giselle found a wooden bench they could use in dress and undressing, and putting on shoes or boots.

Mrs. Victor began to tag their choices, and also wrote the pieces they wanted on a form. "We have people who will deliver these furniture pieces to your apartment tomorrow after 4:00 p.m. They will bring everything to your apartment. When they ring your doorbell, they will tell you a code word. This is for your safety, as well as theirs. Therefore, you will be safe and so will they." She smiled and patted Marlene's arm.

"That's a very reassuring idea. I like that." Giselle nodded.

"Good. Come up and sign some paperwork." Mrs. Victor said and then we'll get your beds changed out tomorrow."

As the girls went back up to their apartment, Giselle glanced at her watch. "It's after 7:00 p.m. Do you want me to go home now and return after work with a load of my stuff, or could you stand me sleeping in that king bed with you tonight?"

"Neither of us needs to go out anymore this evening. Let's make some dinner from what I brought, and both stay here tonight. Then when we get the new beds in, and we can clean up and really get comfortable. We'll have the weekend to settle in and move things where we'll find they will fit best. I also brought my vacuum." Marlene touched the small door in the hallway. "It's in here."

Chapter Twenty Six

Downtown, now, Taylor let himself into his avenue apartment. He had stopped and picked a few items at a local deli. He wasn't used to shopping for food on a regular basis. He knew he would have to go out, perhaps on Sunday morning and do some major shopping, but he hadn't worked that activity into a regular habit. He first changed from his suit and tie, and found some more casual clothes to change wear doing chores.

Another new chore he would have to work into his schedule was doing his own laundry. While he had been living with Marlene, she had been taking care of that little chore. It had to be done, and right now. And he was the one to do it. Luckily this apartment building did have a laundry room in the basement.

He sat down and warmed some of the food he had brought home, ate it and then gathered up the clothes, plus sheets and towels that needed washing. At least he had a jar of coins he had brought with him from the Sugarhouse apartment.

Once he located the laundry facility, he found another man down there washing some clothes. He also noticed there was a TV mounted above the sorting table. It was turned on to a basketball game. Keeping up with the college teams in the area was not his habit. He also hadn't followed NBA lately. When he still lived with Roz and Eric, he would sit and watch a basketball game with Eric now and then.

Yet, he didn't want to leave his laundry to anyone coming into the laundry room with his clothes unattended. So, he settled down in a chair and began to watch the game. When he asked the man about each team, and what city they were from, the other man stared at him as if he were from another planet.

"Buddy." The guy said "You must not be a sports fan. Right now, the NBA is the 'hot ticket' to watch."

Taylor, who didn't want to appear strange, began to ask a question now and then. By the end of the game, he remembered when he and Eric watched these games fairly often. He found himself remembering what he and Eric had enjoyed about basketball.

Finally, the other man turned to him." My name is Frank Parkland, and you are- - - -?"

Taylor stood and walked to the man and put out his hand. "I'm Taylor Rosenbaum, and a new tenant to this place. It's a pleasure to meet you."

"Which one did you move into? I've been in here soon after the renovations were complete. It's a great place to live. Even if you're planning to live here less than a year. I like it here, close to everything."

One of the dryers clicked off, and Frank moved to it and began to empty it. Methodically he began to sort and make stacks of clothing on the wide counter. Then he picked up a large canvas bag and filled it with the clean clothes. He also picked up two other bags and walked to the door. "See you some other time. Again, I'm Frank Parkland."

Taylor smiled and returned his attention to the TV. *Seems like a pleasant fellow. One more reason to enjoy living here.*

Now it was Taylor's turn to begin sorting and folding his clean clothes. As Frank had said. "We all must have clean clothes, now and then."

Once Marlene and Giselle made it back to their apartment, they found twin beds with creme 'leather' head boards in the bedroom. Even with two beds the room, it was large enough for them to move around easily.

"Tomorrow, I need to bring some paperwork and a few books from my office. What do you have to put into our 'office'?"

"I actually have a filing cabinet, but it's not by any means full. You can have a drawer in you need it." Giselle answered.

"Hey, to have a filing cabinet would be great. I could at least, use a drawer. "I have a locker at work, but having my things here would be much more convenient. Thank you for offering."

"We'll need to go bring it over tomorrow night. Will that work for you?" Giselle asked.

"Sure. How soon can you come here after work?" Marlene asked.

"I'm off about 4:30 p.m." Giselle said.

"Okay, I should get here, no later than 6:00 p.m.

"I can open a can of soup, or we can grab some for dinner on the way back. Marlene suggested.

"Let's save the outing for the day after tomorrow, and get things set up in here as soon as possible."

"Good idea. I like things in order as quickly as we manage to do it. Then the rest of our day turns out better." Marlene said.

As Taylor was showering, he thought about going to Colorado Springs and again meeting Edie Franklin, now Fletcher, again. *What would she be like after twenty years. She would be at least 50 years old. Would she have put on weight as Roz had? Did she still work as a nurse? That's right, Eric r had mentioned that. What he should do is take a few days off and drive over there and bring Eric back to Salt Lake. He better call Eric tomorrow night and find out if he has a release date from his mission yet.*

Eric would probably want to go back and live in the family house. All of his belongings were still there. What were his son's plans? Attend college, most likely. He realized how much he had missed Eric. It would be great to have him home again.

The next afternoon, he called Roz at the hospital but she had not returned his call. Yet now, he had had an appointment with patients that morning. The woman aged 67, had fallen and had a severe break in her lower leg. The doctor who had performed surgery the day before, wanted to wait for the swelling to go down before he cast the leg. However. Taylor had been called in, because the patient; Marilyn Jenkins seemed to be having problems with reality.

Taylor went into see Ms. Jenkins that mid-afternoon. A nurse went into the patient's room with him. "She's sometimes somewhat awake, but other times asleep or at least is groggy and cannot remember why she's in the hospital."

So, Taylor went into the women's room. "Good afternoon Ms. Jenkins." He said.

Her eyes fluttered open. "Who are you?" She asked in a low voice. "Who's this Mrs. Jenkins?" She asked.

"Why Mrs. Jenkins is your name. You do remember that you have a husband and three grown children."

She pushed up on her elbows. "Would you put some pillows behind me? Now who are you? I'll bet another doctor. What's your name again?"

"Of course." Taylor pushed two pillows behind her and eased her up. "Is that better? Yes, I'm another doctor, and my name is Dr. Taylor Rosenbaum." He said as he studied her. "Do you remember your accident? Can you explain what happened to your leg?" He asked.

"Rosenbaum, huh' One of those Jew boys, that went to college." She touched her wrapped leg under the covers. "When the accident happened, I was riding my father's horse. He told me not to ride bareback, but putting the saddle on her (the horse) took too long. But why do I have so much pain in this leg now?"

"Okay, you don't recall stepping in front of a car in the grocery store parking lot?" Taylor asked.

"What are you talking about?" I hurt my leg jumping Sadie. I hope she didn't get hurt. No, I'm sure she's okay. After my brother Howard put me in the car, and drove me to the doctor's office. I'm sure my sister Sylvia took her back to the barn."

"Well." He said. I have information about a Ms. Jenkins. And this information concerns a woman named Marilyn Smith Jenkins, 67 years old. And this woman broke her leg walking behind a moving car, pushing a grocery cart."

"I know! You're one of those doctors who was sent here to not allow the insurance company to pay for my broken leg. Well, they just better pay the hospital, or my Dad will sue them."

"What about your husband? He will be the one to deal with the insurance company." Taylor asked her.

"What husband! I'm only 22 years old; Much too young to marry. I have to have a teaching degree before I can get married. That's a rule in my family. But my poor sister, Vivian broke the rule by marrying that young soldier. And now his rich family won't accept her. Poor girl, she's on her own. At least she got a job, and she and another girl put in for an apartment. They are so hard to find in this post war era." She took a breath. "Did they draft you? Did you have to serve in a veterans' hospital?" She asked him.

Taylor couldn't help but smile. *Where did this woman come up with a post war scenario? Did some trauma cause this break with reality?* "I'll return later to chat more with you again soon."

As he walked out of the room, He went back to his office to write up a report, but realized he needed more information. So, he turned back to Miss Marilyn's room and found her having a snack. "Well, I'm glad we had this talk. I may see you again tomorrow." Taylor walked out and went to find her primary physician; Or at least to find more information about this woman.

Chapter Twenty Seven

Taylor requested a meeting with Marilyn Jenkin's husband. When he reached the Jenkins' house, he managed to speak with one of the daughters. "Good afternoon." Taylor said. I'm Doctor Rosenbaum assigned to Marilyn Jenkins' case."

"Yes Doctor Rosenbaum. I'm Cara Jenkins a daughter of Ms. Jenkins. Is she getting any better? Has she remembered her present life?"

Taylor could hear the anxiety in her voice. "I just left your mother's room. Right now, at the present time she does not seem to remember her adult life. At least being married and having children. She spoke about an accident riding a horse."

"Yes, my father and I visited her last night. She did not acknowledge my father has her husband or me as her daughter. She asked me if we had a college class together. I am attending the community college. But she never did as a young adult."

"Did your mother attend another community college at some previous time?" Taylor asked.

"Yes. She actually went to a community college in Arizona. She has a degree from Arizona State University. She taught evening classes at the college that I now attend."

"This is very interesting. Somehow. she wants to amend her past with your experience. She sees your experience and somehow wants to have done the same, but prior to your birth. She is remembering being a young woman, and she wants to have some of your experiences now." Taylor said. 'Since the damage to her leg is ongoing, she will be here in the hospital for another day or two. Did she grow up with horses near her?"

"Yes. My grandfather had a ranch/farm in Southern Utah, and I believe he had one or two horses. But after my grandfather died, my Uncle Brad took over the farm, and grew crops for animal feed. The farm is near Cedar City. I've only been down there maybe three times. My father is a professor at another college, as well as an investor for his family. That's as far away as you can get from raising crops and keeping a horse or two." She laughed.

Later that afternoon Taylor had a conference with Ms. Jenkins' family, Cara Jenkins, Jacob Jenkins, an older brother, and their father. They discussed Ms. Jenkins elaborate delusions of her life as a young woman. Then Taylor asked. "This information could be very important. Having this background about her is very useful, but how much of it is true?"

Cara spoke up. "Mom probably did ride a horse or two. I don't remember a story of her falling off one and having an injury. Maybe she did, but I could call Uncle Charles and see if he remembers Mom having an accident falling off a horse."

"Let me know what you learn." He reached into his pocket and handed her a business card. "When I visit her again, I'll be able to understand her present delusion. The hospital will release her as soon as they put her in a walking cast."

That evening he called Eric again and they were able to talk for several minutes. "Good evening son. How are you doing this day?"

"Hi Dad. I found out that two new missionaries are coming in from Atlanta, Georgia. They should be here in about two to three weeks. Then Elder Mendoza will be released. You want to come and pick me up, don't you?" He chuckled. "You want to come and visit Edith Fletcher, while you're here."

"Well, yes, I do. During the Iraqi war we worked closely as a surgical team for several months." He cleared his throat.

"Okay. And - - - - - you want to meet your son. That's okay. I can understand why. He's a good guy and is in college and has a job. I'm too busy to really spend time with him. And also, you would like to see his mother too. Oh, and they are very curious about you, also." He laughed.

"Okay. I'll try for some time off in about three weeks. Keep me posted when you think they will release you. It will be great to see you, too. I was in Colorado Springs many years ago, just after I was drafted into the army medical corps."

"I have to go to a meeting in a few minutes, Dad. Talk to you in a few days. Bye."

Taylor sat back in his leather chair, and smiled. *It's time for an adventure. However, I should talk to Roselyn and tell her of my plans. At least I'm planning to bring Eric home in a few weeks.* Just then his phone rang, and he picked it up. "Hello?"

"Dr. Rosenbaum. This is Harrison Wilcox, Ms. Jenkins. surgeon. She tried to get out of bed, and further injured her leg. She told my staff that only you knew how to treat her injured leg."

"Oh Boy! I'm sorry, I'll come up to the hospital immediately." Taylor found an older jacket in the front closet, grabbed his keys, a bottle of water and left for the hospital.

Once he arrived, he put on a protective gown, gloves and went into surgical room #3. They had her 'asleep' and the attending physician and Dr. Wilcox were cutting away the dressing. The three MD's soon learned the damage was not serious; Just a small bleed, and soon it was sewed up and they decided that a walking cast would further protect the leg. They sent her back to her room with instructions to contact them. Then they left for the cafeteria.

While discussing the case, Taylor who had missed supper grabbed a sandwich with his coffee. The other two had cookies with their beverages. Again, Ms. Jenkins release was on hold. The hospital had just opened a twenty bed 'nursing facility' for patients that were not ready to be released to go home, but were in a convalescing situation. It was mainly because Ms. Jenkins had no family member who could be with her. They all had jobs or were in college. Her attending physician would speak with the family that evening.

Taylor dragged back to his apartment. For some reason he was exhausted. He knew he would have to talk with Roselyn. He was sure she had plans for Eric's homecoming.

After a light dinner, he gathered up his courage and dialed the Rosenbaum number. After two rings the phone was answered.

"Good evening, you've reached the Rosenbaum's." The cheerful voice answered.

Taylor answered. "Is this that pretty young girl who is a senior in high school?"

"Oh hi Dad, How have you been these past few *weeks*." Shanna answered in a business-like voice.

"Oh, I'm good. May I speak to your mother?" *for a moment he remembered discussing his cases with Roselyn. He always enjoyed doing that.* Moments later he heard Roz.

"How are you this evening, Taylor? What is it you want to discuss?"

'I'll get right to the point. When do you expect Eric to be released from his mission?" I spoke to him yesterday, and I am planning to drive over to Colorado Springs and pick him up."

"Really! He has not spoken to me about this plan. You're planning to drive over and bring him home? Usually, the Church Missionary System puts returning missionaries on a plane or train to their home town."

"Well, I've spoken to him several times, and he seems to think his mission president will be okay if I come and pick him up. In fact, Eric is looking forward to it."

Roselyn automatically frowned, but then the thought came that Taylor *was* his father and legally had the right to go wherever and bring his son home. "I suppose if you two have discussed the fact that you will pick him up, I'll just inform the Stake President, of your plan to bring him home. Traditionally, Eric will have to give a talk in Church about his missionary experiences. Most likely it will be two or three weeks after he arrives home."

"Once he settles in at home, I'd love to hear of his experiences. You'll have to keep me informed. So, how are you and the girls doing?"

He asked, and worked to sound neutral but interested.

"We're doing okay. As you know we had quite the winter. Have you been up skiing? Oh and I found out that you have moved. I suppose you grew tired living with that *airheaded young thing* you left us to move in with."

"That's what I first learned about you Roz. You're very good at meeting new people and analyzing them." He chuckled. "I suppose I will have to admit you were accurate in understanding Marlene and my fleeting interest in her. Chalk one up for Roz." He laughed. "Yes, I found a very nice apartment in the lower Avenue's. It is close to my downtown office, and larger enough for my present needs. Change of subject. Will you have an open house for Eric once he gets comfortable back home?"

"It will be up to him, as to what he wants to do. But I imagine he will want to go back to the university, either a summer session or will look for a job, and then enroll in the fall. If it works out that you do drive him home, I'm sure you two will discuss his plans on the way home." Roselyn said.

"Speaking of professions, are you still working at the hospital?"

"Yes, why?' She asked.

"I have a very unusual case that I've become involved in. The woman I was asked to do a consult had a bad accident and broke her leg; A below the knee facture. However, I was asked to see her because, she did not remember her present life or acknowledge her husband or her family. I would like you to go and speak with her, and I would like your professional opinion concerning her delusions."

The medical personnel have put her in a walking cast, and she is to be moved into the new wing of the hospital. It's an area where the patients cannot yet be released to go home, but need less special care."

"Oh, I've been over there on one occasion. What is her name? Hold please, while I get you scheduled for tomorrow." Roz set the phone down, but quickly returned. "Okay, give me her name and room number."

When Roselyn reached Ms. Jenkin's room and she found that she had requested a shower, and so one of the attendants offered to get into the shower with her. The new walking cast had been wrapped in a plastic 'sleeve' they were down the hall working in the 'sit down' shower. While there, Roselyn received a call from a doctor concerning another consult with another patient.

Roz explained to the floor nurse that she would return later.

Chapter Twenty Eight

Because of the long consult with another doctor, Roselyn didn't arrive home until nearly eight o'clock. She found a chicken sandwich plate with some coleslaw left by Ellie in the fridge. She was grateful, but exhausted. But after her supper sandwich and a cup of tea she felt somewhat revived.

A few minutes later the phone rang. Roselyn reached over and picked it up. She scowled at the instrument. *It's probably for one of the girls.* But she was surprised when she recognized the masculine voice. "Hello." She answered.

"Ah, Roselyn?" Luke Landre said.

"Yes. Is this Luke? How are you this evening?"

"Yes, good, and 'good' to talk to you. The 'guys' want to get together and rehearse for another event. Not a funeral this time." He laughed self-consciously.

"When, where and for what?" Then she let out a giggle. "I sound like one of my daughters."

"There's a new junior college and it just opened up south of Provo. They are having a ribbon ceremony the first week in June. The College Board wants to have an opening week end. This is to attract the young people that could possibly be interested in enrolling as students the summer season. They are holding a dance. They want us, our foursome to be the 'half-time attraction."

"An older group from the 80's attraction? Why not find a group closer to their age?" Roz asked.

"I believe the 'powers that be' don't want any crazy behavior; Just a band and a group singing some 'old' favorites. Hey. My girls went through some of the old music books we used to use. They picked out five we could sing that wouldn't embarrass them. I think they heard us." Luke said and laughed. I spoke with Sam, and he said we could use his studio Wednesday late afternoon. How does that work for you?"

"If I don't have a 'long consult', I could leave by four that afternoon."

"What if I pick you up by five in the afternoon Don't worry about supper, Roger's wife said she would fix some dinner for us.".

"That should be okay. I'll call you if I get snarled up. I don't have your cell phone number. You'd better repeat it to me." She yanked her phone from her purse. "My number is- - - - -" She repeated it to him.

Next, he rattled off his to her. "Okay, I'll call you before I come by to pick you up. Bye for now."

She held the kitchen phone in her hand for a long moment, smiling. Luke used an old phrase *Bye for now.* He always said that to her at the end of a phone call. Maybe that is how he ends all his phone calls now. But the phrase still reminded her of them as a couple so many years ago.

In Colorado Springs at the mission home, the bishop received a phone call from the Stake President of the Atlanta, Georgia West Mission.

"Good evening the Colorado Springs Mission President answered; This is Riker Carlton, Atlanta Mission. I have two new missionaries, flying out tomorrow afternoon, to Colorado Springs as replacements of those missionaries you are releasing this week."

"What time should we expect them?" The mission leader said.

"Probably after six P M. Their flight leaves around two fifteen. It's about a three-hour flight. Their names are: Justin Jones, a young black, and Gregory Whitney. Both of them are fine young men. Neither has been to Utah before."

"I'm ready to release Elder Rosenbaum and Elder Alverez. Elder Rosenbaum's father is coming to pick him up. His father was in the military during the Iraqi War. And I believe he was stationed here at Camp Carson. That's probably why he wants to come to Colorado Springs; Old memories."

That evening Taylor received a phone call from Eric. "Hi Dad. The missionary system is going to 'set me free' in three days. He laughed. "I'll be ready to leave on Monday morning. What's your patient 'load' right now?"

"Right, I have one delusional woman in the hospital, and usually see a girl who suffers from autism, plus whoever comes into the hospital that needs my attention. However, I can leave Monday morning early, and be in Colorado Springs by early evening. I'll rent a motel room. Find out where a good one is located, and I'll stay there. And from there we will coordinate our time while we are there, in the city. I'm planning to be gone from my patients that week. It will be great to see you, son, and the others we'll meet.

He laughed nervously and cleared his throat. "There is one patient I'll tell you about when we have time to talk. I'm sure you have some interesting people you have met and can share with me their stories. Three days, it will be so good to see you. Love you son. Goodbye for now."

"Wow! Eric said to himself. *My dad is getting soft in his old age. Before today, has he ever told me he loves me? Not that I can recall.*

The next day Luke came by to pick up Roselyn about five P.M. the next afternoon. Luckily, she had been home long enough to change clothes and grab a glass of water. He rang the doorbell, and Shanna answered it. For a moment she stared at the man standing on the front porch. "Oh, hi. You must be here for my Mom." She stared at him for a moment. Then she opened the door wide and said, "You might as well come in." She showed him into the living room. Then she said, "You must be Mr. Landre. I'll tell mother you're here." Then she vanished into the house.

Luke went to the window and stared out at the view of the city. *I had no idea this house had such a great view. He began to see familiar buildings and stretches of familiar roads.*

"Luke. Good afternoon. I'm ready to go."

He whirled around to see Roz standing behind him with a sweater in her arms. "Okay, you have quite a view from up here. Did you buy the house for the view?"

"Not really; I was because of the five bedrooms. But the view is always enjoyable." She slid on the sweater. "We still have cool evenings. Hang on, I'll get my purse." She led him down the stairs to the front door. His car was parked in the driveway, and he walked around and opened the passenger door.

She slid in sniffed and smiled. "This has the scent of a new car. When did you buy it?"

He grinned, and slid in the auto. "Put on your seatbelt" He buckled his own, turned the car around and drove down to the main road. "I've had the car about three months. I was driving a nine-year-old car, with two hundred thousand, plus miles on it. Time for a newer model."

She laughed. "Now I remember, you really liked cars. While we were singing together, you had at least two different ones. You traded the convertibles for an SUV." She patted his shoulder. "That's what I drive, a Toyota SUV." She settled back and glanced out the window.

"So tell me with your new degree, a PhD? Just what types of cases do you handle? What 'crosses your desk?" He asked.

"Sometimes I see traumatized children in the hospital with burn scars, or other injuries. Right now, I have an appointment tomorrow with a woman in the hospital with a severely broken leg. But right now. she has 'lost or blacked out her whole adult life, marriage, children, husband. She has decided that she is only twenty-two." I work to get my patients back to reality."

"Sometimes reality is too painful. So we construct a separate reality. I know that sounds crazy. But just for a day or even just an evening. You can pretend something other than the way things really are." Luke breathed.

'I can understand doing that. When Taylor first left, sometimes I'd pretend that he, especially when he didn't come home, was out of town or working late on a difficult case. But soon I had to face reality that he would never return. The real 'kicker' was when he brought this poor young girl with him one night. She was twenty-six and so uncomfortable to be in my house."

"So what happened?" Luke grinned.

"My girls got a taste of their father behaving like a dumb teenager. And as soon as he left dragging this inept girl with him, they realized how childish his behavior was and, in a way, felt sorry for him."

Luke took a deep breath and shook his head. "Some people have trouble growing up." They stopped at a red light and Luke turned up a street in leading up in the avenues.

"Interesting, Sam lives up here?" Roselyn asked.

"Yes, remember that large sparling house they lived in up above the boulevard. After the first two children left, he and Cynthia found this older house and remodeled it. This one has more class."

A few minutes later Luke drove up 'E' street to a white brick house on the up side of the street. There was a double driveway and Luke parked behind a newer midsized red car. He came around and helped Roselyn out of the car. They walked up four steps to a shiny black front door.

A few seconds later the door opened and Sam grabbed Roselyn and pulled her into a front hallway. "Good to see you; Gorgeous. Good, see you brought Landre with you. Come on in."

Cynthia followed her husband in, wiping her hands on a half apron. "Don't mind Sam, he's excited about this 'gig' he's lined up."

They were ushered into a large living room with two beige sofas and a soft green side chair. And of course, in the corner was the grand piano. "This is the plan." Cynthia said. "We are going to have a 'salad course' now. Then we'll have a rehearsal time. After that the main course will be served. Living with a 'music man' for over twenty years, I realize singing and playing on a full stomach is not the best."

She stopped and looked out the window. "Oh, here comes Roger. I'll set the first course on the table."

Chapter Twenty Nine

When Cynthia answered the door, Roger came in carrying a guitar case.

Sam jumped up grinning. "Have you taken up a string instrument, Roger?"

"Well, it's easier than carrying in a drum set. Besides I know that one of your kids plays the drums." He looked around the room. It looks like everyone has arrived. What's the plan?"

"Come sit down we're having a salad course first." Cynthia said.

Roger's eyes widened. "Okay, lady of the house, we'll go along with your plan."

After salads, ice water and some rolls warm from the oven, they all went downstairs to a music room. There was a set of drums, another piano, this one was an upright. "Okay, Sam asked. What music did everyone bring?"

"I brought a few 80's love songs my daughters' picked out." Luke said, and opened a portfolio and he set the music them on the piano. 'I have a stack of some music I played in the 80's and early 90's." Sam said. Let's sit down over here." He gestured at a kitchen set with four chairs across the room.

They all did as Sam suggested and spread out the sheets of music they all had brought. "Okay, let's see what you all have here." Sam stacked it up and began to look through each song. "Hey, you want to do 'Eye in the Sky?"

"Why not? Last week, wife and I went out to a steak eatery and the song was played as we ate. I don't know what musical service the restaurant had, but they played it. I also heard another song; 'Don't matter to me.' Didn't Roz and Luke do that song together?"

"Yeah, that's a good reverse love song." Luke said. He grinned across the table at Roselyn. "Here are the songs my girls put on their stamp of approval.' Luke pushed a stack of music across the table.

'I found a few, too." Sam said. All of you take a look and see what you want try rehearsing. He picked up a small stack and went to the piano. Roger went to the drums and picked up the sticks and sat down. They decided to get serious.

Three hours later Cynthia yelled down the stairs. "Time for a break. Get up here for the main course."

They all eased back upstairs to the dining room table with a big chicken casserole, and more hot rolls.

Roselyn took two bites of the main course. "Hey Cynthia, I want the recipe. And did you bake the rolls?"

"Me bake rolls? In another life. I bought them at Reams."

"Baked or purchased, Bring out some more." Sam yelled.

Soon it was getting dark. Roger glanced at his watch. "Guess what, the time at the tone will be ten twenty P.M. Work tomorrow, people."

The three of them left a few minutes later. As Luke drove down from the high avenues to the seven hundred east, street he smiled. "That was a very good rehearsal. It was also fun to sing and play again."

"Yes, it was, it really was." Roselyn answered. She glanced out the side window." Even with daylight savings in the summer, once it's dark. It's very dark."

They talked about their busy lives. Then Luke turned on the car radio. And an old song came up, and Luke began to sing some of the lines.

Roselyn couldn't resist, she began to sing along with him. Then they heard a favorite; *Africa* "I absolutely love this song." She said. And began to sing along with the radio.

Luke joined in. After it ended, they laughed together. "Did we ever do the song; Africa?" He asked.

"I don't think so. But we should, because it a great love song." He said. A very few minutes later he drove up into the cove where Roselyn lived. He parked in her driveway, climbed out, and helped her out. 'You know what. I've never had a look from the last house on this cul-de-sac." He took her hand and they walked over to the little place between her house and last house next door.

"There's a little path." She said and took his hand. A little below the edge of the lawn she guided him down between the houses. They moved together past some trees. "Here sit down." She led him to a small bench.

"I always knew it was a wonderful view." He whispered, and slid him arm around her.

She turned to him and he kissed her. It began soft and easy, but soon the kisses became more torrid. Roz eased back and touched his face, and felt the growth of whiskers. "Are you going to grow a beard?" She asked and giggled.

"I've thought about it. Does it bother you?" He asked in a soft voice.

"Not really. I just remembered when you grew one when we were in college. Wasn't there a beard growing contest back then?" She touched his chin and gently kissed it. Then another kiss on his mouth and it deepened. He held her tight, and his hand ran down her back.

"Well, it's a lovely night, and when we were in college we could neck, but we were pretty inexperienced. But now we have no bed handy to continue this rather intense activity. Even though we're older and have a comfortable bed right there in my house, but there are also two nearly grown-up girls in there, too." She sighed.

"I understand. We also have three grown children at my house; Plus, two fifty- something reputations to protect." He put his forehead against hers. Offering his hand. they walked back to Roselyn's front door. "Well, this evening has been very revealing. An 'eye opener for both of us; Pointing to the future of us." He took her in his arms and they stood linked at the door for several seconds. Then he turned and moved quickly to his car. Almost in a flash, she heard the car door slam, and a few seconds later she watched it disappear up the street. For a long moment she stood and watched the moon rise. She shook her head, but couldn't stop a smile. They really still had it for each other. After twenty something years the spark was still there. *Eat your heart out Taylor. I'm done with you.*

A few hours earlier, Taylor Rosenbaum was pulling a suitcase and some other bags from the trunk of his car and carrying them into a motel room in Colorado Springs. He had driven for close to ten hours from Salt Lake City to this town he that had spent several months in, over twenty years ago. He remembered that he had been released from the Army Medical Corp at that time. He then returned to Salt Lake to a wife and a two-year-old son. That son was now being released from an LDS mission. He had spent the last six months as a missionary in this city.

Taylor was very tired, and wanted to take a shower, and maybe take a short nap before picking up his son, Eric. Once he had all his belongings in the room, he checked the air conditioning, began hanging up his clothes.

He decided to call Eric now and they could plan their evening together. He called the mission home and finally managed to speak to Eric.

Hi Dad. Did you just get in town?"

"Yes. I rented a room for us in a motel called the Central Springs. I just managed to unpack. What are you plans for the rest of the day?"

"There giving Alverez and me a farewell party in a few minutes. You could come and pick me up in an hour or two. Or you could rest up and pick me up first thing tomorrow morning."

"I think that I will take a shower and then a nap. What time is good to pick you up tomorrow morning?"

"Any time after ten A.M. I'll be ready. Let me give you the address." For a moment Eric moved away from the phone, but then came back "I'll read it. Do you have a pencil and paper, or you can put it into your phone."

Eric slowly repeated the address. "Did you get all that? It's close to a large Stake House. I'm sure you've seen them all over Salt Lake."

"I think I've passed a couple since I've been here in Colorado Springs. Enjoy your farewell party. See you tomorrow morning." Taylor set down his phone, and for a moment slumped down into a desk chair. He felt the fatigue from driving several hundred miles. He flipped open his suitcase and began taking out clothes and hanging them up in the closet. Next, he picked out some clean clothes, but felt the heavy fatigue of driving all those miles.

After his shower and a change of clothes, he was still tired, but now he was hungry. He would go to the motel office and ask for suggestions to find a place to go for some dinner. As he walked up to the office, he felt the pleasant warmth of late spring evening. As he walked into the office an attractive older woman turned away from her computer.

"Good evening may I help you with something?"

"Yes, do you have any suggestions where to go for a quick supper?"

"Why, yes." She reached under the desk and handed him a flyer with the names and address of several restaurants, or fast-food places. She set the flyer on the counter top and turned it toward him. "There's a Denny's to the east two blocks, and here, - - - "She pointed to another place. This is an Applebee's half a block on the east side of the street."

As he studied the flyer, she watched him. "Thank you, this is very helpful." He picked up the flyer and left.

He chose the Applebee's and was not disappointed. After a hamburger and a salad, he drove back to the motel. Now with a full stomach, he could barely keep his eyes open. What energy he had left went to arranging the bed the way he liked it. He had chosen one of the queen beds, so he took off his outer clothing, tossed them on the other bed. Leaving one small lamp on, he shut off the other lights, locked the door, and slid into bed. Then he found a comfortable position and fell asleep.

Chapter Thirty

When Taylor awoke the next morning, for a moment he was disoriented. But after gazing around the room, he remembered he was in a motel room in Colorado Springs. He glanced at the clock on a small table next to the bed. It read eight-thirty A.M. There was also a small coffee maker on that table and some packets of coffee. Soon he had made coffee, and stood staring in the mirror and sipping the brew from a paper cup. While he dressed, he drank the rather non-descript liquid.

Once Taylor was dressed and ready for his day, he decided to call Eric. When his son answered, he could hear conversations in the background. "Are you ready for me to pick you up?" he asked.

"Yes, any time. "What's the plan? Do you want to go over to Camp Carson?" The son asked.

"I did bring my old identification. We could try as see if we could get in." The father answered.

"You're probably hungry." Eric said. "Go get some breakfast then- - - - -. Suddenly Eric responded to someone in the mission home speaking to him. "Never mind, just come and pick me up. My mission president has some contacts at the 'Base'. He thinks we shouldn't take my suitcases and books to a motel room now. Come and get me, and then we'll go over to Camp Carson. He said "We can get some food at their coffee shop." Eric rattled off instructions to get to the mission home. "See ya when you get here."

Less than thirty minutes later Taylor drove into a parking place in front of a large house close to an LDS Church building. He left his car and walked up to an attractive brick house with a large front porch. Taylor rang the doorbell, and in a timely manner the door was opened. A middle-aged man answered. He smiled and extended the glass storm door for Taylor to enter.

"Mr. Rosenbaum." he said. "Please come in."

Eric stood a few feet away. But then he come to his father and threw his arms around him. "Hey Dad, you're looking good."

Taylor stood back a gazed at his son. He was taller than he had been when he left Salt Lake two years before. He also seemed to have 'filled out' seemed stronger, with more muscle.

"Have you been working out?" Taylor asked still with his hand on Eric's sleeve.

The Stake President stepped forward. "These young men do a lot of walking, and we do encourage some other strengthening activities. "I'm John Morrison. And we hate to release these fine young men, however their strength and testimonies are needed at home at this particular time of confusion in our country."

Eric turned and shook hands with the other young men in the room. "Communicate with me from time to time. And keep working hard, and hang in there." He gave a small salute. "Let's go Dad." He pulled on a jacket and led his father out the front door. "I'll return for my things later."

Father and son climbed in Taylor's car. As they drove down the residential street, Taylor turned to Eric. "Where to?" "I didn't bother to eat anything yet. Can we get some food on base?"

"I have passes to get on base. Let's go there now, get you some breakfast and we'll take a little tour. You'll see how the world has changed in the past twenty years."

They drove north and soon they could see a large airfield to the right a few blocks later Eric said. "Turn down this lane, Dad."

At least a half mile or so, Taylor drove along a tree shaded road. But then signs directed them to the front gate and they were forced to stop. At the entrance booth a man in uniform stood, and slid, open a tall narrow window. "Identification, please." He said.

Both Eric and his father took identification from their wallets plus Eric handed the passes his mission president had given him.

The young man in the booth scanned information, and then stamped the passes and handed the information back to Taylor. "Have a good afternoon." he said, and the gate went up and he waved them through it.

As Taylor followed the road into the base, he was amazed at the changes to the area. Many new buildings stood where twenty years ago were just fields of dry grass. "Look at all the new buildings." He said almost to himself. He pointed at a large structure. "That has to be new housing. Wow, each unit seems to be fairly large. Do you know the capacity of the base now? What types of training expertise have they dedicated this base to? Is advanced training being done here?"

"The army doesn't broadcast what the training mode is for this base, but I've heard rumors that they are doing rifle and marksmanship work. Especially when the soldiers are is a in combat situation, and also from helicopters. Turn left and follow this road for a half mile. We'll go eat at the commissary."

Taylor could see a large circular building straight ahead. "Just what is this building?" he asked.

"Food." Eric laughed. "Groceries, restaurants, fast food. It's all in there." Park as close as you can."

Taylor drove down a lane keeping in sight what seemed to be a large main entrance. He found a parking spot and pulled in. Soon they were walking into the building. The first thing he could see was a grocery store, with doors that slid open as people approached them. And also exits that closed as people with carts full of food walked toward the outside doors. "Do we go in the store?" he asked.

"No. We walk to the right down this hallway/" Eric grabbed his father's elbow and guided him down the wide curved hall. They lost sight of the food and grocery store. Next, they walked by some offices, and other short halls leading more to the interior of the building. Again, following the curve of the building, Eric stopped at a glass door with large windows on each side. Printed on the glass door, in large print was the words; Coffee Shop.

Eric opened the door. "Come on in Dad. We go in here." He waved his arm at a room to the south.

Eric pushed open the door and Taylor followed him in. Almost immediately a trim woman, possibly in her mid to late thirties approached them. She was dressed in a yellow shirt and slacks with a white apron edged in yellow and red trim..

"You interested in breakfast, lunch, or dessert? Follow me." She led them down a curved room with booths on the both left and right. There were a few of them occupied but the next one was empty. "This okay?" She asked.

"This is fine." Taylor said. And slid onto a bench, and Eric sat down on the other side.

The server set down menus on the table and said, "I'll be back to take your order in a few minutes." She turned and walked quickly away.

Reading the menu reminded Taylor of the food offered at an I Hop, or a Wendy's restaurant; Just good average- American cuisine. "I think I'll have eggs, bacon and pancakes. What looks good to you, son?"

Eric glanced at his watch." Breakfast was early this morning, so I'm going to have a hamburger, fries and a coke."

The waiter came back at took their orders. Then they settled down and began to chat. "By the time we get back to the motel, it will be mid-afternoon. We can organize your belongings and make a plan to pack the car. Taylor suggested.

"We have one stop before we drive back home." Eric said. "But I need to check on what time is best." He smiled and shrugged, punched in a number on his phone and listened. "Are you having a good day?" He asked the individual who answered the phone.

"Yeah. How about you?"

"When's the best time for a visit?" Eric asked.

"Okay. The subject of interest won't be home until about 'four bells'." "How about around five P.M.?"

"I'll see what I can do. Call you back if there is a snag. Or if there is problem on your end, give me a jingle. Later then." Eric closed his phone."

"What was that all about?" The father asked.

Eric cleared his throat, was silent. But then he glanced down the open area, and could see their waiter walk toward them carrying large tray.

She set it down on the booth table. "Here's your food.' She set a mug, and a large covered plate by Taylor. She then set a plate in front of Eric and a large glass of a beverage. She lifted the covering on the plate; "One deluxe hamburger with fries, and for you sir; breakfast." She filled the mug with coffee. Do you want cream?"

Taylor smiled up at her. "No, just sugar." And he slid the sugar container across the table near his plate of food. 'Thank you, it all looks good."

She stepped back and picked up the tray. "I'll come back with more coffee." She turned and moved quickly down the hallway.

After a forkful of perfectly scrambled eggs, Taylor smiled. "I didn't know what to think of this place. Now I'm impressed. Have you eaten here before?"

"A few times. I've only been here six months." Eric said and sipped his drink.

"Did you ever find out why you were transferred?" Taylor asked.

"I'll talk to you about the situation later. Right now. I'm going to eat."

After the good food, they wandered into the huge grocery area. "Have you bought any snacks, or beverages to take in the car for the drive home?" Eric asked.

"No, not yet. What do you suggest?" Taylor grinned at his son.

"Well- - - -, I know you like to keep your car interior clean. However keeping the car clean is difficult. So let's grab some snacks, and drinks that are easy to handle." Eric went for sodas and some granola bars. And paper cups, and a roll of paper towel.

His father shook his head and laughed. "I had forgotten about the appetite of the average twenty-two-year-old. Anything else do you think we'll need?"

Eric stood and gazed around the store. "I think this will be sufficient." He turned and marched to the check-out area.

They walked back to the main area and as out through the main entrance into brilliant sunshine of the late spring day.

Chapter Thirty One

"Hey Dad, Let's take my belongings over to your motel and relax for a few minutes. I've been up since six this morning."

At that suggestion, Taylor yawned. "Perhaps that's a good idea. By the time we drive back there it's going to be nearly two P.M. Taylor drove straight to the motel and managed to park in front of their motel room.

Soon they emptied the car and took everything into the room and hung up the dress clothes and stacked the rest wherever they could.

Eric sat on one of the beds. "Wow, a queen bed. For two years I've been sleeping on bunk beds of one sort or another.' He took off his jacket and hung it up. Then he dropped on one of the beds. Next. he took off his shoes, and yanked out a pillow from under the bed spread. *Too much light in here.* He mumbled, got up and closed the drapes, pulled off the bed spread, and lay down on the bed. A few minutes later he got back up and took off his dress pants and hung them up with his jacket. Once back on bed he pulled up the spread and used it as a cover.

When Taylor came out of the bathroom, he found his son asleep. *Good idea, I could use a nap too.*

Later that afternoon, Eric's phone rang and brought him out of deep slumber. "Hello?" He answered still half asleep.

"The object of our affection just arrived home. And as to her normal behavior, she then took a shower and now she decided on a nap. So we're good for an hour or two. Can you get over here by six P.M. As I said, we're good for an hour or two."

"My Dad is asleep, too. I just checked the time. What do want to do? Should we meet at the eatery we chose, or should I just drive up to your place. What do you think will be best?"

"Just drive up here, and we'll let them decide what they would like to do. I'll call about the time you should be on your way here."

"Good idea. See ya, when we get there." Eric grabbed some clothes and headed for the bathroom.

A while later, Taylor knocked on the bathroom door. "Eric. Are you getting hungry for some dinner?"

"Yeah, I'll be out in a minute. We have one errand to take care of first. I'm getting casual. Just wear what you had on, okay?" The bathroom door opened, and Eric came out. "Be ready to leave in a few, okay Dad?"

"It's your town. I'll be ready soon."

As they walked outside, Eric swung around and faced his father. "It would be better if I drove, okay?"

"Of course, as I said before, it's your town."

Eric drove them into an older neighborhood. It had large older, but well cared for homes on larger lots. Finally, he drove into a cul-de sac to an older dark brick house with a wide front porch. "We need to stop here for a few minutes." He said and climbed out of the car. Next, he dashed up the three stairs onto the porch. For a moment he waited for his father to join him.

Eric pushed on the doorbell, and a few seconds later the front door opened. Taylor, somewhat slower than his son, just made it to the front door, and watched as a tall young man opened the door. He pushed open the screen door, and the young guy swung open the heavy front door, and held it open for his guests.

"Welcome Bro" he said and grabbed Eric in a hug and dragged him inside. Next. he swung the door wider, and gave Taylor entrance into the house. Then he gave Taylor a hug and said, "Welcome- - - -Father."

Taylor stared at this young man. "What did you say?"

"I said. Welcome dad. If Eric is my half-brother, then you *have to be* my father." Just at that moment Edith came bustling up from the basement carrying a sack of food. She turned and stared at the man talking to her son. "Jonah, who are you - - - -She glanced up at the man half turned away from her. "Jonah who is this- - - - -! She stared at this tall older man, and then recognition blazed in her eyes and mind. "Taylor! How did- - - - - -?"

Then she heard Eric say. "I brought him, Ms. Fletcher."

For a long moment her mind flashed back to lying on sweat soaked cot with this man wrapped around her. She could almost feel the shuddering orgasm that he had just given her. She took a deep breath, blinked and then she found a smile. "You just drove all the way over here from Utah to pick up Eric? I knew he was soon finished with his missionary service, but I thought they would just put him on a plane and- - - - -?"

"No I wanted to come back here, visit Camp Carson. We did some of that today. I wanted to meet my son."

"Well, here he is. Jonah, meet Taylor Rosenbaum."

Taylor came around and took Jonah's hand, shook it and then enveloped him in a big hug. "It's good to know I have such a handsome son, who already knows my other son."

"Well, as you see I have the makings of dinner on my hands." Let me get started on this food." Edith said.

'No Mom, the guys have other plans." Her daughter said. "So go back upstairs and get your shoes, because we are going out for some dinner."

"Is that the plan? We go to a restaurant for dinner?" Edith stepped back and studied this long- ago lover who gave her a son. She wanted to take him somewhere quiet and talk to him and ask him a million questions.

Instead, he came closer and took her hand. "Come Edie, Let's go with our children and 'go along' with their program. "We'll talk later."

"Yeah, let's go Mom. Here, I'll take the sack of food and put it in the fridge." Jonah said.

"Oh, let me go change clothes. I just have on jeans and an old shirt." Edith said.

"You're fine, Mom. We're just going down to Denny's." Jonah said and put his arm around Edith's shoulder.

Soon the five of them were sitting in a large curved booth. It seemed comfortable for all of them, and they could see each other. The waiter brought them each a menu and then left. "I'll be back to take your orders in a few minutes."

For a few minutes the conversation stopped, and each of them seemed to be studying a menu. Finally, the server returned and took their orders. It seemed everyone ordered 'burgers, and salads, the most popular orders. Edith broke the trend, because she ordered, set down a credit card, soup and a salad.

Too soon for some and not soon enough for others, dinner was over. Taylor grabbed up the bill and went to the check-out counter and paid the ticket. They all had come in one car. Edith's Toyota SUV. Once in the driveway, they all followed Jonah into the house and sat down in the living room.

Teresa, after five minutes or so of stunted conversation, jumped up and said, "I have a final in American History tomorrow. I'd better go study for a while. You all have a good evening. 'Nice to see you again, Eric. and to meet you, Mr. Rosenbaum." She turned and the people in the living room could hear her dash upstairs.

"Eric, come upstairs with me. I want to show you one of my physics books. Maybe you would understand the concepts." Jonah asked.as he jumped up and moved toward the stairs.

"Physics, huh? It's been many months since- - - - but okay." He glanced at his father's face and followed Jonah up the stairs.

"It seems that all the children have left us to pursue other interests." Taylor said. He stood and took a few steps to Edith sitting in a rocking chair. "Come, show me around your house." He took her cold hand in his and pulled her up. "How long have you lived here?"

"We, Herb and I found this house a few months after Teresa was born. We had been living in a small apartment, actually just a one bedroom. We tried to get some better housing in a military apartment building, but couldn't qualify at the time. So, we went to a real estate company, that would help people working on base, or for some army people who needed to find permanent housing. We finally found this house, but it needed lots of upgrading. Let's go into the kitchen. I made a dessert, and could use some coffee." she said. Then she led Taylor into a large country kitchen located across from the living room.

Chapter Thirty Two

Taylor glanced around the room. "This is a good room; a kitchen, combination family room." At first, He sat down on a dark plaid sofa across from a long bar separating the food preparation area from the family area.

She began to make a pot of coffee and set it on the stove. She lifted coffee mugs, sugar and creamer from cupboards above her head, and set them on the bar.

As the coffee perked, he pulled out a bar stool and sat down across from where she stood.

Soon she picked up each mug and filled them with the brew. "Do you want some cookies? There is a good bakery across from the office building where I work. Sometimes on my way home, I stop and buy a bag as I walk to the parking area. The kids like them."

"I don't even know where you work, or what you do?" he said.

She gave a little laugh. "I'm a nurse, and did work at the base hospital. But a few months ago, the military opened some medical offices downtown. This is mainly for mothers and children of the military. We have some medical people, especially for military families in those offices. The clinic is to offer medical services to women and children who live off base. Then they don't have to drive to the base, just for a sore throat or a check-up or for an advancing pregnancy. Many families live 'on the economy'. And the base buses all the kids to local schools. A few years ago, there was a big conflict about 'base' kids and the normal Colorado Springs children. So the military in their lock-step way of doing things, decided to pay the local school district to bus the kids living on base to the local schools. This was especially important for secondary schools. Military kids seem to have more discipline in their lives than the average teenager. This carries over into sports. Colorado Springs began to win regional championships with military children involved in sports."

"Did your children go to regular public schools then?" He asked.

"Yes, and I also have always taken them to the local Methodist Church, too."

Edith came and sat down by Taylor and sipped her coffee. She touched his sleeve. "I have to say that seeing you walk in my house was a big shock. Our sons communicate through their cell phones. To meet him, I actually sought Eric out. One late morning, actually it was Christmas morning, I was driving home from a long shift at the hospital. I glanced over and noticed him standing outside the Mormon Church building. Instantly I knew he belonged to you. Physically, he resembles you and has many of the same mannerisms you do."

"I'm proud of him. To dedicate two years of his young life to teach people about a new religion amazed me. I never had much to do with this unusual religion. I have to say their mother took them to church every Sunday. No alcohol or smoking in my house. And as a medical person I couldn't argue with that."

"Then why did your marriage break up?" She asked.

"I suppose I felt a little ignored. She- - - - Roz began work on an advanced degree in clinical psychology. She became so focused and spent so much time and energy on getting this advanced degree. And as a result, she packed some extra- - - - - began to gain weight. Our sex life suffered. I suppose about that time, I strayed, and had an affair with one of my secretaries. And Roz kicked me out." He sighed, and shook his head.

"Would you go back to her?" Edith touched his arm.

"No. actually now, I can enjoy working with her. She has trimmed down, and lost most of the weight she gained. She looks good. Sometimes I use her as a consult on some of my difficult cases. She also has a beautiful singing voice, and what I've heard from the girls is that she is back singing with a rock group she was involved with while in college. I heard them sing a few years ago. And all four of them are still active with music. We just had too many basic differences concerning our very different lifestyles."

"Well, I am really impressed with Eric. I'm really glad I 'found' him. He's a good example for my two kids."

"To change the subject, I did check up on you from time to time. Then I learned you married and had two children with your husband. But years later, I heard about the death of your husband. The information about you and your family didn't seem correct. That you had a son way before you married. Finally, I realized that Jonah could me my son. Then when Eric told me about Jonah, and knew he had to be mine."

"Was that part of the reason you broke up with your wife?" She asked a bite in her voice.

"Maybe a small part, we just quit trying to be a couple. I moved out several months ago. So I suggested I would drive over here pick up Eric and meet Jonah, and see you again. If I've done something you are unhappy with, let me know and I won't bother you. But I can see Jonah and your daughter might need some help along the way. As they grow up these kids have it rougher than we did. This nation is in trouble, and I'm praying some smart, dedicated leaders will move to straighten things out. I'm well aware of how the pandemic shook up the world. But that situation is getting better, with little help from the politicians."

He seems so intense. *Maybe he's grown up a little too.* She glanced at the clock above the counter. "Oh, my gosh, it's after nine P.M. and tomorrow is a school and workday. Are you going to drive home tomorrow?" She asked.

"Yes, sad to stay. I've appointments the first of next week, and Eric wants to register for the summer quarter at college."

"And my children have school tomorrow, too. Look, before we go back to the parenting duties, call me once you get back to reality. I'd like to hear from and about you, again. She stood up and kissed his cheek. But he pulled her into his arms and really kissed her. Finally, she stepped back slightly and off her stride. "That was- - - - -that was something to explore further."

Just then they both could hear quick footsteps on the stairs. "Hey dad, we'd better go. They have school tomorrow." Eric said.

"You're correct, and we have a long drive tomorrow. I'm very glad that I can share the driving chore with you." Taylor walked close to his older son and slapped his back. Then they turned to the large front door.

Edith came close to Taylor. "I'm glad you could come for a visit and meet Jonah, and we could see each other again."

They all shook hands. And as Taylor and Eric walked to his car, Taylor turned to Jonah. "I'm certainly happy to meet my other son."

"And it's good to have another Dad." Jonah said and waved.

"We'll talk later." Eric said and put his thumb- up in a gesture.

"Yes, we all will." Jonah said and waved.

Edith came near Taylor, and gazed up at his face, and whispered "Come back to me." Then she stepped back and waved. For a long moment, she stood on her porch and watched her former lover and his son drive down the street.

While returning to the motel, Eric and Taylor were both quiet for a long while.

"You're pretty quiet, Dad." Eric said.

"This trip has given me much to think about." Taylor said.

"You're correct on that one. Tomorrow we'll return to SLC and another family." Eric said. "Big changes in my life, and perhaps some changes in yours, too?"

Taylor nodded. "This trip has turned into several question marks in my life. Right now, I have thoughts bouncing around in my head, too. However, first on the list, the event first of all is getting you home. The event is getting you home so that you can make plans to return to college. Other events on your schedule will be a Church mission report. I possibly could help your mother with anything she needs. Keep me in the 'loop'. I'd like to hear your report."

"I'll call you as soon as I know which Sunday it will be on." They were silent for a few minutes. But soon Eric reached the motel parking lot, and parked as close to their room as he could.

Soon both father and son were lying in their beds. Taylor listened to his son settle in, and he could hear his breathing ease into sleep mode.

But for Taylor sleep did not come so easily. He had many sides to his normally well-organized life. Seeing Edith again shook up his routine, even the comfort of living in his new apartment. And being Taylor, the first thing he must do is divorce Roz. He knew she had moved on. She had returned to singing with the rock group that she was involved in while in college.

Chapter Thirty Three

At this same time, in a high school building in a town north of Salt Lake, Roz, and the three others who make up the eighties rock group, now calling themselves; *Vintage Rock* were on stage at a high school reunion. The audience was mainly adults who had graduated from this high school thirty plus years before.

What the alums were listening to was *their* music. Rock music they had listened to and loved, while attending that school and beyond. The band was playing just what they wanted to hear. And they were reacting with spirited enthusiasm.

Roselyn and Luke began a duet of a popular love song. After applause, they then eased into an older but really popular the love song; *Africa,* it was about a lonely man living and working in Africa, But now he was on his way to pick up his lady who has just arrived at the local air field, close to where he now lived. It tells of his love for her.

The other two of the group playing piano and drums kept the background music exotic. The audience's reaction was wild. Cheering and clapping went on for a long time. And screaming: "*more, again, more!*"

Close to midnight the concert came to an end. And the group who had planned the reunion thanked them and paid them well.

As they packed up their music, the four of them were sort of on a high. They began to walk back to Sam's big SUV. He swung back and faced the other three. "That went really well. As I played the piano, I could feel us 'gell' together. I think we can do this again, soon. Anybody have any objections?"

"No." Luke said. "Especially now, since we are at the end of the school year, I'm sure there are other reunions around the state, happening this summer. I could feel the energy, too. It was great fun to do this. Maybe the word about us will spread."

They all began to walk back to the parking lot and search for their cars. Since they had come early to set up, their vehicles were close to the rear doors of the school.

"Ah here we are. People are streaming out to leave. We'd better get in line and find the freeway." Sam said.

"Over here." Luke called out and grabbed Roselyn's hand. They reached his car, and he opened the passenger door for her, and set the sack of music in the rear seat. He jumped into the driver's seat and began to back out and soon found a line of cars leading to a main road. In a few minutes they were on a main road and found the freeway entrance, and he drove south.

"Roselyn glanced at the clock on the dashboard. "Wow, it's past twelve P.M. Time really flies when we're having fun."

"It was fun, wasn't it?" That's why we have to find another 'gig".

"I wouldn't mind doing another show. On another subject, have your children said anything about our group getting together to do this 'Gig'.

"Not a word. They, all three of them are wrapped up in doing their own thing. My girls' graduation program happened two nights ago. And Stratton has already registered for summer college classes. Summer is here, whether we like or not." Luke said.

"You mentioned that Stratton has registered for a summer term. Where is he going?"

"Just over to the junior college. Both my girls have jobs now, but perhaps they will decide to go with their brother for the Fall semester."

"Eric mentioned he wanted to get into a summer term, too." But I don't know what classes he needs to take this summer. When he arrives home, we'll have to sit down and take a look at what classes he needs to take."

"Give him a day or two to 'deflate'. Believe me, he'll need it." Luke said.

"Yes, big changes. I received a phone call from Eric this morning. Taylor drove over to Colorado Springs to pick him up., and they're driving back tomorrow. So they should arrive tomorrow evening."

Luke and Roselyn were quiet for a few minutes. Then he asked. "Have you thought about us? When we're singing together, I begin to feel, well-- as we did for each other back when we were in college."

She traced her fingers along his right arm. "I don't know if I can put it into words- - - - -but when you kissed me the other evening--- I felt, those old- - - - -. How can I say it, the longing, the passion I felt for you so many years ago."

"I know the Church says no sex, but that was twenty-five years ago. Now we've lived in two marriages and had six children. I loved Caroline. We had a good marriage. But she was not, really very outgoing, rather shy, and had some personal issues. When I began dating her, I wanted to go to medical school, but that would have put off the marriage for a few years. Her father took me out for dinner one night, and told me that Caroline loved me. She had not dated much after she came home from her mission. He would help me with the finances of college, if I changed my major and went into Law."

"My goodness, he offered you a new career, and would pay for it? Now I remember. I watched go you off to UCLA, and you never said as to why you were changing schools. Rather, you called me and told me to date other guys, and not wait for you. Boy was I hurt, and angry. Then your friend, Bob called me and asked for a date. Was that part of the plan?!"

"Now I think about that whole crazy evening. I just remember that you and I had been in the park one evening. It ended with a monumental fight we had that night. Bob took me home, and a few weeks later he introduced me to Taylor Rosenbaum. I had begun my career working with patients in the hospital and the kids in the school district."

"Yes, that's right. You had a girl come in that was self-destructive.

And Taylor called and said that he came to visit her. But by then not only was he an MD, he was working on a degree in psychiatry. I was still working on the law degree and dating Caroline. Things between Caroline and I began to get serious."

"Back then Taylor wasn't so far into that area of expertise, that he would discount my ideas. He was good to work with. When I had a patient, we would discuss it.

Then after a few weeks he asked for a date. And we hit it off, so to speak. By then, you were out of the picture, and engaged. Why shouldn't I date a Jewish guy?" Then she watched him turn the car into a park that was a little more than half way home. "What are we going to do here?" She asked, her arms folded across her chest.

"This car is a hybrid. I just need to get social electrical charge Just a short one. It won't take long" Luke drove right to a group of chargers and already two cars were hooked into charging stations. He climbed out and set the car to charge. Then he slid back into the car.

"How often do you have to do the charging thing?" She asked.

"When the car needs it. This won't take long. It's not fully drained. It's late and after about a half hour we'll be okay."

Because each charging station had good lighting, Roselyn glanced at her watch. "Are these charging stations open all night?" She asked.

"I'm not sure, but we are being filmed." He laughed. "So it's pretty safe here."

"Okay. I guess I won't get into trouble if I'm out past midnight. I actually haven't noticed if my girls watch when I get home; Most likely because I'm never out this late."

Luke began to laugh, but then she laughed, too. "This whole situation seemed so crazy. "Are we going to have twenty-year-olds watching their parents?" Will they set us a curfew?" Then they both began to laugh, but a few seconds later he reached over to kiss her. Soon they were necking like a couple of seventeen-year-olds.

With pulses racing, they finally they broke apart.

"We need somewhere to meet! This groping in the car is ridiculous."

He complained.

"I agree. But as you said last time, we have two fifty-some-thing year olds' reputations to protect. Add to the fact that you are a new widower. And I'm sure that Taylor will want a divorce quite soon. What will your kids say if we start to date?"

"Hmmm, you 're right on that one. Hey, I've got an idea. Now that Eric will be home soon, let's let the kids know that we are singing together again and having a great time. Let them come up with a plan for us. When you announce that Taylor wants a divorce, listen to their comments. Let them make some suggestions about much you and I will be spending time together. And how our relationship could develop." he said.

"But right now- - - - -." He pulled her out of the car and leaned her against the side and started a loving assault. Stroking and exploring her body.

"Whoa! Wait a minute. If you're going to undress me, we'd better get back into the car."

"Ah, but I find your breasts are fuller than before. I'm just checking to make a comparison." His hands continued their exploration.

"Okay. Let's get into the back seat." She suggested and opened a back door. "The back isn't much larger than the front. Oh, and one of the cars just left. How much time- -- - - -?"

As his mouth came down on hers, his hands pulled up her tunic, and began stroking her back, sides, and then breasts.

She slid away and crossed her arms to impede his stoking. "Let's stop this for a minute. I understand it's been quite a while since you've had sex. So long has it been?"

"Okay, I get what you are doing," He took a deep breath and let it out slowly. "Ms. Therapist. It's been, well Caroline's illness began four or five months before she died. And she passed on at least three months ago. So it's been a long, long time. What about you? When did Taylor leave?"

"About the second week of December is when he moved out. So it's been quite a while of nothing, for me, too." She reached up and kissed his chin. "I'd love to have an affair with you- - -however, we either need to be tremendously sneaky, or figure out something else. I don't just want a night in the backseat of your car, but a whole weekend. Most of it in a hotel room, with diet coke on ice."

Then he began to laugh and laugh, and then cough. "Okay." He said with a strangled laugh. "I get the message, but don't you think we could find a good non-alcoholic bottle of wine to refresh us? Even right now I want you, in 'want you' in the worse way."

"I know!" she said. "Let's let the kids decide if we should begin to date. Hey, what was that click?" she asked.

"Oh, a signal that my car is fully charged. I need to go out and stop it and hang the charger up." He slid out and walked around to the charging station. A few minutes later he opened the rear door of the car and helped her out. Then he opened the front passenger door for her to climb in.

For a moment she worked on 'putting herself back together. Bra hooked, tunic zipped and hair combed. He glanced at the clock in the car. "It's pretty late. I guess we'd better go home."

Right about that time, Ellie Ann received a phone call. She had to reach for the phone across the bed sitting on her nightstand. It was Stratton's voice she heard.

"Hi Ellie, I understand that our parents are back singing together again; And also that they're back singing with their college rock group friends."

"Yeah, they had a 'gig' in Layton, for a high school reunion. They're going to be late."

"I understand. I'm glad my Dad can have some fun for a change. Mom's death has been tough for all of us. Have you heard the two of them sing together?"

"Yes, I heard them rehearse the other evening. They are really good, and they seem to be having a good time together? I'm really glad, because Mom has been in a kind of funk since my father left. Do you think they would enjoy doing things together besides singing?" Shanna asked.

"All my father has done since my Mom died, is work. It was really tough on him to watch her go downhill. Maybe the two, your Mom, and my Dad could go to dinner or do something fun."

"You know, now that the weather is warm, we should have a barbecue. I mean all of us; My sister and I, your sisters, and Eric when he gets home. Eric will soon be home. In fact, my father drove over to Colorado to pick him up. They should be here tomorrow night. I'll have Eric call you either tomorrow, or the next day. I'll let you know when they make it back. Talk to you later. Bye."

Ellie sat down and began a grocery list for a backyard barbecue.

Chapter Thirty Four

The next day was a Saturday, and the phone rang at eight A.M. When a very tired Roz answered, she received a message from the hospital. "Apparently, Ms. Jenkins, the woman who had 'blanked out' her adult life beyond the age of twenty-two, is now remembering some of her later adult years. She is to be released from the hospital tomorrow." Nurse Graham said. "Is it possible you could come up to the nursing facility where Ms. Jenkins is now located? Her physicians want to have a conference with you, Ms. Rosenbaum. Especially since Dr. Rosenbaum is out of town."

"Okay. What time would be good for a meeting?" Roselyn said and yawned.

"Sorry to have to bother you. You sound tired." Nurse Graham said.

"That is true, but I'll manage. What time should I be there?" Roselyn asked.

"They suggested eleven A.M. Can you make it up here by then?"

"Yes, I'll hurry." Roselyn threw back the bed covers and went to a drawer for some underwear. "Shower, here I come." She mumbled.

Once Roselyn reached the new 'short stay' annex it was easy to find Ms. Jenkin's room. Waiting there was her bone specialist, Dr. Graffe, and the patient's husband, Harlen Jenkins.

Roselyn walked in. "Good morning, everyone." She said and nodded.

"Are we all here now?" Mr. Jenkins grumped. 'Are you people going to let me take my wife home today?"

"First I want to talk to Ms. Rosenbaum." Ms. Jenkins said and really pulled herself up in her bed. "I know about how to treat my leg." She waved a hand at Dr. Graffe, the 'bone man'. "You sent some information, a booklet, on how to take care of my leg." She pointed at him. "And you Ms. Rosenbaum, you told me the truth, you and the Rosenbaum guy. Is he really your husband?"

"More or less." Roz nodded and smiled. "He went to pick up our son in Colorado, and he should return late this evening. Now that everyone is here. Let's talk about you, and what you have remembered about your married life."

"Okay, if that's what I must do to leave here and go home." Ms. Jenkins said. "Two nights ago, I had a really interesting dream of sitting in the car there with my husband, and we were driving a long distance to California. And we reached a town called St. George. And I asked him if we were in California yet? And he said no, we were stopping to buy gas and get some lunch. Then we stopped and I got out, and later in the dream we were sitting in a restaurant eating, and I asked why we would have to drive another long way. Next in the dream I said I wanted to get a motel and stay here, where we were. He said no, we had to keep driving. Then we sort of argued, but next I remembered the motel in St. George. The place had a swimming pool and you could look up and see the red cliffs in that part of Southern Utah. In my dream I remembered I liked that trip." She closed her eyes.

"I must have gone back to sleep, but when I woke up and remembered the whole trip, and even who was home with our kids. So then I started remembering other trips, and some of them when we took the children and some when we didn't."

"Was there some incident or TV programs that caused you to remember that trip?" Dr. Graffe asked.

"Well, I did watch a quiz show on TV yesterday. There was a woman who won a trip to Palm Springs, California. I think we did go there one time, but the next time we took a trip to the desert town. We had the kids with us. St. George was far enough in the car for them."

"I think you are well into recovering your memory, and I'll release you to go home. However, I'd like to see you in my office in a week or so." Dr. Graffe turned to Roselyn. "Is that all right with you, Ms.

Rosenbaum?"

"Yes, you can release her, but my- - - - -, Dr. Rosenbaum will want to speak with her, too."

"Okay, let's get you out of here and, I guess you'll need a wheelchair to leave. I'll go get the car and drive it close to this new entrance?" Harlen said.

"Yes, a nurse will wheel you down to the south entrance." Dr. Graffe said." Don't forget to call my office for an appointment. Come, I'll walk down the hallway."

Roselyn, since she was in the hospital complex, decided she would check her schedule for Monday. She had a new afternoon appointment scheduled to see a teenage mother, baby, and her parents. The young girl wanted to take the baby home with her. Her parents were insisting that she put the child up for adoption. As Roselyn studied the information sheet, she asked for the other notes concerning this case.

Two interesting facts were important. First the infant was large and at the last minute a C-section was needed to save the child. Second; the infant boy showed to be mixed race. Most likely that is why the girl's parents wanted the baby to be adopted. Roz, asked to speak with the charge nurse. Checking Ms. Sheila Hernandez pager, she was quickly located and she met Roz at the front desk.

When the woman arrived Roselyn introduced herself, Sheila turned to Roselyn. "Let's go into the nurses' lounge and have a chat."

"Sounds like a good idea." Roz said and followed the woman down the hallway. As they entered the large room, the nurse turned to Roselyn, "I'm Sheila Hernandez. Do you want some coffee, or a soda?"

"Coffee will be fine. Oh and I'm Roselyn Rosenbaum." She went to the coffee machine and grabbed a paper mug and filled it, then they sat down at a round table.

"Do you have any thoughts on why this girl wants to keep the baby? And how old is she?"

"All the information so far, is I have is just what I was told. We were to make arrangements for the agency to come and pick up the infant.

I met with the girl's parents, right after she delivered. Her father was insistent that the infant needed to be adopted. The girl's mother was not as convinced as her husband. They are upper middle class, white. But from the conversation, not only they do not want the girl to raise a mixed-race child, they have plans for her to go to college, and get an education. To be the best she can be. They don't even want the baby to go home with her or be in 'their' house."

'Wow! In a way, I can see why they feel the way they do. But I'd like to know why she decided to have an affair. Or was it the results of a 'one night stand?"

"That is why I need you to speak to her. Perhaps she'll talk to you. Really talk about her situation and the best way for her to move on with her life." Sheila said.

"When would be a good time to chat with her?" Roselyn asked.

'The last time I checked on her, she was sleeping. The delivery was not the easiest. That is why we are keeping her for another day. I'd bet you should try to talk with her later this afternoon. Also, the hospital won't release the infant for twenty-four hours."

"Thanks for your info. I have two daughters and thank goodness neither one of them seems to be that interested in a particular young man. Of course, who knows?"

Because of Roselyn's late night, she was tired, and went to an 'in house' bunk room. She curled up on a lower bunk, in a room provided for medical people. Once she reached the room, she found both upper and lower bunks empty. She chose a lower one and cat napped. She woke a few minutes after four P.M. She freshened up, and went to find the new mother. Her name was Amelia Stone.

When she pushed the door open, she found the young girl sitting up drinking from paper cup. "Good afternoon." Roselyn said. "I'm Roselyn Rosenbaum. Could we have a little visit?"

"What are you, some social worker?" Amelia grumped.

"I suppose you could classify my work in that category." Roselyn said.

For a moment the girl did not speak, just glanced at Roselyn. "I'm sorry for being bitchy, but I feel awful."

"I'm sorry you feel like a woman who has just been through a rough delivery."

Amelia smiled, and then shook her head. "You must have kids. How many?"

"Three, but they are all young and, on the way, to be grown up. At least they would tell you that." Roselyn said. "Oh by the way, I'm considered sort of a counselor around here. Can you tell me why your parents want your infant to be adopted and not go home with you?"

"Cause my kid is part black, and they can't stand to have him in the house." The girl snarled.

"Do you think they would react this way if you child was white?"

"Maybe, I don't know." She sighed and sat back against the pillows.

"May I use another term to understand this situation? Now think back a few years. What did your family consider important?" When could you be sure that your living conditions back then could remain that way?"

Amelia frowned. "You mean like always having food in the house for snacks and dinner? And a clean place to sleep. Somethings like that?"

"Yes. What did your parents provide for you and your, - - - - 'You have brothers and sisters?" Roz asked.

"Well yes. We always had food and something to eat for dinner, and breakfast, too. Oh and we always had afternoon snacks."

"Do you think this was important for them to provide food, and a place for you and you siblings to sleep, clothing to keep you warm, and to send you to school when you were old enough to attend?"

"Okay, I see what you are getting at. If I brought my child home to raise, I'd be in charge of him. Okay, I'm not even seventeen yet. So, they would be sort of in charge of him, too. But, he's my kid!" She yelled.

"I know it's really difficult to think about the future, right now. However, let's say your parents let you bring your infant home. Soon or later, you'll want to return to school. Who will tend your child while you are in school?"

"I can home school. I can graduate that way. That way I can take care of him."

"True. But do you think you'll enjoy being home all the time, and not seeing your friends. What about the father of your child? How old is he, and does he know you even had his child?"

"I haven't seen him for a while. He's maybe two years older than I am. He was thinking of going to Idaho. He loves the outdoors, and he wants to work in a national park."

"That takes college plus extra training. We're looking at least three or four years. Has he made plans to do that? And there is another factor. Have you thought about the fact that he may not want you around. What if he doesn't want to worry about you or even want you and a toddler with him? He'd have to provide a good place for you and your child to live."

The young girl dropped her head, and tears ran down her face. She sniffed and sneezed.

"You are emotionally very tired right now. Why don't you rest for a while. I can come back later or tomorrow. The hospital won't release you until you are healing properly. I can come back tomorrow morning. "Here: Roz reached into her pocket and handed her a card. "On this is my name and both home and cell numbers. Call me if you want to talk more."

Roselyn stood and patted the young girl on her shoulder. "Tomorrow is another day. I know it's difficult to think about your life in a year or even a month. If you decide to trace down this young man who fathered your child, let me know. I may be able to do that." Roz quietly left the room.

Chapter Thirty Five

Roselyn sat in her office going over the report she was writing about her visit with Amelia Stone. She planned on visiting her again the next day. Suddenly, she heard the door from the garage bang into the front entrance of her house. It slammed into the wall in the front hallway. She jumped up and watched Eric come into the front hall and drop a large suitcase on the floor. Then he turned back out through the garage door. She hurried out of her office, down the stairs to the front hall.

This time it was Taylor who came in and carried a stack of hanging clothes and dropped them over a dining room chair. The door opened again. This time it was Eric carrying a large sack and started up to the kitchen.

"Eric! Can I help you?" She yelled.

He stopped, set down the sack, and grabbed her up in a large hug. "Mom! He hugged her tightly "So good to see you. Glad you're home. Dad's helping me with all my gear. Am I still sleeping downstairs?"

"Yes. I cleaned up your room a few days ago. You can carry all this stuff down any time you want." She waved at the bags and sacks on the floor.

"I'll start hauling it down now. "He picked up his large suitcase and banged down the stairs.

Then Taylor came in with another load, and she pointed him downstairs.

More quickly than she realized all of Eric's belongings had been cleared from the floor and carried downstairs, hopefully all into his room. Taylor who had been helping Eric, came in and gave her a quick hug and for a moment stood staring out the kitchen window.

"Where are the girls?" He asked. "Oh, do you have some coffee. It was a long drive." He dropped into a kitchen chair.

"Hang on I'll get you a mug." She poured the remains of the pot warmed it and set some cream and a spoon in front of him. "As I recall, that is a very long drive."

"At least we missed the late afternoon traffic snarl." Taylor took a long swallow. "Oh, thank you. You still make great coffee."

Roz went to the refrigerator. "How about a cinnamon muffin?" She glanced over her shoulder. "I found these," She waved at the box. "In a new bakery located down in the shopping area."

"Oh. I could use something tasty." He took another sip of his coffee. He watched her grab a small plate and set a muffin on it. Next, she set it in the microwave.

"Here, this is from a new bakery. One of two new stores now located down in the shopping area near the freeway exit. This comes from 'Sal and Sim's Bakery." She sat down across from him. "How was your trip, and has Colorado Springs changed much since you and I were over there?"

"It's like any other large city in the western part of the U. S. It's grown, and boy has Fort Carson changed, and enlarged. Eric had been on base and could guide me around. The growth of Fort Carson makes it half again as large as it was when we were there. I suppose now there is always a war going on somewhere in the world. And as a nation, we need to be ready for whatever happens." He shook his head and yawned.

"Where are you living now?" Do you have several miles to drive? *Right then she could once again worry about him, without just being angry. I guess this is because of my feelings for Luke.*

Suddenly the front door opened with a bang, and Shanna charged up the stairs. "Where's Eric? Stratton said he's home." She stopped and took a breath. "Oh, hi Dad. Did you guys drive all the way from Colorado Springs in one day?"

"Yes girl. Come give your ole' Dad a hug." He stood and grabbed her in in his arms. "So is school out for the summer?" What are your plans?"

"I sort of have a job at a daycare. I took an early childhood class at school and a woman who owns a day care came to class and kind of recruited a few of us. So- - - - -I sort of signed up, and I start Monday. I'll try it and see how it goes. Who knows I may like working with little kids?" She stopped, took a breath. "I bet Eric is downstairs." She mumbled and dashed down the stairs.

"On that note, I'd better go before I fall asleep. The coffee helped. Thanks Roz. Taylor stood and went to the stairs. "See you soon."

Roselyn went to the top of the stairs and watched him go out through the garage. Several seconds later, she heard the sound of his car going up the street. *I guess that I'll be last to greet my son after his two years away from home.* She turned and began to add the dishes to the dishwasher. *Darn it I forgot to tell Taylor about the Stone girl. But very soon I need to go to bed.*

Before she could change into her bed clothes there was a knock at the door. She opened to see Eric standing there.

He grabbed her up into a bone crushing hug. "Mom, how, you doing? I didn't forget you. The girls had to tell me about their plans for a double family barbecue."

"Well. how are you doing? Are you ready to assume a normal life?" His mother asked.

"Yeah. My sisters will drag me back into society. And Stratton will help. I thought about a lot of things while driving back from Colorado. I know I want to get back into school this summer. I'm not sure if I'll stay with the major I began college with; Maybe something else. Right now, I came upstairs for some ice water and a hug from you. I know you must go to the hospital early. So. goodnight, I'll bore you with my stories tomorrow."

She watched him charge down the hallway to the stairs, and he was correct, she did need to go back to the hospital early.

The ten miles to Taylor's apartment in the avenues seemed to take longer than he thought it should. However, finally he reached his underground garage, parked and took his large suitcase up to his apartment. He dropped the suitcase in the hallway next to his bedroom door. His next chore would be a shower, some clean pajamas, and two fingers of whiskey in a small glass to relax him.

As he tossed and turned in his bed searching for a comfortable position, he thought about Edie. He still couldn't believe it, but he still loved her and wanted to be with her. Yet he knew there were many steps in which to achieve that goal. In his mind he thought about moving his practice to Colorado. He needed to first divorce Roz. Then find out about the laws of practicing psychiatry in Colorado. Another route could be the United States Army. For a long time. he remembered the emotional stress of being in a war zone. However, fatigue took over, and the next thing he became aware of was light coming in through the shutters in his bedroom. And the dull sounds of morning traffic.

At about that same time, Roselyn stirred out of a dream and realized that light was coming in from the large window in her bedroom. She glanced at the clock on her nightstand, and numbers read eight-eleven A.M. She slid out of bed and headed for the bathroom.

Forty-five minutes later Roselyn stood in the kitchen and finished off the last half of a bagel with a slice of turkey and cheese melted on it, along with coffee and half an orange. She was still amazed that she was eating breakfast, after many years of skipping it. But she felt better eating smaller more frequent meals, and it paid off. She had lost twenty-two pounds since Christmas. And she needed to buy some new clothes. But soon she was backing out her car from the garage for the drive to the hospital.

Once in her office she picked up the report she had written after interviewing Amelia Stone. She went out to the elevator and went up to the maternity floor. She checked with the floor nurse to see if anyone was visiting Amelia.

Chapter Thirty Six

"No, her physician came in a half hour ago to check her progress concerning the C-section. I was about to take her in some breakfast. You can come in as I carry in the tray."

They found Amelia curled up lying on her side. "Amelia, would you like some breakfast?" The nurse asked.

"What is it? I mean what did you bring me?" She asked and pushed up to a sitting position.

"Here, let me help you." Roselyn raised the top of the bed and pushed some pillows behind the girl. Then stood back and allowed her to try and sit up.

"Hi, Ms. Rosenbaum. Yeah, I could eat some food." Amelia allowed Roselyn to straighten her nightgown. And get the pillows behind her so she could sit up comfortably.

Roselyn grabbed the tray table and set it in front of the girl. Then the nurse set the food tray on the table. Roselyn then took off the cover from the tray and asked. "Do you want some milk, first?"

"Sure." Amelia took the carton and a straw and soon was sipping the milk through the straw. "We have this kind of milk at school." She glanced at the tray. "What else is there?"

Roselyn took the cover from the tray. "It looks like pancakes, bacon and scrambled eggs. Oh, and we can get you another milk if you need it." She handed the girl a fork. "Do you want some catsup on your eggs?"

"Sure, eggs are so boring without it."

Roselyn opened the small packet of catsup and sprinkled the

contents on the eggs. "Eat these while their still warm." She turned around and realized that the nurse had left the room. She found a chair as sat down close to the young girl's bed. For a few minutes she sat quietly and watched the girl eat.

"Hey, sometimes hospital food isn't so bad." She forked up a large portion of pancake and chomped it down. "You should try these pancakes, - - - -not bad."

"You have a good appetite. Eating well will help your body to heal more quickly."

"My stitches still hurt, but not as bad as yesterday. My mom came up to see me last night. Amelia stopped talking to chew and swallow. "We just talked about having babies and how rough it can be sometimes. Do you know she was teaching school when my older brother, Jim was born? She said she went home from school on a Friday, and she had him on Sunday. That year, she only missed the last three weeks of school."

"Wow! I quit my job about a month before my son Eric was born. He was born in March. And it snowed all the way to the hospital." Roselyn said, with a laugh.

"I'll bet you weren't laughing then." Amelia said. "How old were you when he was born?"

"I was nearly thirty."

"Thirty!? How old were you when you got married? And how come you were so old?"

Roselyn gave a small shake of her head, frowned, but laughed. "I met my husband when I was twenty-five, and married him a year later. He was in medical school, and we needed my pay check for rent and food. So we put off having any children until he could support us. But back then nearly all young men had to register for the 'draft' or join the military. Because he was in medical school, I was the major source of our income."

Amelia sat back and shook her head. "Do you have other children?"

"Oh yes. I have a girl two years younger than Eric and another girl who will be eighteen in August. She just graduated from high school."

"Is she planning on going to college?"

Roselyn nodded.

Shaking, "That's what my Mom wants me to do. And I guess having a baby to take care of would make things a mess." She put her head down, but then picked up her long hair and flipped it back on her shoulders. Then she shook her head and tears creased down her cheeks. "Do you know who would adopt my baby?"

"No, but that is why people adopt. Whoever adopts your child will be financially comfortable. Think of some woman who for one reason or another hasn't had a child. Maybe she's older than thirty. Now there is a healthy newborn available for adoption. She is going to be so happy, that she could have a baby of her own to care for."

"Would she be a black woman?" Amelia said. "My mom kind of said something like that."

"Possibly, more than likely, or maybe her husband is mixed race. Most everyone in this world have had certain bad situations or sadness in this life. It's just the way it is. But as you grow stronger, you can find a place in your life that calmness, and doing things successfully makes you a better person."

"I guess I'll go home without my son, but Mom said I should do things that the average sixteen-year-old should be doing. Building your life with the building blocks that I should be adding to my life at sixteen, you can't use the ones available when your reach age twenty-five."

"Your Mom is a wise person."

"So are you. Ms. Rosenbaum, so are you."

Chapter Thirty Seven

Taylor returned to his office that morning and checked his calendar. He had an appointment at ten A.M. with a woman who had a son suffering with autism. This child had not had any schooling and at age thirteen did not speak, but just cried and threw tantrums when he wanted something.

He had been referred to a specialist and wanted Taylor to substantiate the fact that the boy needed to be put in the estate hospital for the mentally ill. In the other doctor's report, he had stated the boy's behavior had not improved in a private school for autistic children. He had been enrolled for less than a month and had become a disturbing influence on other children in his class.

After reading the reports about the boy, Taylor didn't believe that much could be done for the young teenager. However, Taylor believed that God put everyone on this earth for a purpose. And perhaps this boy's reason for being here was not only to help him, but those people he came in contact with. The appointment had been changed to one P.M. at the hospital in a secure environment.

When he met the woman, The mother of the patient, he was surprised that she was British. But she had married to an American, and their son was born six months later. Now, when the mother and the boy came into the hospital Taylor had arranged to take them to the workout room.

He met them at the front entrance to the annex, and drove a luggage cart to take them through the corridors to the gymnasium on the first level.

The boy wore a restraining belt. So that an individual could control him with a belt would keep him from running away. This would force him to walk along at a normal speed and force him to remain with the adult restraining him.

"I'm Dr. Rosenbaum. Please sit down on the cart, and I'll give you a ride." Watching the boy, Taylor realized that the boy understood and seemed to be curious enough to 'go along for a ride'. So. when Taylor showed him where to sit and belted him in, he cooperated.

Taylor drove slowly enough to watch the boy's reaction to being in the hospital. When they reached the workout room, a young orderly was there working out on a treadmill. He stopped and jogged over to Dr. Rosenbaum and his patient.

"Good morning doctor, and who is your patient this morning?"

"This is Whitney Granger, along with his mother, Ms. Granger. I thought this morning we could introduce Whitney to some of our exercise equipment. Whitney this is Fred. He will direct us to the equipment. Hop on Fred, and point us to where you want to begin."

"Let's start with the strength training weight bands." Taylor drove over to the strength bands. "Ok, Whit. Can I call you Whit?" Fred said and offered his hand to the boy. "Let's start with the ten-pound bands." He put the boy's hands on the handles that pulled on the bands. "Now, I want you to pull first with your right hand and next with the left. Fred put his hand on Whitney's and pulled gently. "Now you pull as hard as you can."

At first the boy dropped the bands.

"Oh come on, look at that muscle." He squeezed the boy's left bicep. "You try it again. This time, the boy actually gave it a pull. "Good, but you must really give them a pull. There, that's better."

Across the room, Ms. Granger turned to Dr. Rosenbaum. "It's good that Whit is enjoying this exercise, but does that have to do with him learning to talk?"

"If he wants to come back and exercise again, he will have to ask to do it. Watch, now Fred is going to take him to the treadmill." Dr. Rosenbaum said. For ten minutes or so Fred took Whitney around to different exercise areas. The last one was a jumping area completely covered with a net, and the net could be closed.

"Now Whit, to protect you, this jump cage it is covered with a strong net. So that if you fall down, you won't fall out. Do want to try it?" Fred asked. "But you have to ask. You must tell me. You must say 'TRY'."

Whitney stared you at the young trainer.

"I thought you like to try the jump cage, but I guess not. The trainer began to push away from the 'cage."

Whitney put his hand on Fred's arm. Fred turned back to the boy. "What do you want?"

"Ugh!" he grunted. Then he slowly said. "Tr-y!"

"Okay!" Fred said and wheeled back to the jump cage. He helped the boy into the cage. "Now before you jump, spread your legs a little. Now, rock back and forth until it feels comfortable."

Fred watched. "Now rock back and forth from foot to foot." Whitney did as he was told.

"Good. Okay. Just do what you feel comfortable with." Fred stood outside of the 'cage and issued commands until the boy tried different steps and started to actually do little jumps. After about five minutes or so, Fred said. "It looks like you're getting tired. Now, I'm going to say. Stop, and you must stop."

Dr. Rosenbaum and Ms. Granger watched Fred wheel Whitney back to where they were sitting. She came close and said, "Did you enjoy jumping?"

The boy nodded, as his mother helped him down from the cart.

"Okay. Did you like exercising with Fred?" Dr. Rosenbaum asked.

"The boy nodded, and a tiny smile creased his face. He tugged on his mother's arm and nodded. "Is that what you want to do, Whit. Come back here? Can you tell me in words?

Various expressions flitted across the boy's face. First a frown, then his eyes widened. And he said, "Try!"

"Good, how about you come again next Saturday? We will check

Fred's Schedule so that he can be here to help you." Dr. Rosenbaum had the boy and his mother climb on the cart and he drove to the hospital entrance. "See you next week."

"Whoa, that was quite the experience. Before today the boy hasn't said anything?" That's crazy. I have a niece who has autism. But she talks to her parents, and sometimes to me." Fred said.

"That's what they told me, that Whitney does not talk. So now we have an appointment for next Friday. It's going to be interesting if he really wants to do exercises." Dr. Rosenbaum said. He waved at Fred and walked quickly to the elevators.

At Roselyn's house Shanna and Ellie Ann were working on a potato salad. They had also made a large Strawberry and pineapple gelatin salad.

"What else are we going to eat at your barbecue?" Roz asked.

"We're doing hamburgers, and Crista is going to grill some hot dogs if anybody wants them. And we're just serving ice cream cones for dessert. "Oh. and Stratton and Eric are in charge of the drinks."

"What time is all this going to take place?" The mother asked. "Are where are we meeting for this picnic, and did you finally decide what time?"

"At the Landre's, about six P.M. They have a better back yard than we do."

"True." said Roselyn. "Okay. I need to check my exchange and see if I need to go up to the hospital. Roselyn went upstairs to where her cell phone was in her purse. As she scrolled through the messages her phone rang.

"Hello? She was somewhat familiar with the number, but did not expect the voice she heard.

"Good morning Ms. Roz. Are you ready for the picnic this evening?" Luke said.

"Roz laughed. "Luke this isn't your home phone, is it?"

"No. I sneaked out and drove over to my office. I did have some work to catch up on. You want to join me?"

"Are you going to tell me that you have a sofa in your office?"

"Well, yes. You could come and try it out with me." He took a breath, but then laughed.

"Hmmm, I don't think that is a good idea at the present time. We need to be ready to be somewhat friendly with each other this evening. Let the children, yours and mine, do a little match making."

"You really think we need to go through all that?" He gave a sigh.

"That's what this barbecue is all about. They are doing a little matchmaking. They are worried and want us to be interested in having another romance. Think of us as twenty-year-olds would do. They want us to be happy in our later years. You're a widower, and I will soon be divorced. They don't want to have to 'take care of us' The six of them want us to take care of each other. And in the long run, take care of them too."

"The older three are thinking as twenty- plus year olds would do. They want stability from us. So they can begin to take care of themselves. And if you and I are in a stable relationship, they can quit worrying about us and continue to grow up the way they should. When you think of this whole family situation, it makes sense."

"Exactly." She laughed. Be extra friendly to me. From their point of view, if we bond it's to their advantage. While we're still the adults in the family. How do you want to proceed? I think we can behave as good friends that have an investment in each other, because we sing together Then perhaps in a few days you can call me and ask for a date. What we do on this date is 'up for grabs'." She giggled.

"I see. Rent a motel room and watch a movie while we're there. We'll have to tell them what we did. A least in general terms. This makes me feel as if I'm nineteen. Which I was, thirty-something years ago. Boy, to have that energy we had back then. Okay, I'll be attentive, to a degree. More than likely, I'll be grilling the hamburgers." He chuckled.

"That chore will keep us both of us out of trouble. This whole activity is going to be a 'hoot"

Chapter Thirty Eight

They all met at six-thirty at the Landre residence. The girls had two large picnic tables covered with bright red and white print plastic cloths. Luckily, the early June evening was not too hot and there was a slight breeze.

As Luke began grilling the hamburgers, Stratton began filling a large oval serving dish with the meat as it came off the grill. Luke also lightly grilled some of the wieners for 'hot dogs'. The girls began setting out salad makings and dressings for the hamburgers and hot dogs. Soon they were in line 'filling their plates with the evening's 'bounty'.

Roselyn made it a point to 'save room' at the end of one of the tables for Luke when he finished grilling the meats.

When the two families were combined there were eight individuals. Right now everyone seemed to be noisily enjoying the food and the company. School had only been out for a few days, and so it was a time for relaxing and talking about what each individual had planned for the summer.

Because it was early June it didn't become dark until after nine P.M. Roselyn was the first to pick bowls and plates and walk back into the Landre house. "Come on people we're losing the light. Let's get this cleaned up. Tomorrow is a Sunday, and we all need to switch gears and get ready for church tomorrow."

"But Mom." Shana whined "We just got out of school!"

"I know, but we are expected to be at our Ward at ten-thirty tomorrow morning. Especially since Eric just returned from his mission." She turned to Luke. "What time does your ward meet on Sunday?"

"We have the late time this year. Twelve noon until two P.M. Roz is right gang, we'd better start cleaning up. I'll put the left- over meats in freezer bags, and you can come over tomorrow, Roz and take some home." He turned and grinned at his 'new', lady. Yet he had been in love with her for over thirty years.

Taylor Rosenbaum trudged into his apartment. It was a Saturday evening, he'd had a long day, and he was tired, but also frustrated. Even when he was living with Marlene, when he returned to their apartment, she would have some sort of dinner for him; or some suggestions about where they could go out for dinner. This time of year, there would be a concert or a film she knew about. A place where he could relax, and perhaps a restaurant or bar near where they could just go for a drink.

What did he have to look forward to? A quick supper he had to fix for himself, and a trip downstairs to do his laundry. He knew there were places where he could order -in something for dinner. Right now, he wished he were in Colorado Springs having some dinner with Edith.

He searched his refrigerator and found enough greens for a salad. He also found a partial bottle of wine. He would order a pizza and worry about his laundry tomorrow morning. His big frustration was how he could return to Colorado Springs, and also have a viable income while living there. Somehow, he needed to return there, and search and find a position to still earn his six-figure income.

In the back of his mind, he knew it meant starting a practice in either psychiatry or surgery. But right now, he went through a list of restaurants to find a pizza place that would deliver.

After a long day at his office, Taylor was more than happy drive to his apartment. He was more than glad that he only had to drive the short distance from his offices. He was still tired from his long drive from Colorado. As he climbed into the elevator from his parking area to his apartment, he was relieved and happy to be home. He did enjoy living in this apartment.

When he walked in, he almost tripped over his suitcase still sitting in the entrance area of the apartment. That was another chore he needed to attend to. Yet as he dragged his luggage into the bedroom, he just pushed it into a corner. Perhaps after a nap he would find enough energy to attend to unpacking and make a trip to the laundry area in the basement. This was one of the irritations he now had. If he was still living with Roz, she would have taken his clothes downstairs and put them in the washer.

He took off his outer clothing, hung up his suit and shirt shook out the comforter on his bed. He closed the bedroom shutters, lay down and pulled up the comforter. Right now. he was glad he had purchased a good mattress and springs for the bed, and he soon fell asleep.

It was more than two hours later when he woke up, and it was dark in his bedroom. *What time was it?* He turned on the bedside lamp and glanced at the clock on the nightstand closer to the window. *Seven-forty-six P.M.* Wow? He had been asleep over two hours. Now he was hungry. He pulled on sweats and thumped into his kitchen. Next, he stood staring at the contents of his refrigerator. It was 'sparse pickings' A small piece of lettuce, part of a tomato. That could possibly be salad. But all he could find in the freezer was a hunk of frozen pizza. Right at that moment he wished he could return home to Roz's house and eat some supper. But he had moved out more than six months ago. Then he recalled the conversation he had with his attorney about divorce proceedings. He wanted to get the divorce moving along as soon as possible.

He found a bottle of diet soda in the cupboard. Filled a glass with ice and proceeded to warm the left- over pizza. A trip to the supermarket tomorrow would be necessary.

Sunday evening Roselyn called the Landre house, Crista answered the phone. "Good evening. I wondered about what plans were for dinner?"

"Hi, Ms. Rosenbaum, Stratton threatened to go get a pizza. Why did you have something in mind for us?"

"I just made a large vegetable salad. Why don't you have Stratton call Eric, and they can order and pick up enough pizza for all of us. I think I have a variety of sodas, too. Do you think that will be okay for everyone?"

"Yes, Ms. Rosenbaum. That sounds great. I'll tell Stratton right now."

Close to an hour later the six children and two adults sat in Roselyn's kitchen and or dining room, and feasted on pizza, salad and one of the girls had purchased a large box of- - - - '*ice creams on a stick*'.

The three high school graduates, after supper, had gone into Shanna's room to discuss their plans for work during the summer, and gossiping about some boys they all knew.

Luke, Roz Stratton, Eric, and Ellie Anne, sat out on the balcony located off the kitchen and dining room enjoying the pleasant evening. Soon, Ellie had a phone call and left to go to her room. Eric and Stratton went down- stairs to Eric's room, but soon had the TV on in the family room. They were watching a stock car race. When the program switched to a commercial, Stratton asked Eric. "Did you miss TV while on your mission?"

"Yes, especially the NBA Basketball finals. We did get to watch part of last year's Super Bowl, but that was because we were in Mexico. That mission was not as strict as the Central Colorado's Mission. Life moves more slowly in Mexico. But then again it was much hotter there, too. Not much fun to wear good slacks and a white shirt all the time."

"Did you ever find out why they closed part of your mission 'south of the border'?"

"I think some of it had to do with the open borders between the U. S. and South America. Some of the people we worked with would get a chance to come into the U. S. I don't think they knew what they were up against once they got here. There are villages down there that are nearly empty. Think about it. It would be like many of the people in the States on our northern border deciding to move into Canada. There would be a border war. The problem is that the Mexican cartels are using the mess to flood the U. S. with drugs. And there are too many people here dumb enough to buy them, get 'hooked' and then overdose."

"You're absolutely correct. There are people walking into schools, and shooting them up, killing kids. Give me a job, and I'll sit in the entrance with a rifle across my knees just waiting for them to 'try' anything." Stratton said.

"Hey Stratton, don't laugh. There is a group of young guys in Colorado that have an organization something like that. Maybe it's because of the army base over there. Some are probably 'army brats'." They are really upset the way people are behaving around the country, young people, close to our age. When I read or hear about that it makes me proud of our police around the country and what they face each day; Plus, angry at all these criminals killing children or just some poor woman in a supermarket. And don't get me started. My Mom has some really strange 'patients' at the hospital.

Some of the dumb things they are teaching at schools these days. We're lucky to live here is Utah. Most the school districts still have people with common sense running the schools."

That evening Taylor sent another E-mail to his attorney friends asking for help with a divorce from Roselyn. He explained it was a 'no fault' separation. The only situation would be money. He knew with all three of his children soon would be in college. He would need to help the family financially. It wasn't that Taylor was poor. His practice was lucrative, and he had made some good investments over the years. He sat at his desk mulling over his present situation.

Then he tried another idea. He pulled up his army papers, read then over, and began a letter to the Army General who was in charge of Fort Carson Colorado, at this time. Perhaps they could use a doctor of psychiatry on the base, or even another surgeon.

He would love to hear Edith's voice over the phone, yet he really didn't have any news to tell her. He'd wait to see how the information that he was sending to Fort Carson would be received. How the powers that 'be' would react to his information? He sighed and realized he was still tired and *bored* that evening. It would be fun to see his children and listen to their gossip. Rather he searched his refrigerator and found a partial container of ice cream. He got out a spoon and began to eat from the container. Something that he would chastise his children from doing, what he now was doing. . Taylor was not a sports fan, but he now sat down in his living area and found a stock car race to watch. but soon he dropped down on his sofa. Just a short nap before the ten 'clock newscast. He woke close to midnight, shivering lying there only in his pajamas. He staggered into the bedroom and fell into bed.

Monday morning came early in the Rosenbaum household, Roselyn was up and so were Eric and Shanna. She was to report to her new job at the day care center, and Roselyn needed to be at the hospital at nine A.M.

Eric, used to being up early. was toasting bagels and making up a jar of orange juice. The only individual still in bed was Ellie Ann, and she soon dragged into the kitchen. She gazed at the family. "Boy, you guys are noisy. How can anyone get any sleep around here?"

"We all have places to go and things to do. Don't you have a job starting today?" Eric asked, and took a bite of his peanut butter covered bagel. He shook his head.

"Not until tomorrow, but since I'm up, I do have some laundry to do. But to do that I need to fortify myself with some breakfast." She grabbed a box of cereal from the pantry, and half a banana from the counter.

Eric set his dishes in the sink, "See all of you later. I need to go over to the college and register for summer school."

Roselyn went back to her office and grabbed her bag. "See all of you this afternoon. I'll call if I run into some situation that I will need to see to."

Chapter Thirty Nine

Taylor woke early, and decided that he could do some laundry, before he was expected at his office. While he was downstairs in the laundry room, his cell phone rang, and one of his patients needed to be seen in a few hours. He managed to get some of his clothes from the dryer and hurried back upstairs to his apartment. It was fortunate he had remembered to take his cell phone down to the laundry with him. As he was stuffing his newly washed load into a dryer, the phone rang. "Hello?"

"Ah, good morning. I hope I reached you before you went to your office." Edith said.

When Taylor heard her voice, his breath came out more quickly. Somewhat shallow and a little faster. "Good morning. To you."

"It's really great to hear your voice. Are you on your way to the clinic?"

"Well, I'm already on duty. It's quiet around here for a few minutes. I thought I'd take a break and grab some coffee." She cleared her throat.

"It's very nice to hear your voice. You said clinic. Is that the one you work at that is in downtown Colorado Springs?" He asked. (*I sound so ridiculous)*

"Yes. Most of the nurses take a weekly shift here, Meaning a week every month. In a way it's less stressful, but sometimes we find a serious problem with a child. At times it's medical and sometimes perhaps an emotional situation. Life is somewhat stressful for these military families."

"With the mess in Washington right now, there are many more families having problems than there were before the covid pandemic. We see it here, too. But how are you and your family doing, in general?"

"My children are pretty resourceful. But Ellie is in college, and Eric wants to go to college and Shanna just graduated from high school. She already has a job at the Day Care."

"My daughter, Teresa just graduated from high school. I didn't realize these two, your daughter and mine, are the same age." Edith said.

He laughed. "Oh, I already sent a letter to Fort Carson, enquiring about a medical position in the military. I don't know when I'll hear from them, but I'll let you know if and when they communicate with me."

"Then you'll let me know? I'll call right away." Edith cleared her voice.

"Since my children are somewhat older than yours, and their mother is a good parent. Eric is nearly twenty-three, and I also have a daughter close to twenty-one. At least that is what she reminds me of.

"It's coming up soon."

"Oh Taylor, when I saw you, I didn't realize how much you meant to me. Even at our age having a loving partner is so important. I've been a widow for over three years. I- - - - feel that I've missed so much - - - - -,"

Then Taylor could hear voices in the background.

"I've a new patient. I'd better go. Talk to you again, soon. Good bye."

Taylor sat there staring at his cell phone. **I can't sit here dreaming of Edith. I'd better get to the hospital, and soon. For him, Taylor's time at the hospital was pretty routine that day. He did see Roz hurrying into an elevator that early afternoon. He stopped by the hospital cafeteria and managed to pick up a prepared supper to reheat once he made it home.*

When he arrived at his apartment there was a large package waiting for him in the reserve box. He grabbed it and hurried into his apartment and set it down on his desk. The return address was Fort Carson, Colorado. For a moment he just stared at the bulky package wrapped in tan paper. But he took off his jacket, hung it up and sat down at his desk. Then he took tools from the desk to carefully open it up. There was a cover letter, and a stack of documents. He quickly surveyed them, but then went back to the cover letter. The jist of it, offered him a position as a medical doctor, with beginning salary of

$91,500 per year with the rank of Major of Medicine. He would be contacted about housing. There was brochure included showing and describing some recent condos constructed on the base.

He was so excited he slid some other papers to the floor, but quickly picked them up. *Who should he call first, Edith? Roz? The hospital?* Finally, he forced himself to calm down and begin to think through what this change in his life really meant. First of all, at the present time his income was now more than one hundred thousand per year. He had children to help with their college expenses. He would need to speak to Roz, and soon.

Logically, he now began to think through his obligations. First, he owned this apartment. And it would sell easily. Second, he would most likely live with Edith. He jumped up and began to pace his living situation. Who should he talk to first? He'd been married to Roz for over twenty-four years. Even though they had been married more than 24 years, and they would soon be officially divorced More than ever, right now, he viewed her as a friend. He would call her right now.

The house phone rang three times, and he was about to put it down when it was picked up. He heard a young feminine voice.

"Hello, Rosenbaum residence."

"Is this Shanna? This is dad. Is your mother at home?" This is, you know, Taylor."

"Oh, Hi dad. Mom and Mr. Landre are out looking at a house. When Mom gets home, I'll tell her you called."

"Why are they house hunting?" Taylor asked. *What is going on over there?*

"Because we're joining families. Us and the Landre family. Mom and Mr. Landre are getting married. So we're all joining up. I'm going to have a roommate sister. We all looked at another house yesterday, but it was too small. This one they're looking at is bigger and has three levels and four garages."

"When did all this happen?" Taylor asked in a surprised, but a rough, gruff voice. "I'm very surprised. When did all this happen?" Taylor asked. Trying not to sound angry, but he was, and very curious too. "I didn't mean to upset you.". How are you doing, now that school is out?" He took a deep breath. "So when did all this happen, come about. I mean, the joining of the two families?".

"Ah, this weekend. Sunday night we all got together. You know Mom and Mr. Landre were in a rock group years ago. They have had two concerts lately. Anyway, we had a family conference and Mom and Mr. Landre used to sing together, and they kind of liked each other a lot. Back then. Sort of in love when they were in college.

So, they decided to get back together, but not just singing. And when Mom got your divorce papers, she told Luke she could marry him. But first we all had a family conference. And everyone decided that we could form a Landre-Rosenbaum family." She giggled.

"Right now, Crista, Stratton, Eric, and Ellie are visiting some houses with a lady that sells, houses, real estate lady. It's going to take a real big house for all of us." She giggled again.

"Yes, I'm sure it will." He said softly. He cleared his throat. "Tell your Mom, I called. I'm planning on going out of town. I'll phone her later. Do you have a summer job?" He asked.

"Yes, I'm going to work in a daycare. It's at the elementary school. I can get some college credit while doing it. I like little kids, so it might be fun."

Taylor hung up the phone, but then sat there twirling a pencil, and in his head he thought. "I have to hand it to you, Roz." He said almost to himself.

"She has always been good at beating me at my own game."

He stood up and walked into the bedroom and dragged out his good leather suitcase. Time to plan a trip to Colorado Springs.

While Taylor ate some supper, he thought about what he must do to 'cement' this new position into place. The first thing he needed to do was to sell this apartment and he knew just who to call.

About three years ago he worked with a very beautiful woman who was an executive with large real estate company. They met in an unusual way. One evening. Roz was working and he promised the children a pizza. He went to an older restaurant that had famous pizza. At least some years ago when he was still working at the hospital. As he waited for the food, the woman rushed in to pick up her children's supper.

It had begun to rain, and with it, wind. He jumped up to hold the door open for her as she struggled to close an umbrella, juggle her purse, and hold the door to walk in. They both receive a blast of wet cold air, and once in the shop stood there laughing.

"Dinner for your family?" he asked.

She laughed and nodded. "If I can get home without dropping it on the concrete outside."

"I believe that, between the two of us we can load two pizzas into two cars."

She placed her order, and when both pizzas were ready, he had her pull her car up to the entranceway, and he placed hers in the back. Then she pulled over and helped him get his food into his car.

"Say, we need to meet here more often, especially on rainy evenings." He underlined.

'Not a bad idea. Just park your car for a moment, and get into mine, and we now can at least exchange phone numbers."

"Good idea." He answered back. He climbed into her car and for a better part of an hour they flirted but managed to exchange information. She was the first female in many years, that temped him to have a little extramarital fling. This one was short lived, but fun. At the end Taylor realized that he had a struggle with marital fidelity.

About three years ago, Taylor hired a new secretary. Six months later they drifted into an affair. She was a widow, and much of their time together was pleasant and. he felt somewhat helpful in her life at that time. He had been somewhat helpful to her in resuming a normal social life. .

Chapter Thirty Nine

About an hour later Luke, Roz, and three of their children returned home with bags of hamburgers, drinks and French fries. "Did you get time to check out some houses?" Shanna asked. As she opened the bags and began putting the contents on plates.

"We went through two. One was larger and we could all have a room or share a larger room, but there was not enough parking for all of our cars. Do you realize that between six kids and two adults we have six cars! Stratton said.

"The poor real estate lady about had a fainting spell when she watched the parents and five young people troop through the house. It was a pretty good, one but lacked enough parking."

"Hey, let's eat, I'm famished." Eric said.

"Get out of the way." Ellie ordered. "I'm getting out some plates and utensils. I'll set plates and eating tools, condiments on the table. If you want to go outside to eat, go through the kitchen door. If not find a place to eat in the dining room."

"Okay soda. Let's do as the girl asks." Eric said. He chose a sandwich some fries, and turned and poured a glass of soda. He carried his food to the table.

Sitting outside on some lawn chairs, Luke and Roz discussed the houses that they had visited. "The first house we went through was, with some minor remodeling would work, but the location and the lot size was a big problem. too small and the location for remodeling is not good. Actually, no matter what we try, the lot is too small." Luke said.

"Yes. Even though I really liked the second house, the lot won't accommodate all the cars this potential family has. I think a house in a newer area would be better. While at work tomorrow, I'll call the real estate company, and have them send me some materials from their last home show" Roz said.

"I'll see what I can find, too. Luke pulled her to her feet. "The sooner we get something to live in the better. Otherwise, I'll have to sneak you off for a 'private date'.

She laughed and leaned against him. "I'd like nothing better than a sneaky date. However, we have six young people observing our behavior. We must set a good example. Difficult as it is. You'd better gather up your 'three'. Tomorrow brings work or school for all of us." Roz stood and gathered up the bags and napkins and started upstairs to the kitchen.

"It's time for everybody to go home. Tomorrow is another day, and after work, I'm going out with another realtor, named Adele Sanderson. She thinks I should take look at an older house in Granite Heights."

It was late in the afternoon, before Roz arrived at the address given to her by Adele. It was an older home on a cul de sac. About twenty blocks from seventh east where Luke lived. Luke had a court case, yet he still had not arrived home at around six p.m. that next evening. She then met Ms. Sanderson at the address given her. At first Adele took Roz around the property, showing her a new area. Not only a with a triple garage, but another long parking area along the north side of the house.

"As you can see, there is lots of parking. Now let's go in through the garage. Roz noticed that that the kitchen was good sized, and had been remodeled. A large bar which included a dishwasher, which had been built into the original bar as well as a new utility storage. The living room was to the north and had a fireplace on the south wall.

They walked down a south hallway to three average sized bedrooms and two baths. A wide door on the east side opened up to a stair way. Adele led Roz up a set of stairs. "There was always a finished attic up here, So the adults decided to build a master bedroom, bath and den. Right now, its dim and stuffy up here, and they added an air conditioning unit and heat vents". She allowed Roz a chance go through the master bedroom closet. She led Roz back down. "Now we go down into the basement."

They walked back down two flights of stairs to the basement. The first room Adele showed Roz was a large bedroom, with a long walk-in closet. "This was the older boys' room. The smaller room next to that was for two younger children." She turned to the north "Now we'll go into the TV- room. On the south wall was another smaller room. "This is the room the father used as an office. So there are two bedrooms, and across from those bedrooms was another bathroom."

"Wait a minute." Roz stopped. "You've shown me three bedrooms on the main floor, One, no two upstairs, and now two down here. How many people lived in this house?"

Adele turned to Roz with a laugh. "There were nine children in this family. I mean they are all still 'around'. But this house had nine children, two parents, and they all moved to Mesa, Arizona. At least all but two. The oldest boy, joined the military and the oldest girl married." Adele grinned. "Do you think this house will accommodate your family?"

"It certainly seems large enough. But now we must have Luke take a look at the house as well as the garages." Roz said.

"Okay, Lets go back outside." The two women marched out and Adele opened up the garages. They were the standard size and had some useful shelving built along one side. Plus, there was enough room for their large freezer at the rear of the double garage. "I must have Luke also examine this place, and perhaps also the two older girls must see it.. Let's go get a soda or some other refreshment the day is becoming quite warm."

"Let's go over to the office. It isn't far from here." Adele led out and, Roz followed in her car. Once at the office, Adele took Roz into her office. "Sit down, and I'll go get some refreshment." She pulled some paperwork from a filing cabinet. It was a folder about the house they just had visited. "As you can read, the square footage is over 4,245. It could be even larger; Do you think the parking will be a problem up here.?" Adele asked.

"Luke will have to see it. Plus, the two older girls. "I really like it. Roz said. "Now we'll need to check out some other details. It is not too far away from major roads to the college, or other jobs the kids have this summer. Let me take the description sheet and explain it to everyone in my household." They walked to Adele's car and ten minutes later Roz drove into the Landre driveway. She picked up her phone and called Adele."

"I must explain this house is Luke's and his three children. When they all arrive home, we'll talk. We may call you as early as this evening or perhaps tomorrow. Thank you for showing the dwelling to me. The more I think about its location, we may want another 'house tour."

Since it was a Saturday, nearly all three of Luke's children worked that day. She left a note on Luke's desk in his den' locked the front door and went out through the garage. She drove ten minutes or so from his house to hers. Once she walked into her house, it was quiet. She realized that she seldom had a Saturday away from the hospital. It was strangely quiet. What should she do now?

What were the general plans for supper? She kept a meal list taped to the inside of the pantry door. What had they decided on? The list said Snyder's pizza and tossed salad. She glanced at the floor of the pantry and noticed several bottles of soda. Next, she opened the freezer section of the fridge and found ice cream bars. It was good to have some dessert for later. But right now, she decided on a nap.

Chapter Forty

All four girls were at the Landre house sitting, in Crista and Cauleen's room. "I know they went out looking at houses last Saturday." "That means that they plan to unite the families." Cauleen said.

"So that indicates they plan to get married," she said with a slight frown.

"Anyone object to that?" Eric said as he walked into the girl's bedroom. "Look at the situation in this way. They sang together when they were in college. I heard that they were pretty; sweet on each other. They're in their fifties. I know that's not old, But I'm sure they would enjoy a good family, love relationship. I mean adults are living to their eighties. Why not?"

"Mom went out with the real estate lady this morning; I know she'll ask a few of us to go see the house soon. I'll go if she asks me." Said Ellie.

"Okay to represent the guys in the family, I'll go with Ellie." Said Stratton. "What do you want to do. Wait for Mom to ask us to look at the house, or call the real estate woman and ask her to meet us up there. And I know it's up somewhere east." Ellie said.

"Okay, Ellie and I will go take a look at this house." Stratton said. He turned and went into the kitchen for the phone.

Less than an hour later Stratton and EllieAnn got out of Stratton's car and climbed up to the front door and knocked. She glanced around. "Well there is this a three car garage. That's a good start, having enough parking. Oh, here comes the woman I believe her name is Adele Sanderson."

From the end of the cul de sac she came walking. "Are you two part of the Rosenbaum family?"

"I'm Ellie Anne Rosenbaum, and this is Stratton Landre."

"Good to meet both of you. Let's start with the front door." She opened the door, and they walked in.

"Oh, look a great fireplace." Ellie said. And then she walked to the front window and gazed out at the rear yard. "It has a good-sized back yard. Hey Stratton, lookout here, there's a picnic table and chairs shaded under a shelter of sorts."

"This is good." He followed Ellie out through the family door out to the back yard. Walking around the yard, he stopped and put hands out as if to measure the width and size.

Meanwhile. Ellie walked back into the kitchen and was gazing around and checking out the kitchen and the breakfast bar. Also, she noticed a long kitchen table there, with eight chairs surrounding it. "Hey all of us can sit around this table all at once."

"Okay, I'm going to check out the bedrooms on this level." By pacing out each room, he carefully checked the size of the bedrooms by pacing each room. Next, he walked into both bathrooms to also measured width and storage space. Then he turned to Adele. "Is there a master bedroom suite?'

"Yes. She grinned. "Follow me it's upstairs." She started up the stairway to the third level. Once she made it up, she walked into the larger of the bedrooms. "This is the master bedroom and bath. The smaller bedroom was the former owner's sewing room. But she added a good-sized storage closet."

By then Ellie had stomped up the stairs and was gazing at the larger bedroom. "Ah, this is the master. I see a great closet. I'm checking it out." She turned to Adele. "So, the lady of the house sewed?"

'Yes, she did. I'm sure she did a lot of mending, too. Let's go down to the basement and take a gander at more bedrooms.'" Adele grinned.

The two females bounced down to flights of stairs to the basement. They walked into a sizable family area with a TV on the south end with two sofas for TV watching. There was also a large closet under the stairs. "In here is a place for Christmas decorations or, whatever you want to store down here. Now to the north end are two more bedrooms and a bath. And over here is a good place for bookcases. There is also a 'cool' room. A place to store food."

"Well, I'm impressed. I think this house would be a good place for the eight of us to live. Now we just need to have a wedding. What happened to Stratton? Let's go find him. Also has Stratton's father seen this house? I know you took him out last week to see, what, two other houses? Let's go find him."

Adele called out to the young people. "Is there anything else you want to know about this place?"

"Yes." Stratton said as he walked up to her. "How many people lived in this house, and why did they sell it? Plus, what is the price of this place.? Oh and have you looked at our house we are now living in, and what would be the market value of Ellie's house? Have you come up with a list price for ours?"

"Questions, questions?" Adele laughed. "Let's, go back to my office and we can answer your questions. Come on follow me."

Once they were in Adele's office, she pulled up their files on both houses. And she already had the file of the house they had just left on her desk. "Okay, she said.' "Sit down and I'll pull up the present file from the computer." She turned to her computer.

"The Landre house was inspected and priced at $,759,500. It will need a new water heater in a year or so. Other than that, the house seems to be in good repair."

'I thought that it would be more toward eight hundred thousand or so."

"Well it is a good family house.. You'll find similar sized houses in your neighborhood."

"What about the Rosenbaum house?" Ellie asked?

"Because of the location. Yet it has more square footage than your house, Stratton. There is still some mystique about living above the boulevard." Adele said.

"Okay then. What would the Rosenbaum house be worth?' Stratton asked.

"I'm not sure, forty to fifty thousand more. People sometimes buy the view. And that house also has the back yard pool. "

"Okay then, between the price of both houses, can we afford the house you showed us" Stratton asked.

Adele nodded and grinned. "Easily. Don't worry about that. Just go home and start packing."

"Have they decided about that house already?" Ellie asked?

"Pretty much. They felt it would house all of you. And by selling both their houses they can easily afford this one."

"They just can't or should not move in together if they're not married." Ellie choked.

"Hey, don't worry about it. I'm sure they have a plan. Come on, my Dad kind of let it come out that he had always had somewhat been in love with your Mom."

Stratton stood up. "Thank you, Adele for showing us the house. Now we know what our future housing could be. It will be much easier. Come Ellie, we have jobs and chores to begin at home. Moving a really boring, but an important job. It's not only the way you pack, that makes it much easier when you must begin to move in but, helps you to stay organized."

Stratton drove Ellie home and as she climbed from his car, she said. "Find out what you can, and I'll do the same. It would be great to have everything moved before Fall Quarter begins."

"You know what, I think all six of us will be in some sort of higher education come Fall Quarter. That's kind of scary, and expensive." Ellie said. "We all need to take a look at each of our finances. Of course, most of us will go to the community college. Except for me and Eric. Stratton, are you finished with junior college?"

"Yes, and so are the twins. I may need to pick up possibly two more courses before I decide where I should graduate from." He laughed.

"That sounds weird. I'll most likely go to the University or to the new Utah university. So, I guess that if the parents decide to buy the house that we looked at this morning. It won't matter which college I attend."

As Roz was driving home from the hospital, her cell phone rang. "Hello?"

"Hey lovely lady, I just received a call from Adele Sanderson. Three of our of our children, Ellie, Eric and Stratton had her show them the house we looked at two days ago. Apparently, they approved of it."

"After long thoughtful consideration, I think the house we viewed that day will be a good place for both families. Now, the word is that the parents, us, have to get married.! This is necessary because we have to be financially responsible. So, we just have to get married! How do you want to approach this?"

"Are you serious? Let's elope." She giggled. "No, I've given thought to this situation we find ourselves. Do you want a wedding, I mean with invitations, in some ward house. I am not looking forward to all that. We could all go to Las Vegas, and rent a chapel, but they are all getting into a summer half-semester in various colleges. For legal purposes we need to marry. Mainly to sell houses and buy this place that they approve of. Come on, you're an attorney. Let's get the legal stuff done."

"You are right. This isn't a big romantic affair." He took a breath, and chuckled. "Although I can't wait to get you in bed with me."

"There is that one little action we should attend to. What about this house? The Master bedroom seems to be adequate. Okay, think of something and I will too."

Chapter Forty One

At this precise moment all six of Luke's and Roz's children were having an emergency meeting of their own, Roz's children were called, because the meeting was being held in the Landre twins' bedroom.

"Okay, plan one is that we need to get those parents of ours married." They can't seem to come up with any plan, so my sisters talked, and we discussed the idea of a kidnap scenario. I spoke with Eric and he okayed the idea. It will take all of us in two cars. I'll drive one car and Eric will drive the other. Another. idea came up as to how to drug them. The parents, I mean. Eric has a medical friend. Ellie has a friend that grows tropical plants. We planned on two bouquets. One for each parent. Allow them to sniff the flowers, and will put them to sleep. Then Eric and I will each drive a car with a parent in each. We will drive to Wendover, Nevada, It's only 90 miles. Now all of this will happen on Wednesday evening. We can get to Wendover in two hours or less. So plan on staying overnight".

"Why did you plan on doing this on a Wednesday night?" Shanna asked.

"Because it will be a slow night in Wendover. And there is a wedding Chapel, and a motel there. Okay that is the plan. So be ready."

Wednesday evening came and a little before eight that night. children were ready to carry out their kidnap plan. They told the parents that they were all going out to dinner. The bouquets were ready, and they seemed to work. With Luke in the back seat of their family car and with one of the twins in the rear with him then, Roz in the rear of her car with Ellie and Eric will drive, with Shanna in front.

They left around 7:30 p.m. and Stratton drove his father's car with Crista in the rear with her father. The traffic thinned out about fifteen miles going west They communicated through cell phones. The idea seemed to be valid, and an hour and a half later they were well on their way to Nevada, where a marriage could be performed with just a valid driver's license. To tie the knot The traffic thinned a bit as it became dark. "How many miles have we left to go?" Ellie asked. "Dad is becoming restless."

"Did you see the 'rest stop sign?" Eric asked. "I read one on the right side of the road. REST STOP, 17 miles: We we'll be there in twenty minutes."

Then the cell phone rang. And Shanna picked up. "It's Cauleen, they want to pull into the rest stop."

"Okay." Eric sighed. He slowed down a little and began to search for the rest stop on the left side of the road. Finally, he stopped, signaled left and drove across the road, in his rear-view mirror, he watched Stratton do the same.

Once both cars parked and they stopped, the females began spilling out of both cars and managed to locate the women's rest room. Stratton climbed out and stretched. The rear door of his car flew open and out staggered his father and he turned to cling to the rear of the car. "What—where are we?" Luke gazed at the highway sign. "Wendover, what- - -?"

Stratton came up and put his hands out steady his father. "Ah, we sort of drove to Wendover, so you and Roz could get married." He dropped his head, but then stood straight and gazed at his Dad.

"It's time to bring all the members of this family together. Legally, I mean. We all want this. And we are all here." Stratton turned and watched his friend Eric bring his Dad Luke over to him. Luke turned to see Roz standing by the back door of their car, being held up by Ellie.

"The children gave us a push in the right direction. Let's drive into town and see what we can find." Luke said. "In fact- - -," He pulled out his cell phone and dialed a local number. He turned away to talk, but the children gathered around him. He stepped back and closed his phone. But then the children stepped back.

"Okay gang, we are driving to Wendover. Take the second right turn onto Desert Road to the Wendover Chapel, next to the 'Desert Chapel. It's next to the Desert Treasure Motel. They are waiting for us."

Everyone climbed back into cars. And in less than half-an hour they arrived. Luke walked into the motel office, and waved Eric and Stratton to follow him. Twenty minutes later the three of them came out holding keys.

Roselyn went into the women's area in the chapel and combed her hair. And smoothed out her slacks and blouse.

"I'm sorry if you/re upset about this kidnapping situation, but it was the best plan we could come up with." Ellie said, and hugged her mother."/ "But we need you two to get married!"

Twenty minutes later they were all in the wedding chapel and with only the information on their drivers' licenses. Luke and Roz were legally married. In Neveda, married and everywhere else..

"I'm sorry this scenario came so quickly, but it was the best we could come up with in so little time." Eric spread out his arms.

Luke turned to the children. They turned to him, "We just felt that everything would be better if you two were legally married."

"It's okay, because Luke and I couldn't come up with anything better. Right now, we need to get into rooms and all of us need a good night's sleep." Roselyn said.

The motel manager passed out three keys. One for a family suite, for the girls, one for a regular two beds s for the young guys, and the bridal suite for the newly married couple. Luke and Roz. "Oh, by the way breakfast is on us at ten tomorrow morning. Good night to you all."

They all glanced at the numbered keys. Ellie walked over to Eric and asked for a family suite key. "I just need to get my overnight bag." Now all of them went to the two cars for their belongings. On their way to their designated rooms. Ellie grabbed a shopping bag and handed it to her mother. "Here. You may need this." She said. And gave her mother a hug and handed her a small bag.

"Thanks girl. You just have a good night's rest and we'll see you at breakfast." She followed Luke to the motel room.

Once in the room, Luke ushered Roz in and found that besides the bed area, there was a sofa and chair close to a large TV.

He dropped down on the sofa. But then walked over and touched the large bed with an attractive coverlet on it. "This looks pretty comfortable." He stood over her, and glanced down, "I know, this is slightly crazy. Are you okay with this, or are you feeling as slightly unsettled as I am?"

"You could say that and be very accurate. Right now, I have two, possibly three thoughts rolling around in my head." I can't fault the kids, they just want to live in a comfortable house and get on with their lives. So, with that in mind, I'm going into that bathroom and get ready for bed. I'm tired." She picked up her purse, and the bag Ellie had handed her and marched into the bathroom. A few minutes later she came out wearing a lovely light green night gown with a lace bodice.

"Is that what Ellie gave you? That. Is very, nice. I won't take long." He fairly skipped into the bathroom. She could think of many things she wanted to ask him. Was now the time? She sat in front of the TV and found there were multi- -music channels available.

She tried a different setting and found some soft [elevator] type music available. She found a good channel and turned to it. Put it on softly. Then her phone rang. She grabbed her purse sitting on the coffee table. "Hello?" "Oh hi Taylor. Did you make it to Colorado Springs?" She listened. "Good, no I'm quite involved at the present time. I'm glad you made it to Edith's. I know it's a long drive. Good luck. Say high to Edith for me. Bye."

He came out from the bathroom and wearing a short robe. Something he could wear to a swimming pool.

"Did you think to bring a swim suit?" He asked.

She slid into the right side of the bed. Wasn't that the female' s side? Like the man always driving the car? Left side. How did the English figure their whole side thing out?

When he came near her, he reached and pulled her into his arms.

"Wait a minute, she needed to go back. She scrambled to the end of the bed and stood there. She shook her head. "Before I get in this bed with you, I need to know why you walked away from me, and started dating Caroline."

"YOU really need to hear about Caroline, now?"

"Of course, now! Back then I thought we were in love? And one evening you call me and tell me to date other guys?"

He stood there and shook his head. "I was desperate. I was low on money, and my Dad couldn't help me much anymore. Somehow Mr. Kendrick told me that he would pay my tuition into law school if I would take Caroline to a ball game or dance at the university. She had been home from her church mission for nearly a month and had no dates. And, her mission was difficult for her."

She was shy and hadn't done well with some of the people in the ward, or some of the other missionaries.

"I didn't think dating her a few times would be such a big deal. But to her it was. She was a sweet girl, and tried everything to please me. Then her father called me and told me I was doing a great service to the family. Apparently, I was helping their family. Because I had pulled Caroline out of her depression. Even my mother thought I was a real 'hero by helping Caroline."

"Was it that bad, dating her?" Roz asked.

"No. She was easy to please and even my mom thought she was a kind, sweet girl. Then, one night I saw you out with Taylor. You seemed to be having a great time. You were dancing together, and looked really good and seemed to be okay."

"Yes, he was a good date." Roz said softly. She sighed and walked around the bed and slid in. "I was getting cold standing there in this nightgown." She shook out a pillow and leaned against it. "Come, get in bed. It's getting late, and we'll have to drive home in the morning, or later today."

"Can you get,- - -understand - what these kids of ours did?! They want two things. A comfortable house and security, that we'll give them a place to live, and parents to take care of them."

"You are correct on that one. Even though they are all nearly grown, they want stability, and love, just as we want love."

Luke pulled her into his arms and stroked her back and touched everywhere he could reach. Then wrapping her in a blanket.

"I have been waiting for, many years to hold and love you. It's like when we sang together. It was as if each of us knew what we needed to work for us, and knew what the other wanted. Be my singing partner, and my love partner. Life will be sweet!" He kissed her deeply and now had the one woman and soul partner he needed and wanted lying in is arms.

He had loved her for over thirty years. She would be the love partner, help mate and help him be the second parent to six grown kids!

THE END

Printed in the USA
CPSIA information can be obtained
at www.ICGtesting.com
CBHW032008060724
11149CB00008B/197